A Deal with the Devil . . .

"You cannot go. I need you."

"Darling, many women do."

"If you help me, I can give you the man responsible for betraying your friends. In a week, I can get you into his house."

Her spy's finger dipped into the hollow above her collarbone. "I can get into any house I desire. And why are you still breathing so hard, Princess?"

"I can get you there without any skulking. You can walk in openly and have as much time as you need." Now her lips were inches from his. Heavens, but he had beautiful lips.

"Fine. You have won me over. Now tell me who it is."

"No." She wasn't a complete fool. "I will tell you after you train me."

"Done. I'll give you a week's worth of training. But I am not responsible for your success."

"Agreed. So what are we going to—"

"Tomorrow night. Rest when you can in the daylight because for the next week, Princess, your nights are mine. . . ."

ANNA RANDOL

Sins of a Wicked Princess

AVON
An Imprint of HarperCollinsPublishers

AVON BOOKS
An Imprint of HarperCollins*Publishers*
10 East 53rd Street
New York, New York 10022-5299

Copyright © 2013 by Anna Clevenger
ISBN 978-0-06-223140-6
www.avonromance.com

First Avon Books mass market printing: November 2013

Avon Trademark Reg. U.S. Pat. Off. and in Other Countries, Marca Registrada, Hecho en U.S.A.
HarperCollins® is a registered trademark of HarperCollins Publishers.

Printed in the U.S.A.

10 9 8 7 6 5 4 3 2 1

*To everyone who couldn't wait
for Ian's story*

Sins of a
Wicked Princess

Prologue

$\mathcal{I}$an Maddox watched the backs of the other two members of the Trio as they strode from Sir James Glavenstroke's office. Their little merry group of spies had been officially disbanded. Now that Napoleon was dead, the Foreign Office wanted nothing to do with three former convicts—no matter how perfectly trained.

Both Clayton and Madeline, the other members of his team, had been shocked by the news. Madeline had even been hurt.

And no one hurt Madeline.

Ian waited until his two friends were out of sight before opening the door to old Glaves's office again. Despite everything they'd endured, the other two spies had never been stripped of the nobility that held them together at their very core.

Ian, on the other hand, had never been burdened with it to begin with.

Glavenstroke choked on a mouthful of brandy when he spotted Ian. "What are you doing here? I've said all that needs to be said."

Ian suspected the man liked to think of himself as the father of the Trio. But Ian didn't doubt he'd slit their throats if he deemed it expedient. Or rather, he'd order some poor idiot to forfeit his life attempting it.

Ian lowered himself into the leather chair across from Glavenstroke, propped his boots up on the desk, and picked up a glass of brandy, downing it in one gulp. The aged French liquor was worth more than the entire stipend received by the Trio for their ten years of service.

"What do you want, Wraith?"

Ah, Glavenstroke was nervous, then. He never called Ian by his completely dashing and thoroughly apt spy name unless he was afraid.

Good. He should be.

"I'm not a fool, correct?" Ian asked.

Glavenstroke's eyes narrowed but he shook his head.

"Lovely. I was hoping you'd concur. That makes this much simpler. Perhaps you could tell me why I'm supposed to believe you'll let the three spies who know England's dirtiest secrets waltz away free."

Glavenstroke's head jerked like a horse fighting a bit. "You've proven your loyalty. I could do no less."

"Perhaps *you* could, Glaves. But I suspect some of your friends will soon think better of it."

The older man's face reddened. "What are you suggesting?"

"When the time comes to tidy up all the loose bits at the Foreign Office, the Trio will never be mentioned."

"Of course not. Everyone is grateful—"

Ian crossed his ankles, then reached down to flick a spot of mud from his boots. "You see, my dear mentor, I won't tolerate it."

"Now, listen here! I saved you from Newgate—"

"Truly, Glaves? After all this time it hasn't occurred to you that I was still in that prison cell because I chose to be?"

"You seemed more than eager to grasp my offer when I tendered it."

"Indeed. It seemed useful. And it *was*. The chance to refine my skills. Refine my mannerisms. My language. And learn all those undetectable ways to kill a man . . ."

Glavenstroke surged to his feet and planted his hands on the desk. "You have the gall to threaten me?"

"No, no. Not at all. This is simply an assurance that anyone sent after me will die bathed in their own blood." Ian stood and poured himself another glass.

"But surely you're loyal—"

Ian lifted the glass in a toast. "I am loyal to the Trio." He picked up the decanter. Might as well take the whole thing. "Anyone who threatens us will die. Painfully. Make sure you spread that helpful little morsel of gossip around."

Chapter One

"We named her Juliana after you, of course, Your Highness." The apple-cheeked woman peeled the red, angry infant out of a huge cocoon of blankets and thrust her forward.

Princess Juliana Castanova refused to turn her head to see her aunt Constantina make another tick on the back of her fan. That made the third new baby Juliana this week and the tenth this month. If she ever did manage to regain her country and return home with her fellow exiles, there'd be some confused schoolteachers.

Yet Juliana dutifully accepted the crying creature and kissed her on the cheek. When the crying suddenly ceased, all the gathered courtiers gasped and applauded.

Juliana suspected the baby's reaction had to do with being freed from far too many blankets in the stifling reception room, but as her aunts constantly counseled her—her people had been deprived of a country, she'd be a beast to deprive them of their monarch as well. So she smiled as if her royal blood gave her some sort of divine power over infants.

Then she quickly passed the child back.

The clock in the hall tolled the hour, signaling the end of the public audience. The rest of the hopeful supplicants were herded out the doors until next week. Not that they'd have much more luck then. Smiles, she could give. Money was in much shorter supply.

After the collapse of the monarchy in Lenoria twelve years ago, the Castanovas had been stripped of everything but their personal holdings—which weren't considerable: a single mountain chateau and a hunting lodge on Lake Tuire. The prince regent had granted Juliana a yearly stipend when she and her younger brother fled to London. Thankfully, he'd also gifted them with this house. Otherwise, there'd be no way she could support the fifty loyal Lenorian servants who'd fled with her.

What little extra money she had was used to support Lenorian citizens in London, but there was never enough.

Juliana longed to flop in a chair and bury her head in her hands, but a princess did neither of those things. So instead she glided over to where her three great-aunts sat to the left of Juliana's oversized and less-than-comfortable throne.

Constantina, the youngest of the three elderly women, pursed her lips as she studied the back of her fan. "Drat! That brings the total to thirty so far this year. I believe I owe you a quid. Although you'll have to wait until next quarter for me to pay. I spent the last of my money on a new collar for Lulu. His old one was becoming terribly tarnished." She stroked the rotund ferret curled in a basket by her chair.

Leucretia tapped a finger to her rouged, bloodred lips. Although she was the eldest sister—she'd been the twin of Juliana's grandfather—she still dyed her hair raven black and kept the long plaits wrapped around her head. "Shall we double the wager? I say we won't make it to one hundred Julianas by the end of the year."

"Done! I say our Juliana has great things in store this year and will far exceed everyone's expectations."

If only Juliana could believe that. The Congress of Vienna was over, and her country had been divided between the Spanish and the French. The only thing that kept Lenoria temporarily intact was the lack of Juliana's signature on the treaty.

Which she refused to give.

Yet both countries had vowed to go to war if Juliana tried to reclaim her throne.

So now she sat in London like a ninny while she tried her best to figure out a solution.

Leucretia lifted a sculpted brow. "That is possible. But there are only so many Lenorians of childbearing age in England."

Eustace sighed at her two sisters. "You should not speak of childbearing in front of Juliana. It isn't proper."

Leucretia snorted. "All the babies she kisses must come from somewhere."

Eustace's crinoline gown crinkled as she stiffened. Her nostrils flared but she refused to argue. "You must hurry and change, Juliana. Monsieur Dupre will be here in less than an hour to continue your portrait."

"Am I truly necessary?" Juliana asked. The portrait Dupre painted flowed almost entirely from his own imagination. It looked nothing like her.

But all three of her aunts stared at her with equal expressions of shock.

"Of course you are," Eustace said, her jowls quivering. "Even if Prince Augustus doesn't express interest in you, perhaps one of the other Hapsburgs might. Or if not them, I hear Czar Alexander has a second cousin we haven't approached yet. Of course he is only ten."

Juliana had discussed this topic far too many times to blush at her aunts' frank examination of her lack of marital prospects. It was hardly her fault the options were so few. They needed a prince that wasn't French or Spanish so she could gain his country's support in her effort to regain her throne.

But strangely, she was finding it rather difficult to find someone willing to marry a poor, plain princess without a claim to her country.

"Gregory said Prince Wilhelm will be attending a house party at some duke's country estate. We should all attend." Constantina held down a portion of biscuit to her pet, who sniffed at it once before returning to sleep.

"Gregory is back?" Juliana asked.

Leucretia stood. She always managed to look far more regal than Juliana ever could. "And avoiding you, apparently."

Which meant her brother was most likely in trouble or about to become so. "Which duke is hosting the party?"

Constantina had to think. Dukes were on about the same par as chimney sweeps in her mind. She never bothered to keep track.

"The Duke of Sommet?" Juliana asked.

Constantina nodded happily. "It's been ages since we went to a grand party."

Blast Gregory. Why couldn't this house have a dungeon? She'd told him to stay away from Sommet. Her brother was convinced Lenoria had fallen through the meddling of outside forces. Juliana agreed. But while she'd become rather obsessed with uncovering the conspirators responsible, Gregory was far more eager to band with anyone who promised an immediate restoration to power.

Juliana knew Sommet only slightly from the Congress of Vienna, but he was a man of grandiose promises and velvet threats. He liked to think himself a man of influence. But Juliana had found he abused his influence over those weaker than himself.

Like Gregory.

Juliana had no desire to spend any time at his party. "Isn't Prince Wilhelm fifty?"

Eustace sniffed. "Forty-five. But my own dear Albert was fifty-three when I married him." And he'd died three years later, leaving Eustace to mourn him for the past fifty years. Not something Juliana wanted to replicate.

"Let's try Prince Augustus first." He, at least, was her age, even if the most flattering reports of him called him a sniveling pudding of a man. "And I'd better change if I'm to meet with Dupre." Juliana picked up her skirts and hurried as elegantly as she could from the room before her aunts tried to change her mind. If she didn't adore them so much, she might be able to better resist their advice. But as it was, they were so well-intentioned she had a difficult time denying them anything.

The corridor was only slightly cooler than the air in the reception room, but Juliana would take any reprieve she could get. After glancing around to ensure no one was watching, she tugged at her heavy velvet bodice. London wasn't the best place to be in July. If the invitation to the house party had been from anyone else, she might have accepted, simply to escape the smell of the city.

Juliana retained only select memories of Lenoria, but she did remember there was always a breeze in the summer. And the air smelled of flowers and rain, not of soot and refuse.

A familiar dark head appeared then disappeared around the corner ahead. "Gregory!"

There was a long enough pause that she was certain her brother had decided to run away—in which case she'd have to give chase, even knowing the scolding her aunts would give her once they heard.

But then Gregory reappeared. He didn't slump— he'd been raised by the same aunts, after all—but he did avoid her gaze. "Juliana. I was just going out."

"It can wait."

"No, it—"

Juliana lifted a regal eyebrow and her brother silenced. Being the ruler of an almost nonexistent country did have some advantages. "I hear you have been spending time with Sommet."

Gregory flushed and brushed a heavy lock of his chestnut hair from his eyes. "He has plans to help restore Lenoria."

"Plans that involve plotting without the consent of the current ruler of Lenoria?"

Her brother scowled, making him seem far younger than his twenty years. "What choice do I have when the current ruler won't do anything to reclaim the country? It's been almost two years since the war ended. We were supposed to be home by now."

Juliana flinched, but she wouldn't let her brother goad her. "Sommet is a manipulator and a liar."

Gregory's tone turned pleading. "You don't know him like I do. His plan will work. By winter, we could be back in Lenoria. You could finally be taking care of your people. Do you think the Spanish or the French will take care of them?"

"*How dare you.*" Sommet might be able to manipulate Gregory with his lies, but she refused to be manipulated as well. "I give everything to my people. I spend every minute of every day agonizing over each one of them."

"Agonizing isn't the same as acting. And since you aren't the ruler of anything, I don't know why I'm listening to you."

He strode past her down the corridor.

"Gregory."

But he didn't glance back.

Juliana yanked out the pins securing her heavy gold crown in place and tugged it off as she walked the few remaining feet to her room. Not feeling any less suffocated, she tossed it on her bed. "Darna?"

Her maid was nowhere in sight. Juliana knew she should sit quietly and wait for her to return. But she wanted out of the blasted gown. *Curse Gregory anyway*.

She *was* acting. She was just acting cautiously. Acting rashly for the sake of action would be worse than no action at all.

Wouldn't it?

She reached behind her and fumbled with the buttons. Her aunts wouldn't allow her to wear the dress again regardless. Apparently, being seen in the same dress twice would cause her subjects to lose faith in her ability to rule or some such nonsense.

You are Lenoria now, Leucretia would say. *Make her glorious.*

The buttons refused to come undone. Normally she would have given up and waited for her maid, but instead, she grabbed one corner of the closure on the back of her dress and yanked.

Two pearl buttons popped loose and rolled across the floor. She glared at them, then peeled her bodice down, tugged out of the sleeves, and wrestled with the rest of the dress. The fabric was so stiff that when she tossed it on the floor, it sat there full and awkward before slowly deflating.

She kicked it once for good measure.

"Perhaps I should announce my presence before you get more naked," a low, rumbling voice announced. "Or violent."

She stumbled back with a shriek as a man stepped from beside her wardrobe. He was tall and broad. Handsome. Dark-haired and scarred.

And suddenly at her side with an agility a man his size shouldn't possess.

Before she could take a breath to scream, his hand clamped over her mouth and his other arm wrapped around her waist, sealing her to the hard wall of his chest.

Chapter Two

Ian was slightly frustrated. And not from the surprisingly soft feminine form writhing against him.

No one had told him the princess was insane. Not that it surprised him. Half the royals in Europe were stark raving barmy. A little too much cooing in the same nest.

But the intelligence he gathered was usually flawless. He'd been told that Princess Juliana was formal, cold, and plain.

None of those words applied to this woman.

Her hair was brown. That much, at least, his sources had gotten right. But he'd been told her eyes were brown, not the color of burnished copper. Her face was perhaps a trifle narrow, but the sharp angles of her cheekbones lent it elegance.

And when she'd ripped the dress from her body . . . He smiled at the memory. One of the best things about being a dishonorable scoundrel was that he didn't have to feel guilty about that entertainment.

All of his leads pointed to this woman. Over the past two years, someone had betrayed the true identities of the members of the Trio to their worst enemies. The betrayer had covered her tracks well. But eventually they had all led here.

To the princess in his arms.

He didn't wince at the sharp kick to his shins. It never occurred to women to wear useful shoes. But when she followed that with an attempted bite to his palm, his estimation of her rose a little.

"Who gave you information on the Trio?"

Someone had betrayed Madeline to a vindictive Prussian bastard and Clayton to a group of violent Russian revolutionaries. Their true identities weren't something this princess could have pieced together on her own. Someone from the Foreign Office must have handed her the information. He intended to find out who and for what price.

He had to know how many pounds of flesh to carve, after all.

He pulled his knife and flashed it in front of her face. "I'll let go of your mouth and you will tell me your answer. Now, before you decide to be annoyingly brave, know that before you can draw in a breath, I'll have slit your throat, but not enough to kill you. No, just enough so you can no longer breathe to scream. Then I'll slice you open, starting at your pretty little toes, up to your belly, where I will play with your entrails while you watch." As far as threats went, it was one of his better ones.

It was a risk. Some people fainted entirely at that point, but he was growing impatient with the endless labyrinth of people and dead ends that had clogged his search.

Juliana nodded against his hand. So he slowly lifted it.

"I have no idea what the Trio is."

Ian added another tick to his admiration at the cool composure in her voice, but he tightened his hold. Not enough to leave marks, but enough that her breathing came in spurts. "Come now, Jules. You must know the name of the group of spies who toppled your country. You wanted revenge. I can understand that. Admire that, even. But, you see, our two goals unfortunately conflict at that point. Now, if you value your skin, tell me who gave you the information."

She'd been shivering, but the motion suddenly stopped. "What did you say?"

"Which part? It was a rather long monologue."

"A group called the Trio was responsible for the uprising in Lenoria?" The outrage in her voice actually sounded genuine.

"The letter sent to General Einhern came from this house. And one year ago in June, three Russian revolutionaries came to this house, where they were given information on a friend of mine." Clayton and his new wife had managed to survive the Russians, but it had been a close thing. Ian wouldn't let them be at risk again.

"The Trio is English, then?"

He barely dodged a foot stomp. And he had to shift quickly to keep from slitting her throat too early.

"I thought the French were behind it because we wouldn't side with Napoleon. Or the Spanish because—" She growled. "And I've been sitting in London all this time. In the very lap of the bastards responsible for my parents' deaths." Her sharp elbow hit him with surprising force, but not enough to make him more than wince. "Well, I wish good luck to the people who are hunting the Trio and wish *you* to the devil."

This interrogation wasn't going the way he'd anticipated. He'd interrogated many people over the years. Men. Women. Even children a time or two. He always obtained the information he needed.

He'd also become quite good at knowing the truth when he heard it.

And she was telling the truth.

Damn.

Like a cat drowning in the Thames he floundered one more time. "My information isn't wrong."

"I'm afraid it is." For the first time since he'd entered, she sounded disdainful and condescending. Like a princess.

What the devil had he missed? His information was not wrong, but he wasn't about to bicker with her, wasting time until her maid returned from the little crisis he'd arranged.

"I wasn't even here last June. I'd been invited to Brighton with the regent."

Ah. *Double damn.*

If that was true, then holding her at knifepoint was a rather large waste of time. He sheathed the knife and spun her around so he could study her face. "I can check that claim."

"Go ahead." Her strange amber eyes could have frozen the devil's horns.

"Someone in your household is responsible," he said. One of the letters had been written on parchment from her desk. Ian had verified it personally. And those revolutionaries *had* come here. Somehow he must have put the pieces together wrong.

She inched back. "Unfortunately, you're not going to get the chance to find out who."

"I will."

She grabbed a candlestick from the table and brandished it in front of her. "Not after I scream. My soldiers will gut you."

Ian laughed at her naïveté. With a single grab and twist of her wrist, the candlestick was in his hands. "Your soldiers consist of five lads playing dress-up with rusty swords. They can't stop me from coming back whenever I choose. You won't even be able to prove I was here in the first place."

Her eyes narrowed. "Then *I* will shoot you."

He tucked a finger under her chin. Blimey, but her skin was soft. "Aren't you the most darling thing?" Spunky. That was the word. The princess was spunky.

Juliana slapped his hand away and he returned it to his side. She was not *darling*; she was nearly a ruling sovereign. "I'll double the security on the house." Had she just spit as she talked? But she was beyond caring. She'd spit on this man's grave.

"Because your security was so efficient in keeping me out the first time, Jules?"

If he didn't stop grinning, she'd punch him.

"You will address me as Your Highness."

"I make it a rule never to call any undressed person by their title."

That was it. She swung for all she was worth. His grin actually disappeared before her hand hit.

Ouch.

She winced at the impact. She might have broken her wrist.

His strong hand clamped over hers, and she blinked her eyes open. Had she really closed them?

She'd punched his arm. Not even his face.

He tucked her hand behind her back, tight enough that she couldn't move unless she wanted to dislocate something. "Very good, Princess. But don't fear, when I return to your less-than-castle, you won't even know I'm here." His lips lowered until they were inches from hers. "And while you're lying in bed thinking about my hard chest, you might ask yourself why you never did bother to scream."

He spun her away in a quick maneuver that made the world tilt. She had to catch the table to keep from falling.

When she whirled back around, he was gone.

Chapter Three

Ian wanted nothing more than to climb into a bed. Not just any bed like most nights, but a soft bed with blankets that were made from bunnies covered with goose down.

Despite his boasts, the princess's house had been more difficult to get into than he'd anticipated. He'd had to scale to the third floor before he'd found any windows that could be opened from the outside.

He just wasn't as young as he used to be.

His boots left imprints on the soft Turkish rugs in the corridor outside his room at The Albany. He seldom used these rooms. He generally preferred to skulk with his own kind in any of a dozen hovels in the slums of the city. But tonight, his back ached and a night on the floor of some hole would get him nothing but hours spent tossing and ruminating on a nearly naked princess.

Besides, he had to do something with all the money Cipher had invested for him.

He unlocked the door and stepped inside, already planning what he'd order from the kitchen staff. The price of the rooms was more than made up for by the divine creations that came out of the kitchen. Jean Pierre was a master craftsman when it came to flavors.

Ian eased shut the door behind him.

The hairs on the back of his neck suddenly stood at attention.

The fireplace was lit. As was a candle.

Someone had moved his stockings.

He'd left a pair drying in front of the fireplace when he was last here . . . what, two weeks ago?

What the devil? The hotel staff knew not to enter his rooms. And if someone was waiting to kill him, he doubted they'd light a fire and tidy his clothing.

"Good evening, sir. Your dinner will be delivered shortly."

An elderly servant in an impeccable black coat and a lemon yellow hat containing three ostrich feathers stepped into view.

"Canterbury?"

"If I might take your hat and gloves, sir?"

"What in the blazes are you doing in my rooms?"

"Taking your hat and gloves, sir."

"But how did you find my rooms?" It wasn't often that Ian was baffled, but this did it.

"Mr. Campbell gave me your location, sir, when I inquired."

Curse Clayton. "When I asked you to take that position with Madeline in London, it wasn't because *I* wanted you close at hand." No, he'd known he could trust Canterbury completely with Madeline, but Ian didn't want him. The old butler dredged up far too many worthless memories.

"I believe you made that quite clear at the time, sir."

How much more blunt did he need to be? "I do not need you."

"So you said twenty years ago. And that didn't work out so well for you, did it? Arrested and sentenced to hang shortly thereafter."

By then Ian had been firmly entrenched with his merry band of cutpurses and gutter rats. He'd been living with his gang of thieves on the streets for almost ten years. Yet when Canterbury had heard about the trial, he'd come and tried to speak on Ian's behalf even though it had cost him his position as the Duke of Yuler's butler.

"I survived."

There was a knock on the door. Canterbury answered and accepted a silver tray from the footman. He placed it on the small table and uncovered a plate of beef dripping with savory juices and seasoned with rosemary, mushrooms, and a touch of black pepper. In a nearby bowl, strawberries wallowed in clotted cream as white as angel wings.

"I assumed you'd want dinner when you returned, but if I was incorrect . . ." He started to lift the plate.

Ian grabbed it. It would be a crime to let such food go to waste. And he happened to be an expert on crime. "How did you know that I was going to be here tonight?"

"A good butler always anticipates his master's whims, sir."

"No. I was the spy. Not you. You do not get to deflect me with non-answers."

"As you say, sir."

"No, I want *you* to say. That is the whole point."

"Shall I have the staff wait on dessert, sir?"

Ian glared. "You fight dirty, old man."

"A good butler would never dream of fighting, sir. Now would you like wine or brandy with your meal? I was able to obtain a rather fine bottle of French brandy, if I might be so bold."

"Oh, you might be," Ian muttered. He plopped down in the chair with a sigh. "The brandy, curse you."

"You may wish to remove your muddy coat before eating."

"You are an interfering old biddy, Canterbury. Do not push your rather meager amount of luck. And I don't see how you can take issue with my coat when you look like a bloody lemon peacock."

Ian wished he were the type to savor the meal. It was beyond divine. It was as if Canterbury had somehow reached into Ian's very soul and plucked out the perfect symphony of flavors.

Curse him, anyway.

"Where are you staying?" Ian asked.

"Here, sir."

Ian took another mouthful of the beef. Mercy. He needed to fall down and beg for mercy before he died from sheer bliss. "I've never had this here before. What do they call it?"

"You have had it before, sir."

"Going batty in your old age?" Ian wasn't entirely sure how old Canterbury was. Sixty-five? Two hundred? But other than the slight stoop in the man's once straight spine and his thinning gray hair, one would never have known it.

"No, sir. It was one of your mother's favorite recipes."

Ian set down his fork and stood. "I'm finished."

"Sir, your mother—"

"You can stay here if you like, Canterbury, but don't expect me back."

Hurt flashed only for an instant before it was gone behind the butler's impassive façade. "Very good, sir."

The July air was too hot and humid to clear his thoughts as Ian strode back onto the street. Damn Canterbury. His mother was dead in an unmarked grave at the crossroads. She should be left in peace. After all, it was what she'd wanted. What she'd wanted more than her own son.

A man crept out of the shadows, the menace on his face melting into a gap-toothed grin when he recognized Ian. "Who's your mark tonight, mate?"

Ian let the gutter flow back into his accent. "Off to see Margie."

"A lovely dove, she is."

Margie was a friend of his from his days in the gutter. She'd risen from a two-bit light skirt to the owner of a bawdy house with sixteen *employees.* She kept a room for Ian in the attic when he wanted it. But as far as everyone else knew, he spent many a night in the redhead's arms.

Ian let himself into the small cramped room by way of the window. This room, at least, was untouched. His stockings hung dry and stiff in front of a cold fireplace.

But he didn't feel any more at peace here than he had at The Albany.

Grunts and drunken laughter filtered through the walls. He'd fallen asleep to the noise without trouble many times, but tonight the moans repulsed him and he found himself back on the street.

Where to now? The flat by the wharf would stink of rotting fish heads in the summer heat. Clayton or Madeline both would happily provide him a room for the night. Or he could spend the night as an uninvited guest in any house in London.

Yet somehow he found himself back at the walled garden of a deposed princess.

As he tucked his fingers in the cool vining plants that scaled the walls, his mind ceased caterwauling. And his grin slowly returned to his face.

There were more guards posted tonight.

Good for her.

Too bad they didn't know what to look for. Their eyes watched the gates while he'd scale the wall to the garden, climb the oak tree to the balcony on the second floor, and then follow the gutter to the empty bedroom on the next floor.

He could sleep in the blue guest room three doors down from the fair princess with her none the wiser.

She'd be asleep now. For a moment, the urge to stare at her peaceful slumber nearly overwhelmed him. She'd be tucked in by her maid, her hair fanned out over her pillow. The angry flush would be gone from her cheeks. The animation in her face momentarily at rest.

What did a princess dream of at night? Castles and handsome princes, no doubt. The color of her next ball gown. Or perhaps having Ian clapped in manacles and thrown into the dungeon—she did have spirit, after all.

Ian turned away from the wall. He wouldn't go inside tonight. The information he sought wouldn't be found in darkened corridors and empty guest-rooms. He'd need daylight to question her servants.

He strode away. There was a cot in the kitchen of the Rutting Beaver that would do for the night.

And for the first time in his life, he couldn't wait for the morning to come.

Chapter Four

*J*uliana wanted nothing but to go to sleep, but first she'd had to spend several hours reviewing the security on the house. And now this.

"Gregory, you'll have to stop pacing and just tell me what is amiss."

Her brother dragged his hand through his hair and groaned again. "I'm as good as dead."

She would kill him herself if he didn't start talking. "What? Do you owe someone money? Is it a gambling debt?"

He stopped long enough to frown at her. "I know better than that."

"What then? A woman? Your mistress?"

Gregory sank into the chair in the corner of Juliana's room. "I hope never to hear you utter that word again."

Juliana snorted, glad none of her aunts was there to hear her. "I see the bills for the jeweler. Now either tell me what is wrong or leave me in peace so I can sleep."

"It is Sommet."

Ice filled Juliana's stomach. "What has he done?"

Gregory buried his face in his hands. "You were right about him. He has—he has found a way to have the crown taken from you." He dug his fingers into his scalp. "And given to me."

"*What?*" She might not particularly want to be a monarch, but she'd die before she allowed anyone to wrest it from her.

"It has to do with you being a woman."

"Women are allowed to rule Lenoria." It was always the eldest child rather than the first male.

He swallowed. "Yes. But if the princess is still unmarried by twenty-two, any male heirs have the right to challenge her for the throne."

In 1345, King Hubart had wanted his son to inherit rather than his daughter. He couldn't change the old law, so he amended it.

"You're twenty-four," Gregory reminded her.

"I know how old I am." Juliana took a calming breath. "I fail to see what the problem is. Don't challenge me. Sommet cannot force you. Just deny him."

Gregory actually moaned.

"He *can* force you?" she guessed, dread expanding in her chest.

"He had information on the people who toppled Lenoria."

The Trio. The man who'd been here earlier had mentioned them. His rough voice and gentle hands. "What did you do?"

Gregory scowled for a moment. "It's not like it's

any different than what you would have done. If you'd captured them in Lenoria, you would have had them executed."

Perhaps. Perhaps not. She was eternally grateful that she didn't have that authority here in England. "That's Sommet talking, not you. You tried to have people murdered?"

"*I* didn't try to kill them. I simply told other people they had wronged where to find them."

"How did you know who their enemies were?"

"Sommet." His bravado dissolved. "He kept proof linking me to it. He says he'll reveal it to the government, if I don't obey."

The English would be up in arms at a foreign royal plotting the murder of its citizens.

"They might hang me for attempted murder."

Even if they didn't, the scandal would be enormous. The regent would withdraw his support. They'd lose the house and their small stream of income.

"And if you do what Sommet wants?"

Gregory groaned. "I'd become king. Sommet claims he has the support to free Lenoria."

"Then why won't he do it with me in control?"

Gregory's words were muffled by his cravat as he ducked his chin into his chest. "I may have signed away certain rights to him if he could get Lenoria back."

Juliana gripped her bedpost to keep from strangling him. "What, precisely?"

"The mineral rights in the southern mountains."

A princess does not raise her voice. A princess does not raise her voice.

"Those rights belong to the crown. You have no right—"

Ah. It suddenly all made sense. "If you were king, then the documents you signed would be binding." There was gold in those mountains, and more importantly iron, vast amounts of it if the reports were to be believed.

"Perhaps it would be for the best if I did listen to Sommet, then at least we'd have a country, which is more than we have— *Ouch!*" he cried as she gripped his ear.

"You did *not* just threaten to take my country from me." The mob ten years ago hadn't managed it; she wouldn't allow her brother to.

Her brother fought to get her to release him. "Ouch. Not really, I swear. That's why I came to speak to you in the first place. I don't know what to do."

The fight went out of Juliana, and suddenly she was a young girl leading her sobbing brother out of a castle burning with their parents' bodies still inside.

She placed her hand on his shoulder. "I will take care of it."

Her brother stared up at her. "How?"

"What documents does Sommet have?"

"Letters. Letters to a friend where I explain my

plans to reveal the identity of those spies." He fidgeted side to side.

Juliana frowned. "But how can he release those documents without revealing his part in all of this?"

"I never mentioned him." He scrubbed his face. "I may have wanted my friend to think it was all my plan."

"Do you have any proof that Sommet was the one who gave you the names?"

Perhaps she could convince Sommet that he was endangering himself with those letters.

"No. He always insisted on meeting in person. Nothing is in writing."

Blast. But perhaps if she went to Prinny on her knees and explained about her imbecilic younger brother—

Gregory cleared his throat. "While in my cups, I may have also written a letter demanding we kill the prince regent for sponsoring the Trio."

Juliana sucked in a breath. "That is treason." He truly *would* hang. She collapsed on the edge of her bed.

"Juliana?" Gregory asked.

She had to take three breaths before she could answer. "Where are these letters?"

Gregory shook his head. "At his country estate, or so he claims. I'm supposed to declare the challenge at his house party next week."

"You know the challenge is a formality. If you contest the throne, it will go to you."

Gregory swallowed. "I know."

That explained the rather impressive list of royals and British noblemen that had been invited to the duke's house party. There would be no going back after Gregory acted.

"If I do as he says, he'll give me the papers afterward."

Yes, and she was a dairy maid.

"Surely there's someone we can tell . . ." Her words faded. Who? Sommet was one of the most powerful dukes in the country. And how could she tell anyone without explaining Gregory's part in it all? "We will go to the house party."

Gregory blinked. "You aren't going to cede the crown—"

She cut him off with a glare. "Of course not. I'm going to get the letters back so he can no longer control you."

"How? He won't listen to threats. You aren't— You aren't going to sleep with—"

She smacked him alongside his head. "I'm going to steal the letters back."

Gregory threw back his head and chortled. "You couldn't even get past Cook to steal a tart—" He quieted. "You're serious. Juliana, that is insane. You will be caught, and Sommet is not a man to cross."

"I will get them back. I swear it. And have I ever broken a promise?" She fixed a stare on her brother when he would have spoken. "Ever?"

Slowly, he shook his head.

"You will accept the duke's invitation on behalf of the royal family of Lenoria and tell him you agree to his plan. You will let him think he has won."

A crease crossed Gregory's forehead. "It might be dangerous. How do you intend to—"

But Juliana already had a plan formulating in her mind.

It would either work—or get her killed.

Chapter Five

*T*he thing Ian liked about Madeline Huntford was that she always set a good table for breakfast. None of this porridge and coddled egg nonsense. No, Maddie always had the best. Bacon, sausage, cheese, jellies.

She bounced a gurgling baby girl on her knee. Even though the little girl wasn't quite a year old, she already promised to be a raving beauty like her mother. Raven ringlets and jade green eyes. "Pay no attention to how much Uncle Ian eats, Susie. Someday he will keel over from the amount of food he shovels into his gut."

He eyed her nearly full plate. "You're one to talk."

Maddie grinned. "I'm still eating for two." Her smile faded. "You have funds, do you not? I thought Clayton—"

"I'm fine. Clayton's investments have left me with more money than I could ever spend. I'm just hungry." He was always hungry. He couldn't break himself of the fear that all this bounty would simply disappear.

"Where is your husband this morning? Out harassing good, law-unabiding criminals?" he asked.

Maddie untangled a lock of her hair from Susie's fist and addressed her daughter. "Papa liked Mama's idea that the robberies in Highgate might be linked by the locksmith that arrived to sell them new doors afterward, didn't he?" She stood and plopped the girl-creature on Ian's lap. "Watch her for a moment, so I can eat?"

This wasn't his area of expertise. The child patted his waistcoat with sticky fingers. A feeling rather akin to panic started in his chest. What if he broke her? He needed the child removed, so he smiled charmingly. "Shall I tell you the story of Buxom Betty? She was a friend of mine. She worked a brothel named— Do you know what a brothel is, little one?"

Rather than snatch the child back as he'd hoped, Maddie glared. "Do remember I once castrated a man with butter knife."

Ian shrugged and started to bounce the child, then stopped. Perhaps that was too much for a little baby. But Susie cooed and giggled so he tried it again. "Adventurous like your mama? Well, when you are older you'll have to come visit me. I will take you to all the fun areas of London your stuffy father won't allow."

"What won't Huntford allow?" a deep voice asked. "I am definitely in favor of it."

Ian turned as the last member of the Trio, Clayton Campbell, strode into the breakfast room, his elegant blond bride on his arm.

Maddie smiled. "Clayton. Olivia. What brings you here this morning?"

Olivia smiled at the other woman for a moment, but then her face creased with concern. "We were going to ask for your help finding Ian, but apparently that won't be necessary. We found something odd in the paper this morning."

"*You* found." The pride in Clayton's eyes would have been nauseating if Ian didn't take complete credit for the two of them being together. They'd been rather hopeless in St. Petersburg until Ian stepped in and gave them the nudge they needed.

But still there was only so much a man could take. Ian spoke before they could get lost in each other's eyes or some other poetic nonsense. "What did you find?"

Clayton spread a newspaper in front of him and pointed. "Here."

Ian read aloud the small advertisement. "Juliana offers information on the Trio for sale to the highest bidder. Wednesday evening. Seven o'clock. At the previous meeting place."

Olivia frowned. "It can't be *the* Trio, can it?"

Ian stared at it. What the devil was the woman playing at? The message had to be for him. But what did she want? He had spent all day yesterday confirming that, yes, she had been in Brighton as she'd claimed. Why was she inviting trouble back into her house?

Into her bedroom?

Maddie took her daughter back. "Do you understand this, Ian?

Ian stood, the anticipation in his blood banishing the rest of the effects of another poor night's sleep. "I believe a certain princess can't wait to see me again."

Chapter Six

Juliana paced the length of her room one more time, stopping at the window to survey the deepening shadows in the garden below. What if he hadn't seen her message? It was a gamble—the man might not even be able to read—but it had been the only way she could think of that might reach him. She'd no other ideas.

Well, if he didn't come, he wasn't the man she needed for the job regardless.

She turned to look at her clock again and gasped.

He was here.

Lying in her bed.

In his shirtsleeves. Looking like every naughty fantasy she'd never, ever admit to.

Her eyes darted to where his coat hung over the chair.

How had he—

She hadn't been looking out the window for that—

But she had a more pressing concern. "What are you doing in my bed?"

He lifted a lazy eyebrow, the rugged planes of his face merry with amusement. At her expense. "Isn't this why you invited me?"

"I—"

"Don't worry, most women can't resist me. Though a princess is a first. I bedded a royal duchess once but never—"

"Out." This had been a foolish plan from the start. She knew nothing about him. Not even his name. If she'd gotten the impression that there was something noble lurking beneath his surface, she must have been blind. The man was a miscreant.

"Then I must ask, why do you want me here?" He stood, but prowled closer. So close in fact that she could smell him, a hint of mint and ginger. "I must say I was thankful for all the fellows you had watching for me. I needed a good laugh. Hired extra guards for the occasion?"

She had, actually. She backed up until the silk wallpaper was pressed against her back.

His gaze was so intense she couldn't remember how to breathe. "Was it a trap, Jules?"

Why did that nickname shiver down her spine? She was a princess. She didn't have nicknames.

He raised his hand, caressing her throat, but somehow she knew he could strangle her before she could even scream.

"It was a test." He shouldn't have been able to get in. A servant had been assigned to watch each window. She'd purposefully chosen a time when it was still light out. She had two soldiers planted in the corridor outside her room.

"Did I pass?"

She nodded.

His index finger slid over her bottom lip. She wanted to slap him away. *No one* had ever touched her lips.

That was a rather depressing thought, actually.

His finger paused in the center, dragging her lip down slightly. "So what do I win?"

His eyes mocked her, yet she couldn't look away. She cleared her throat. "How did you get in?"

He shook his head. "It is my turn to ask questions. What do you want, Cinderella?"

"I want to hire you."

"Hire me? For what? Do you need help getting to a ball?"

"Among other things."

His brows drew together at that. "Pardon? That was intended as a joke."

"There will probably be a ball at the house party. I haven't checked. But I need to retrieve something from someone."

He stepped back, and she could suddenly breathe. "You want me to steal something."

"No, I want you to teach *me* how to do it." She'd thought hard about it and she couldn't risk someone else getting ahold of the letters. Then they'd be no better off than they'd been with Sommet.

"My skills are a bit more complex than Latin

conjugations. They aren't something you can pick up in a few hours."

He was going to refuse her.

She couldn't allow that. "I can learn."

He plucked at a bit of lace on her bodice, then flicked at a pearl bob on her ear. "I can see you're made for a life of crime."

"Do not mock me."

He grinned. "Or what? You'll embroider me to death? I seem to recall that your punches were ineffective."

"If you agree to help me, I will give you the name of the man who betrayed your friends."

That silenced him. A cold gleam lit his eye. It obliterated his humor so completely she had to wonder which was his true self.

"You told me you didn't know."

She was a princess. She would not quake. "I didn't then. I do now."

"Then perhaps I'll go find the answer myself."

She couldn't let him learn about Gregory. "I can show you the one truly responsible, not the misguided, confused imbecile that might be connected to my household."

"And why do you think I won't just carve the answers from you?"

That was a very, very good question. A flicker of apprehension licked up her spine. But she lifted her chin. "Because a business deal is far less messy for the both of us."

"Messy?" That brought a quirk back to his lips. "If there's one thing that describes me, it's fastidious. One of the main characteristics of the gutters. What do you want of me?"

"I have two requirements."

"Oh, do tell." He waved his hand in an exaggerated motion for her to proceed.

She clenched her teeth together. "First, you will teach me how to retrieve certain documents without being seen. Second, you'll agree not to harm the person responsible in my household. You will only pursue the true culprit."

"So I let your . . ." He studied her for a moment, then lifted his brow. "Your brother. Your brother, the debauched and foppish Prince Gregory, go unpunished."

"He isn't debauched—"

"Ah, so it was him. I think I'll pay him a visit."

How could she be such a blind fool? He'd been leading her on. And she'd fallen for it.

His head tilted as he watched her. "Don't feel bad for telling me. I'm a professional." He strode toward her bedroom door, but she lunged in front of him.

"He isn't here."

"Do you really think it will prove difficult for me to find him?"

He brushed past her.

"There are guards in the corridor." She hated that her voice was so desperate.

"Really?" He opened the door and stuck his head out. "Hello? Soldiers?"

"What did you do to them?"

He shrugged.

"If you have hurt them—"

His gaze swept her again, surprised, and she felt utterly naked. Vulnerable. "They are unharmed."

Her breath escaped in a rush, but she still couldn't let him leave. Not if she wanted Gregory to go the night without a knife in his back.

"Good-bye, Jules."

She grabbed him around the waist and yanked him back into the room with all her strength. She must have caught him off guard because he stumbled back, falling on top of her.

She couldn't help the small *eep* of pain that escaped; neither could she breathe. She struggled to pull in air. She would *not* suffocate on the floor of her bedroom. That wasn't a dignified death for a princess.

He rolled off her. "What the devil was that?" He scowled. "Are you hurt?" He swore and lifted her into his arms as if she was nothing more than a child. He laid her gently on her bed, the mattress creaking as he sat on the edge next to her. He ran his hands over her ribs, then leaned back. "You're fine. Slowly suck air in. Slow. You've just had the wind knocked out of you."

She wasn't so sure he hadn't broken all her ribs, but she obeyed and, finally, managed a lungful of air. Who would have known he could weigh so much? But then remembering his hard muscles, she shouldn't have been surprised.

"Hell's bells but you're batty." His handsome face seemed pained. But she couldn't have hurt him that much, after all he landed on top of *her*.

"You cannot go. I need you."

His finger traced the edge of her bodice, his lids hooding his eyes. "Darling, many women do."

"*Argh!*" she screeched at him. Actually screeched. It was the most unladylike sound she'd ever made. And why was her skin on fire where he'd touched? "If you help me, I can give you the man responsible for betraying your friends. In a week, I can get you into his house."

Her spy's finger dipped into the hollow above her collarbone. "I can get into any house I desire. And why are you still breathing so hard, Princess?"

He had to be the most arrogant, insufferable beast she'd ever met. She caught his hand as it wandered again toward her bodice and sat up despite her aching ribs. "I can get you there without any skulking. You can walk in openly and have as much time as you need." She shouldn't have sat up. Now her lips were inches from his. Heavens, but he had beautiful lips.

When they weren't smirking. Which was basically never.

"Fine. You've won me over. Now tell me who it is."

"No." She wasn't a complete fool. "I will tell you after you train me."

"How do I know you aren't lying to me?"

"Because I know how fond you are of threats, and I have no desire to see if you'll follow through."

He stood so quickly that she would have fallen off the bed if he hadn't caught her shoulder. "Done. I'll give you a week's worth of training. But I am not responsible for your success."

"Agreed."

She swung her feet over the edge of the bed. "So what are we going to—"

"Tomorrow night." The hand on her shoulder skimmed up to catch her chin. "Rest when you can in the daylight because for the next week, Princess, your nights are mine."

Chapter Seven

Ian paused in the alley, letting his head rest against the bricks. If he'd stayed in that room for one more moment, he would have stripped that blasted, starchy dress from her body.

After his blood finally cooled, he chuckled. She'd tackled him. The princess had just wrestled a gutter rat.

The night was still warm, so he removed his coat and slung it over his shoulder. What could she want so badly that she'd fall to larceny to retrieve it? Letters to a lover perhaps?

The smile disappeared from his mouth.

He walked back to the opening of the alley where he could see the princess's home. After a few minutes, a group of guards walked out. Their shift was over right on schedule. Jules might be worried about security, but she wasn't forcing her soldiers—and he used that term loosely—to work extra hours or double shifts.

Perfect.

Ian followed them to a tavern a few blocks away.

He watched from the shadows as the men drank one round and then another.

One of the guards stood up and left. After another round, two more retired. Good. Those would be the men with families or the more responsible fellows. They were of no use to him.

Soon there were just three.

Light pockets. Drunk. Full of useful information. That was Ian's cue.

He strolled in, tossing his hat onto the table. "A round for all. Lady Luck's been on my side." He plopped down at the table with the soldiers, keeping his posture loose and relaxed.

One of the guards clapped him on the back. "What's your game?"

Ian pulled a card from his pocket and flicked it into the man's empty mug. "That, my friends, is an angel in disguise." He blinked at the men around him. "What regiment are you boys in? The Ninety-fifth?"

The gangly lad straightened. "We're not British. We are Lenorian. The Royal Lenorian Guard."

Ian scratched his stomach. "Is that a bank?"

They looked at each other, aghast. "Lenoria is the most beautiful country in Europe."

"With the most beautiful princess!" the ruddy-faced one shouted, lifting his mug. "Our sacred duty!"

"You guard a princess?" Ian found he was having difficulty feigning sufficient admiration.

These were the imbeciles that had allowed *him* into the house, after all.

"To Juliana!" the three cheered.

"She's pretty then?" Ian asked.

The guards practically shoved each other off the bench in their eagerness to deliver the most praise. Apparently, she was beautiful, graceful, kind, benevolent, wise . . .

None of them had named her stubborn, feisty, or bewilderingly intriguing. Ian felt charitable toward the drunkards once again.

Soon with a few gentle prompts, he had a much clearer view of the occupants of the castle. Eustace was a stickler for propriety and spent all her time at a charity hospital, but she was quick to defend her sisters, niece, and nephew. Constantina was flighty and temperamental, but easily swayed. It was Leucretia, the eldest, who held the real power. The soldiers said her name with a rather reverent awe. Cynical, jaded, and with an epic list of lovers, she was the one who'd guided Juliana into becoming a plausible ruler.

"And this prince you mentioned?" They actually hadn't, but they were too foxed to keep track.

"To Prince Gregory!" The guards toasted again.

His list of adjectives was far different from his sister's. Bold, dashing, fiery, capable of holding his drink, a dab hand at cards, a champion with the ladies.

By the time Ian sauntered out fifteen minutes

later, his suspicion about the identity of the guilty party was confirmed.

He still had a dozen more questions, but he knew to end the interrogation long before anyone realized they were being interrogated.

He might have promised not to hurt the young princeling, but one of the joys of not having any honor was that he didn't feel obligated to keep every promise he made. Promises were a way to make the other party feel enough at ease to give him what he needed.

But for tonight at least, the prince would continue to breathe.

Ian stopped in a dark alley and nudged a pile of rags with his toe. Two sleepy eyes blinked up at him. "What news, Conelly?" Ian asked.

"Wraith?" The old man held out a hand, and Ian's copper disappeared into the folds of the man's filthy jacket. "Ain't heard nothing of interest. Been a few flower girls disappearing over by the theater. Got the doves all in a twitter. Only the little ones been missing."

Icy anticipation filled him. These were his streets. And someone was about to learn that fact. "Any word who's been collecting young ones?"

"Nah, but the beaks raided a nanny house few nights back. Could be they was looking for them girls, too."

If Gabriel Huntford and his Runners were raiding brothels, there was a chance he knew something. But Ian wasn't in a mood to wait until morning. Besides, he had his own ways of finding things out.

By the time Ian made it to the docks, he'd spoken to four more of his *associates* and knew who'd been taking the girls.

Ten minutes later he was standing over the unconscious man, knife in hand. Blood trickled from a cut on the man's face and from the other various cuts to his body.

Ian was quite content to report the owner of this disgusting bawdy house would never reproduce.

Ian bound and gagged the man—or half a man—and wiped his blade on the fellow's coat. If he survived the night, Gabriel and the Runners would find him the morning.

Ian rather hoped they didn't.

A corridor led to the back of the building. Ian pulled his picks from his sleeve. It only took an instant to open the locked door.

The room was too dark to see anything, but the smell was unmistakable. Sweat, vomit, sex. After a moment, he could see six children huddled on lumpy mattresses on the floor. Five girls and a boy.

Hell.

He kept his voice light. "I'm the Pied Piper here to lead you all to safety."

For a moment, none of the children moved.

"Didn't those children never return?"

Ian tried to figure out who had spoken.

"Where I take you can't be any worse than here, can it?"

One of the girls stood; she was the same one who'd just spoken. "I'll go." She couldn't have been more than eleven. She would have been pretty, too, if it wasn't for her black eye.

"What is your name?"

"Apple, sir."

"Good for you, Apple. Who else?"

Slowly the others grouped around her.

He led them past their bleeding captor and out into the street. Most of the children skirted around widely but Apple paused to kick the bound man.

He liked this one.

But as soon as they were outside, Apple bolted, scampering off down the street and around the corner. *Damnation.* He couldn't give chase or he'd risk losing the others.

Feeling rather like the Pied Piper he'd claimed to be, he led them to the house run by three good Quaker women. Though wakened from bed, the women quickly ushered the children inside. They gave orders to the servants to see the children cleaned, fed, and placed into beds.

Ian watched the familiar process with a tired eye. "How many stayed from the last group?"

"Two." Sister Jane said, her round, cheerful face somber.

Ian had sent five. But he couldn't blame the children for not wanting help. They knew better than to trust adults. And for most, life on the street was all they ever knew. They wouldn't like the structure and austerity demanded by the Quakers.

Ian wouldn't have stayed.

In fact, he would have eaten the hot meal and left before the dishes were cleared. Probably would have left *with* the dishes.

Sister Jane accepted Ian's heavy purse with only minimal protests.

"There might be one more if I can find her."

"She's welcome if she'll come."

Ian nodded and headed back onto the street. It took him a good deal longer to find Apple than he anticipated. She was small so he knew she would have learned to hide to survive rather than run. Luckily, Ian knew every hidey-hole and crevice in this neighborhood.

He eventually found her at a much higher altitude than he expected—balanced in the eaves of a rotting warehouse.

The girl was a climber. If he'd met her twenty years ago, he would have recruited her as a budge to scout good targets for his pickpockets.

He dodged the chunk of wood she hurled at his head. "I'm not trading one gent for another."

"Good. I don't want you."

The shower of projectiles stopped. "Then why are you here?"

"To offer you a place to stay."

"In your bed?"

Ian dusted off his jacket. "I could have spent the night with a princess. I don't want a half-grown runt with fleas."

She snorted. "A princess. Was she a fairy, too? Have a throne of gold?"

"Not a fairy. And I didn't get to see her throne, but I hear it is made of mahogany."

"You're bamming me."

"No."

Apple's dark head peered down at him. "She live in a castle then?"

"No. A house in Mayfair. Someone burned down her castle."

"I wouldn't believe her then. Sounds like she's putting one over on you." She was silent for a moment. "No princess would want anything to do with us."

Wasn't that the truth. And even though Ian was dressed rather well, Apple recognized him as a kindred spirit all too easily.

"What'd you do with the others?" she asked.

"I took them to the Quakers on Mill Street."

Apple snorted. "Now I know you are bamming me. That's just a story."

"They'll give you a place to stay, food, and teach you to read if you want it."

"And a jeweled crown and a pony?"

"More like a hot bucket of water to wash in and a bowl of porridge. I already spoke to them. They said they have a place for you if you want it."

Apple was silent.

"Go and watch them yourself. If you like what you see, go in. If not, don't."

"Who are you? A charley?"

"I'm Wraith." Unlike the other members of the Trio who'd chosen their identities after they'd become spies, Ian had been using his for years.

She sucked in a breath. "You're no more real than yer princess. Is it true you waltzed right out of gaol at noon wearing the gaoler's hat?"

Ah, he was glad that story had survived. It had been one of his finer moments. "And his watch."

"But you were just a story. You were gone. Where were you?"

"Hell."

She accepted that far easier than she had his claim of a princess. "Why were you daft enough to come back?"

It was a valid question, but one he didn't have a good answer for. He could have gone anywhere in the world. Yet he'd come back here. To the stews of London. To the stink. To the filth.

"Perhaps because it's where I belong." He might belong to these streets, but he didn't want anyone else to be condemned here.

She inched closer, scaring a roosting pigeon into flight. "Why did you come look for *me*?"

That was also good question. Perhaps because a stodgy old butler had once come to look for him. Ian had laughed at Canterbury's offer of help. He'd been addicted to the occasional riches of thievery, the danger, the freedom.

Instead, he told her, "You talk too much to survive on these streets. Take my suggestion or don't."

"You're not going to force me?" Apple asked cautiously.

"No. I'm giving you an opportunity. You can choose a clean sheet and tough schooling or you can choose to live in the pigeon scat."

Then Ian turned and walked out. If he tried to chase her, she'd be gone. This would have to be up to her.

He had no idea whether she'd agree or not. After all, he'd been too much of a coward to accept his one chance at salvation.

Chapter Eight

"*I* may need more pin money." Constantina made her announcement before Juliana had even made it through the door of the breakfast parlor.

"That isn't possible." Juliana accepted a plate from a footman.

Constantina's bottom lip thrust out. "Leucretia has a new brooch."

"She also doesn't bet her pin money on card games," Eustace reminded her, reaching for the jam. But Constantina grabbed the spoon first.

Juliana took a piece of toast. "We will be going to the Duke of Sommet's house party next week."

Her great aunts stopped bickering over the jam and stared.

"Did you change your mind about Prince Wilhelm?" Constantina asked.

"I cannot afford to pass up any opportunities at this point, can I?"

Eustace nodded. "Quite right."

Leucretia had acquired the jam while the other

two were distracted and scooped some onto the side of her plate. "Why the change?"

She'd known Leucretia would ask. "I spoke with Gregory last night. He says Prince Wilhelm might have more to recommend him than I thought."

Leucretia lifted a brow, but seemed to accept it. "The Spanish ambassador requested an audience with you."

"No."

Leucretia frowned. "I already accepted. You cannot simply ignore the man and hope he goes away."

That was exactly what she'd planned to do. "What time?"

"Noon. That should allow you enough time before you meet with the Lenorian cabinet at two."

Juliana would be happy when she only had one government to deal with. Her cabinet here corresponded with their counterparts in Lenoria, leaving her with far too many people to keep happy.

"What do I tell the ambassador? I won't sign the treaty."

Leucretia clicked her tongue. "You must give him the impression you are considering it, otherwise you risk the Spanish growing impatient."

Her aunt was right. As always. "How am I to do that?"

"Flirt. Flatter. Make empty promises—" Her aunt stopped abruptly. "Perhaps I should join you."

"She shouldn't have to simper," Eustace protested.

Leucretia dabbed at her ruby lips with her napkin. "We're talking about the survival of Lenoria, she will do whatever is best."

Constantina clapped her hands together. "I can flirt."

Leucretia gave her a disgusted look. "We are trying to stop a war not start one."

When the three of them began arguing, Juliana slipped from the breakfast parlor.

"Your Highness?" Her secretary, Renner, approached. She'd long suspected he laid in wait for her, like a hungry tiger. Or perhaps a hungry stork.

Her hope to escape to her room for a few moments evaporated.

"I have sent your acceptance of the invitation to the duke's house party. And here are the lists of Prince Gregory's financials." She took the folder of papers.

Juliana entered her study. He followed, his nervous motions making her long to grab his shoulder so he'd stay still for a single moment.

"Here are the letters containing urgent business." He handed her a stack of about ten papers. "These ones contain useful information, but are not vital." The stack was about twice as tall.

She'd barely managed to set them on the desk when her housekeeper entered. "Your Highness, I have the final seating arrangement for tonight's state dinner ready for your approval."

Renner's nostrils flared. "You'll have to take care of this later. Her Highness is busy."

Her housekeeper planted her fist on her hips jingling the ring of keys at her waist. "Well, the table will not set itself. And the Marquess of Hastings sent his regrets this morning, so that will cause some changes. I need to know if Lady Rinatta should be moved between Lord Malcome and Sir Ulef, or if she'd be better off by the Russian attaché?"

The last thing Juliana needed was more bickering this morning. She'd been plagued with dreams of a handsome spy watching her undress, but then he'd done far more than watch her. He'd reached out and—

She cleared her throat. "I will get to you shortly." She used her most regal tone.

Both servants regarded her hopefully.

"Later. I have some things I must attend to. Alone," she added for emphasis.

They bowed and backed from the room.

After a quick glance about, she opened her drawer. She just needed a little break. Something to take her mind off of the mess she'd gotten herself into with the spy. And her meeting with the Spanish ambassador. And the fact that her seventy-year-old aunt could flirt better than she could.

She pulled out the hat.

She was half done attaching the new trim. Periwinkle.

Her one secret. She made her own bonnets, and her aunts were none the wiser. Ha!

Yes, she was rebellious to the core.

But the small stitches soothed her. This new bonnet would mean a few pounds that could go to her subjects and not into her wardrobe. And someone had complimented the flowers on her coal scoop bonnet last week. Of course, it had been a rather foolish young lord who had called Leucretia's lips *rubious*. But Juliana would take what support she could get.

A knock sounded at her door.

She jammed the hat back into the drawer. "Come."

No one entered.

She was sure she hadn't imagined it. "Come in."

When no one responded, she stood and walked to the door. She peered out into the corridor. No one was there.

Juliana returned to her desk.

She blinked.

There was a red rose in the center of it. A card was attached to the rose. She glanced around the room. "Where are you?"

But her spy was no longer there.

Her spy? Why was he hers? She didn't even want him for anything but this one task.

Yet when she picked up the card, her fingers were weak and unsteady. It contained only one line.

Counting the minutes?

Chapter Nine

"What precisely are you wearing?" Juliana's spy asked from where he'd suddenly appeared in her doorway.

She glared at him, looking up from the hat she was working on. She'd been rather proud that she'd managed to find a pair of trousers with no one the wiser. And she'd managed to secure it between seven different audiences. Tea with the prime minister. And a dinner meant to honor Lenoria's annual grain harvest.

"Were you planning to scale the outside of the building? Swing in through the window?" he asked.

Perhaps. But now that he said it in that tone, she rather suspected that wasn't what he had in mind.

"Sorry, Jules, there's no way you could master that in a week. Can you even manage to climb to the top of your canopy bed?"

Insufferable man. "I could climb to the top of the bed."

"Oh really? Do it."

Why had she allowed herself to be baited?

"Take hold of the bar holding your curtain and pull yourself up. I'll even let you start with your feet on the bed," he said.

She climbed up on the bed, surprised at how unstable it was. She'd never stood on one before, but she doubted he would value that excuse.

She gripped the iron with both hands and pulled.

Her feet didn't leave the coverlet.

"Perhaps if you jump?"

She gracefully lowered herself off the bed. "You'd like that, wouldn't you?"

His gaze slowly traveled down her body. "Yes, I rather think I would."

It had seemed like a good idea to leave her stays off when she dressed for this. Now she crossed her arms. "What *is* your name?"

"So you can write my execution orders?"

"No, so I can call you something other than a smug buffoon!" She placed her hand over her mouth. Had she truly just called him that aloud?

He looked more bemused than offended. "Most call me Wraith."

"Is that your name?"

"It is what I am called."

"Well then, Wraith. Let's see you do it."

"Do what?"

"Climb to the top of my—"

He jumped from the floor, grabbed the bar, swung his body up and around it, and perched in the space near the ceiling like a gargoyle. "Bed?" he finished.

"I hate you."

"Good. I'm not precisely a fellow you should be fond of." He swung off the bed and landed inches from her. "The other street urchins would mock me mercilessly." He reached out and pulled the hem of her shirt lose from her trousers.

She stumbled back, her heart hammering. "What do you think you are doing?"

He didn't even look distracted. "I have given this a good deal of thought. There are many methods of thievery. I think your best option will be to brazen it out."

"What does that mean?"

"You simply walk into the room where the documents are being held."

"That is insane." Obviously, she shouldn't have relied on him. That was worse than any plan she could have made on her own.

"It works far better than you think. My job for the next week will be to teach you not to betray yourself. And how to pick any locks you might encounter."

"Wouldn't it be better if I dressed as a maid and—"

"How will you explain why you're dressed as a maid if you're caught?"

"I don't think—"

"That's exactly it. You don't think." He leaned against her bedpost. "At least not like a criminal. You think like someone who wants to pretend to be a criminal. Two vastly different things."

He might have a point. She'd seen plenty of people ape being a princess and she didn't look a thing like that. At least she hoped not.

"I want you to put on the exact dress you will wear the night you plan to retrieve the letters."

"I have no idea what I will be wearing."

"Pick one."

"It isn't that simple."

"It is. You're a princess. Simply order your servant to bring you a certain dress."

He thought *she* was naive. "It will be a house party. There will be a dozen variables. The venue of the meal, the color of the hostess's gown, the color of my escort's waistcoat, whether there will be dancing afterward."

He shrugged, an elegant motion that brought her eyes back to the broad strength of his shoulders. "Then pick the worst possible one you could be wearing."

She sorted through all her dresses in her mind. "Fine." She made it as far as her dressing room before she stopped. "I won't be able to get into the dress on my own. And I can hardly call my maid in to help."

"I'll help."

Why that— "*Lecher!*" She hissed. Was that why

he'd asked her to change her clothing? "You already saw me nearly nude. Wasn't that enough?"

His drawl was like satin over her skin. "Not nearly."

She threw her slipper at him. "Well, it's all you're going to get."

He prowled closer. "So you're going to tell your maid you've decided to sleep in your clothes every night? Prudery is one of the first things that need to go when someone embarks on a life of crime."

She wanted to clear that smug look from his handsome face. "You're right."

He paused. "I am?"

"Yes, but I warn you, I'm completely naked under this." She reached up and slowly untied the bow that held the shirt closed at the top. It fell open, resting on the swells of her breasts. She took a deep breath, causing it to slip even further.

"Does it always take you this long to get undressed? No wonder you need a maid."

Oh!

Juliana stepped into her dressing room and out of sight before she tugged off the rest of her clothing.

Ian was going to go mad. It was as simple as that. That had been a juvenile taunt, but his other option had been to take her royal virginity against the wall.

Damn, but she was rather glorious when she was flustered.

Even more so when she was angry.

In the throes of passion she must be—

"Are you all right?" Juliana called out. "Did you just groan?"

Certainly not.

She emerged a few minutes later completely swathed in a white linen night rail.

Her full lips tilted like a cat's. "I'll take the letters at night. So this is what I'll be wearing."

She looked so thoroughly pleased with herself that he didn't have the heart to tell her that the best time to steal the letters would be in the day.

He'd let her think she'd won that one.

He pulled his picks from his sleeve. "Shall we start with the locks?"

She nodded.

He knelt at her bedroom door and removed the key protruding from the lock. She crouched beside him, so close he could smell the faint scent of roses on her skin. For an instant, he could think of nothing but lying her down on a bed covered with rose petals, of letting them drift over the curves of her body and settle onto the hollows.

Roses. That was rich. He was lucky if the beds he slept in didn't have bugs.

"So inside this type of lock, there are a set of levers to prevent the bolt from sliding. What a key does is align those levers to the right height so the bolt can slide. Too high or too low and this lady doesn't open."

"Locks are female?"

"Damned finicky things needing to be held just right in order to be able to open."

"They seem rather male to me. They just need a quick twist and they're done."

He nearly dropped his pick. "I see I'm a wicked, wicked influence on you."

Her lips nearly brushed his ear. "Don't give yourself too much credit."

Ian showed her the process twice more. Then had her put her hands over his as he worked on the lock to gain a feel for gauging the tension and selecting the right pick. Only years of practice kept his hands from shaking.

He pulled his hands away. "Your turn."

She accepted the tools from him and lowered her brows in concentration.

"It will probably take a long time to master—"

The lock clicked open under her hands.

"—how to do this. Never mind. Apparently you have more of a talent for crime than I anticipated."

She beamed like a child just given a new treat. "What else can you teach me?"

Chapter Ten

$\mathcal{J}$uliana had mastered the locks by the end of the second night. After learning the door locks Ian had supplied, the small locks on the desks and cabinets had been simple. It was all a matter of patience, and one thing a princess learned at young age was patience.

She was feeling rather proud of herself at the start on their third training session. And giddy. Oh, she knew better than to feel that way. This was a serious endeavor. Her whole country could hang in the balance.

But these past few days had been fun.

She couldn't honestly remember the last time she'd had fun.

She perched on the chair by her window and watched her room. She'd catch Wraith this time when he entered. She'd stacked glasses in front of her doors that would create a clatter if he entered that way. She sat by one window and could clearly see the other.

A horse clattered by below, she only glanced at it

for a fraction of a second, but then Ian was there. Three feet from her, twirling one of her glasses in his fingers. "This was a nice touch. Truly original."

She checked for mockery in his face.

He lifted a brow. "I did mean that."

"Good. I thought it was a clever idea."

He set the glass on the windowsill next to her. "You, Jules, are becoming more and more unprincesslike every day. Quite a disturbing trend."

"I could issue a royal decree if that would make you feel better?"

"Yes, that would actually."

"Would you honor it?"

"Of course."

"Then I decree all spies must reveal their true names to the princess."

He handed her a disassembled lock from his coat and his picks. "Wait," he said when she would have started. He circled the room extinguishing all the candles. "Now go."

She slowly tried picks in the lock one at a time until she found one that was the correct size. "You won't distract me that easily. You owe me your name."

"I granted you a royal decree and the only thing you want is my name?"

The bolt slid open in her hand. "Yes."

He stared at her for a long moment. Only the silvery light from the moon illuminated his face. The scar on his cheek seemed to stand out in sharper contrast. And, for the first time, she noticed lines of exhaustion around his eye.

She longed to trace those lines, but she knew as soon as she did, this quiet moment would be over. He'd make some ribald comment, his smirk would return, and she'd have to respond in kind, as if her heart wasn't beating so hard it hurt. As if her skin didn't feel itchy and too tight.

"Ian," he said.

"Ian." She tested the name. It fit him. Simple, yet not plain. "And your last name?"

"Doesn't matter. It's not mine. It's simply one I picked for the sake of having one."

"But everyone has a last name."

He took the lock from her hand. "In your world, Princess, not in mine."

He was putting distance between them. A process she was far too familiar with. People who kept a respectful distance when they found out who she was. All the bowing. The constant overpoliteness.

Ian had never done any of those things and she didn't want him to start.

"I'm from places fouler than the mud on your shoe," he said. "So foul, in fact, the filth wouldn't even dream of aspiring to be the mud on your shoe."

"You aren't mud. You're a spy."

"Some might argue they're the same thing. Besides, I *was* a spy. I'm currently between positions."

"You are not between positions. If you need money, I can pay you to teach me."

"Ah." He smiled slowly. "Let's not bring money into our relationship. Just a good old-fashioned *exchange of services.*"

Sweet mercy, he made it all sound perfectly wicked.

"Definitely time to move on to our next lesson," Ian said, pointing to the lock in her hand.

She blinked at his abrupt change in topic. "What is it?"

"Over here, Princess." He laced her fingers though his.

She sucked in a breath. Princesses didn't hold hands. Oh, they touched people. She held men's arms. She placed her fingers on men's hands to be kissed. But Ian's fingers tangled with hers, more secure and more tantalizing than she would have imagined.

His fingers were strong and callused to the point of being rough. She'd never had cause to be embarrassed by the smoothness of her hands, but she couldn't help a brief worry that he'd think her soft and useless by comparison.

He led her in front of her dressing table and sat her in the chair. He lit a candle and placed it next to her.

When she tried to turn her head to see him better, he stood behind her and placed his hands on either side of her face, stopping her. "Look at yourself in the mirror."

"I know what I look like."

"You only think you do. Your face gives away every single thing you are feeling."

"No, it does not." She happened to have perfected a stoic, regal demeanor.

Ian lifted a brow. "Does too. Now watch." He caught her face again. "Watch yourself. Not me." His hands skimmed down the sides of her neck. "You are flushing. All delicate and pink."

"I am not—" But she was. She could see it.

His hands continued their stroking. "Your eyelids are heavy. Your eyes dilated."

They were. "I hardly think people are going to be . . . stroking me when I go to retrieve the letters."

He paused and she met his eyes in the mirror. "Shall I use my words instead?"

"*Yes*." Before she embarrassed herself by moaning.

He removed his hands. "Shall I tell you how your night rail taunts me? I have seen women all over Europe in every state of undress. Women from the Orient in silken wisps designed to tempt a man to madness. But this plain linen gown haunts my very dreams until I fight going to sleep each night because I know what my dreams will bring. Dreams of lowering my mouth to your breasts. Of laving your tight nipple through the thin fabric. But what truly torments me is that I know no matter how vivid the dreams, they will never compare with the reality."

Juliana ached. She'd never ached so much in her

entire life. She wanted him to soothe it. She wanted him to lower his hands and—

"See, Princess? Everything shows in your face." Ian stepped away from her chair, grinning. "If someone can read your face, they can tap into your fears. Or your desires. They can twist you any which way they choose.

The air slowly escaped her lungs.

He hadn't meant any of it. She'd nearly offered up her breasts for his sampling and he'd never meant a word. What had she been thinking? Even if he had meant what he said, she couldn't give herself to anyone but her future husband. All the royal families she would potentially marry into would expect it. Some even would demand it be verified.

Ian was simply a pleasant aberration. She'd learn from him, treasure the respite, but nothing more.

"I'm glad you have decided to keep your distance. I have far too many women to keep track of already, and I suspect princesses are difficult to maintain."

Her eyes flew to his.

"All on your face."

That did it. "Teach me how to hide it."

It felt a bit like Juliana was asking him to break a stained glass window. This had always been his reason behind that little demonstration.

Or at least had been his intention at first.

But watching her desire for him play across her

face was the most arousing thing he'd ever been cursed enough to witness.

Thankfully, he'd also witnessed her decision to relegate him back to the rubbish heap where he belonged.

Wise woman.

"The first step is to slow your breathing."

She sucked in a long breath.

"Not so much that it is noticeable. Just a fraction slower. Fear, anger, passion. All of those will change your breathing. By controlling your breathing, you can fool your body."

Her next inhale was smoother.

"Now look back in the mirror. Only a fool would be as awkward as you appear to be."

Hurt flashed across her face.

"Freeze. Do not move a muscle." He pointed to where her brows had drawn together in her forehead. "Emotion first comes out through the eyes and eyebrows. Keep them still." He tapped the groove that had formed between them. "Relax this."

And do it quickly.

The hurt on her face was making him feel rather unsettled.

The change in her breathing was subtle this time. Only someone trained to look for it would notice. The tension left her forehead.

Why did he care so much that it left her mind as well? "For the record, you're rather quick at picking up all of this."

Her eyebrows started to lift in pleased surprise, but then they smoothed and lowered back into a neutral position.

"Very nice. I might make a proper spy out of you after all."

This time, her eyes gave nothing away at all.

Robbed. It was if he'd just discovered his purse had been lifted.

And he knew the response well. He'd stolen many a purse.

But he'd been schooled by a much harsher master, so he knew his face showed none of that, either. "You will want to keep as much of your face relaxed as possible. And whatever you do, don't try to smile. A false smile is one of the easiest things to spot."

"I think I've got it."

"Shall we test it?"

She nodded.

"When I was seven years old, my father died."

No response from her. Good.

"He was a barrister with cases all over England. Or at least that is how he explained why he was so often absent. When we received word that he was dead, it tore my mother apart. But she consoled herself that at least we'd be taken care of. My father hadn't lacked funds."

Her hands tightened on the table in front of her. He'd have to work on that tomorrow.

"But then she found out the truth. She wasn't

truly his wife. Or at least not his legal one. He had
another family tucked away."

She bit the inside of her cheek.

Hell, why was he telling her this? No one knew
this but that damned butler. He could have invented
a story just as easily. Why had he chosen the truth?

"My mother was nothing more than a bigamist
in the eyes of the law. The first wife, of course, refused to pay her anything. We had no money to pay
for the house or the servants. Or even food eventually for that matter. A few weeks later, she packed
our few remaining things. She had me wait in the
entry hall."

Juliana had begun shaking. Or was that him?

"I waited for her for over an hour before the
butler went up to check on her. She'd blown her
brains out."

Juliana gasped and turned to him. She reached
for him but he stepped out of reach.

"Ah-ah, Princess. No reaction, remember?"

"To hell with no reaction." She walked to him
and cupped his face.

He focused on a spot past her shoulder so she
couldn't see into his eyes. Gads, some teacher he
was. He was practically bawling like an infant.

"What did you do?" she asked.

"Took care of myself." Canterbury had tried to
watch after him. But even at seven, Ian had known
Canterbury would never find a position with a
child in tow. And Ian wanted no reminder of what

he'd just lost. "But once again you've allowed me to manipulate you."

"Perhaps I don't care."

"Perhaps what I told you is all a lie."

Her hand dropped away. "It wasn't."

But there was a hint of uncertainty in her face.

"I told you I was good at this, didn't I?"

"No." She sounded more certain this time. "It was the truth."

"And how do you know that?"

"You wouldn't meet my eyes. That is one of your signs, isn't it?"

"Or did I fake one of my signs to trick you?"

She forgot to school her own face and her determination was unmistakable. The clenching of her jaw, the slight narrowing of her eyes. "I am a princess. I believe what I choose to believe."

He tapped her on the nose. "Good for you. Next test." Ian peeled off his coat, then his waistcoat, and finally his shirt.

Ian knew he had a rather fine body, but his innocent little princess looked as if she would devour him bite by bite.

"Your face, Your Highness," he reminded her before the hunger in her gaze caused him to do something rash. This was supposed to have been a test for her, not for him. He'd thought to tease her a bit. This, he supposed, was his punishment for that conceit.

She almost succeeded in banishing the lust from

her gaze. But not from the way her body angled toward him. And the way her breasts had tightened in that accused garment.

Ian strode over to the bellpull and gave it a firm tug before flopping in her bed.

"What—what are you doing?"

"You need to be able to talk yourself out of the situation if you get caught retrieving the letters."

"If my maid finds a half-naked man in my bed—"

"Talk yourself out of this."

"But you haven't taught me what to do."

"So don't open the door. Convince her you pulled the bell by accident."

By accident? Was he mad? Juliana suddenly couldn't breathe. Or was this how he sought to punish her for recognizing the truth in his story?

Her maid would be here in less than a minute. Juliana called her enough to know.

If he'd only put on his shirt she'd be able to think. Heavens, but he was delicious. Sculpted muscles and sinews. Little wonder he'd swung to the top of her bed with no effort the other night. He could probably scale a castle wall without a single drop of sweat.

Focus.

What would she say to her maid?

A knock reminded her the door was locked. "Your Highness, are you all right?" Another knock.

"Yes, Darna. I am fine."

But the doorknob rattled. "Shall I come in and straighten your sheets for you?"

Juliana had to think of something before the woman summoned help. She opened the door a crack. "I rang on accident. I had a nightmare about, um, bells. But now I'm fine." She knew she wasn't making any sense, but she couldn't keep herself from rambling.

Darna frowned. "Let me fetch you some of your aunt's sleeping tisane from your dressing room."

"It's not necessary."

But her maid had already slipped past her.

Juliana sucked in a breath to explain Ian even though she had absolutely no idea what she was going to say. "I—" She turned toward the bed.

Not even wrinkle marked where Ian had been.

Chapter Eleven

*W*ell, that had been an evening Ian didn't want soon repeated. It felt as though his innards had been twisted up in knots.

The last thing either of them needed was for him to forge any sort of lasting bonds between them.

She was a bloody princess.

There wasn't anything linking them together once this task was done. At some point, she'd grow weary of his little parlor tricks and kick his sorry arse to the gutter.

It was far better that he never give her that chance.

Four more days.

Ian kicked at a foul puddle in the street, not caring when it splattered over his boots.

A shadow scurried a little too quickly to his right.

The hilt of his knife slid smoothly into the palm of his hand.

"It's Apple," a small voice whispered. "Can I come out or are you going to gut me afore I can tell you what I came to tell you."

Ian sheathed his knife. "I thought you'd be smart enough to take the escape I gave you from all of this."

The girl stepped into the dim light; her dirty face was even filthier, her hair hanging in lank strands. "I've been scouting the place out."

The girl was clever, he'd give her that. "It's safe. You should go. Or I have rooms at The Albany. Stay there. I have no use for them."

"Me? In the bloomin' Albany? They won't let me in the coal cellar."

"If you can't find a way in, then you don't deserve to stay there. It's better than living in a rubbish heap—as you have apparently been doing."

Apple crossed her arms. "Let's see if you're still complaining after hearing what information I brung you."

"Let's hear it then."

"There's a good deal of blunt being offered for your death. Over a hundred pounds, if the stories are right."

A fortune on these streets. "Why didn't you off me? You found me easily enough."

She shrugged. "That place you rescued us from . . ." Her hands balled into fists. "I don't like owing anyone."

Hell, she might be smart enough for the streets, but nobility would get her killed just as quickly as stupidity.

"Who's offering the money?"

"Don't know. But there are two other boun-
ties being offered. One on a bloke named Cipher
and one on that light skirt Madeline Valdan what
got herself married to the Runner. They mates of
yours?"

Someone had just made a very foolish mistake.
One that would cost him his life. "No."

But Apple's eyes were far too knowing. "So you
say. But from what I hear there's many who are
mighty interested in taking that reward. I wouldn't
venture very far into the darkness. Your reputation might keep a few away but these are desperate
times and all."

Ian took his purse from his pocket and handed it
to her. "Where do the killers go to get their money
if they are successful?"

She hefted the bag. "Grimwald's tavern."

Ian knew of it. More deals were brokered there
every day than in an entire week on the Exchange.
Yet Ian had never had a reason to go there.

It was time that lapse was rectified.

If only he were the type to go in, bash some heads
together, and demand answers. Instead, Ian was
crouched in Grimwald's bedroom, waiting for
the old man to retire for the night. As soon as
Ian had delivered warnings to both Madeline and
Clayton, he'd come to the room in the back of the
tavern.

Unlike the office where the money was kept, Grimwald's private rooms had been laughably easy to enter.

A quick search of the room had given Ian everything he needed to know about Grimwald.

The man valued two things—his tavern and his grandson. Henry, by the name on the bottom of the drawing.

Juliana probably thought he'd never dream of threatening a child. She looked at him with bloody stars in her eyes. Unfortunately, he'd done far worse in his time as a spy. He'd carried out the worst jobs assigned to the Trio. He'd volunteered time and time again. He'd even done several nasty assignments he'd never told the others about.

Not that he'd enjoyed them. Slitting throats was never pleasant business. And some of the information he'd gleaned in interrogations would have been better left in the darkness.

But Madeline and Clayton had been spared.

And even after everything they had done, the other two still practically stank with goodness and nobility.

It was rather a point of pride with him that the other two managed to survive their time as spies with their humanity intact.

If his had been sacrificed, well, it was worth it.

Not that he'd actually hurt the child, but if need be, he'd threaten Grimwald with it.

However, when possible, he tried to avoid too close a kinship to the devil, so Ian finished pouring the lamp oil over the floor.

Soon enough, Grimwald opened the door and walked inside. Confusion played over the man's face as he tried to identify the smell. The moment he did, Ian lit a candle.

"Close the door."

When Grimwald hesitated, Ian lowered the candle toward the floor.

Grimwald shut the door. "What do you want?" His fleshy face was twisted in a sneer.

"Who wants Wraith dead?"

Grimwald shrugged. "No clue."

Ian lit a small puddle of oil.

"Wait!" Grimwald cried. "I don't know. He's using one of me drop boxes."

Ian stomped out the small flame. "Explain."

"I've got these boxes, and if a gent wants a job done, he puts his request in one of the boxes. When the job's done, he can put the money there for his man to pick up. Then there's no need for them to ever meet face-to-face. Safer that way."

"But someone has to buy the box."

"They only have to leave a guinea on the box and it's theirs. I mark the ones in use with a red dot. I ain't fool enough to keep all that information in me head."

The man was a genius. He must make a fortune. Ian lit another small puddle and used Grimwald's panic as a diversion as he slipped back out into the night.

Clayton and Madeline should be able take care of themselves against the riffraff that would be going after them. But as Ian well knew from the knife wound in his back, occasionally even riffraff could get lucky.

Grimwald might be useless, but Ian knew someone who would be far more informed.

His princess was finished keeping secrets.

Chapter Twelve

~~~

*J*uliana's eyes shot open. Her body flashed with the icy tingles that came from being jolted awake.

An echo rang in her ears. But as she froze in her bed, she could hear nothing. It was too dark for it to be the maids. What had she heard?

"You left your blasted cups by your window?"

Ian.

"What are you doing here?" She was too groggy to be polite, even if he looked fierce and intense and so exhausted she wanted to pull him into bed with her until morning.

"Who gave your brother the information on the Trio?"

She sat upright. "I never said it was—"

"It was rather ridiculously simply to verify."

Something in his expression made her wary. "You promised you wouldn't go after him."

"I'm here talking to you rather than him, aren't I? And you might as well drop that sheet. I see you in your night rail every night."

She *was* clutching the sheet to her chest. She let it

fall and swung her feet out over the edge of the bed. She suspected this wasn't a discussion she'd want to have lying down. "We had a deal. You train me, *then* I tell you."

"The deal is void."

His tone was so emphatic, she rather expected him to cross his arms and glower. Instead, he sank down beside her on the bed. Before she could think better of it, she scooted closer, and rested her hand on his knee. "What happened?"

He stared at her hand but didn't remove it. "Someone wants me dead. Not surprising, but they also want my friends dead. That I will not tolerate. Someone put a price on their heads tonight." His sigh was low. "Gads, but I grow weary of this."

"Who wants them dead?"

Oh.

She felt like an idiot. "Hence why you are here."

"Precisely."

"What about the papers I need to retrieve?"

"I'm sorry. I no longer have the time to play schoolmaster. Your love letters will have to wait."

She jerked her hand back. "Love letters? Is that what you think I'm doing?" She stood and walked to the window. "You aren't the only one with lives in the balance."

Ian followed her, his face cloaked in shadows. "Just tell me who betrayed their identities and I'll be on my way."

"No." She couldn't believe the word came out of her mouth.

Ian stiffened. "To which part?"

"Both." She held up a hand. "And do not growl at me. I will offer you the information you seek tonight if you will continue to help me."

"I don't like being denied, Princess." He drew his knife.

She fought to keep her face smooth as he'd taught her earlier. She really knew nothing about Ian. She suspected he was much more dangerous than he allowed her to see.

Yet somehow she knew he wouldn't hurt her.

He stepped closer to her with the knife. "Aren't you going to cower?"

She shrugged. "No."

"I'm not a good man, Princess. I've killed many, many people."

Princesses didn't back down. "But you won't kill me."

He stepped close enough that she could finally see his eyes. They were dark with something she couldn't read. He drew the hilt of the knife down her cheek. The steel was smooth and warm from his fingers. "Why would you believe that?"

"Because you're not a monster."

His laugh was sharp, bitter. "Many people would argue that point." But after a long moment he sighed and sheathed his knife. "What is this deal?"

"We're both after the same man. The man you seek is also the man who holds my documents."

"Your lover is the one who betrayed us?"

She shoved him. "Are you dense? I said it wasn't love letters. The man is blackmailing someone close to me. I need to get the evidence he holds."

If anything, his expression darkened further. "Who, Jules?"

"The Duke of Sommet."

Ian fell back a step. "Son of an eel bastard."

Ian's world tilted slightly before it righted itself.

Sommet.

Why the hell hadn't he forced her to tell him earlier? If Sommet had her papers, she took her life into her hands trying to retrieve them.

Quite literally.

There wasn't real organization within the Foreign Office, just a collection of groups run by various interests. But Sommet managed to have his web spread over all of them, pulling strings and arranging outcomes from shadows even darker than Ian's own.

It was said the prince regent didn't take a piss without Sommet's permission.

Ian may have killed dozens, but Sommet was said to have wiped out entire cities, platoons, countries.

"What the devil are you into?" he asked.

"I cannot tell you."

"Does it have to do with your fool brother?"

"It doesn't concern you." But her hesitation had been as good as a yes.

"So what is your plan then? How do you intend to get us close?"

"He's hosting a house party to which I've accepted an invitation. I had intended to leave at the end of the week. You can come along as one of my party."

"One of your servants."

Her cheeks darkened. "Unless you can think of a better option."

Ah, the refreshing sting of honesty. "No. I've always fancied being a royal footman."

"We can leave the day after tomorrow."

"Tomorrow."

"Impossible. Do you know how difficult it is to move a household of this size? The day after tomorrow will still be difficult. I have meetings that must be moved. Engagements that must be rescheduled."

"Sommet won't be surprised when you show up early?"

"His house party has already begun. But I delayed going because I want to spend as little time with the man as possible."

Ian had never been one to talk anyone out of anything. To each rat its own hole. But he found he couldn't let Jules traipse into that house. "Sommet is dangerous. He just ordered my death. You may wish to rethink trying to steal from him. It won't be easy."

"Do you truly think that will sway me?" She stalked toward him. "How did you get it in your head that my life has been easy?" She stopped inches from him.

Despite the crease along one cheek from her pillow, he still had to fight the urge to retreat.

"You of all people should know. I was twelve when *your friends* toppled my country. When the people they stirred up into a riot stormed the palace and shot my mother and father."

Ian had thought nothing of the death of another king and queen. But now— No. He wasn't about to become all maudlin and regretful. He'd done what he'd been ordered to do.

But he'd hurt *Juliana*.

That knowledge was fresh and new. And it burned as if someone had taken a hot poker to his gut.

"The only reason they didn't murder me and my brother was that they'd already set the palace on fire, and they feared for their own necks." She paused to suck in a deep breath.

Her cheeks were flushed and her eyes practically blazing. Someone should hang him for even daring to be in her presence.

"You may have been a spy, but I've spent the last twelve years ruling an entire country from half a continent away while everyone around me tries to wrest it away. So don't you *dare* speak to me about difficult."

He wanted to pull her to him. He wanted to curse her for this stranglehold she'd somehow placed on him, lashing him to her.

Instead, he applauded slowly.

The fire drained out of her, but rather than leaving her fragile, it left her tempered steel. "Sommet may have threatened your friends, but he has threatened my family and my kingdom. I will stop him."

He should walk away now. He could find out what blasted things she needed from Sommet and retrieve them himself. He didn't need her to get into Sommet's house. He'd breached far more secure strongholds.

Yet somehow, no matter his assurances of help, he doubted he'd be able to convince her to stay away. And if he couldn't keep her from danger, he was damned well going to keep close.

He bowed smartly like the servant he was about to become. "You have yourself a new footman."

Chapter Thirteen

Ian couldn't risk any of his normal haunts tonight. All of them were in places infested with blighters, letches, and muckworms.

And tonight if one of them tried to off him, he feared he'd retaliate in a rather gruesome manner.

And he was too tired for gruesome.

He found himself back at his rooms at The Albany. Yet he hesitated at the door. Damned interfering butler. Keeping a man from his own bed.

Feeling rather disgusted with himself, Ian opened the door and barely ducked in time to avoid a fireplace poker aimed at his head.

He rolled away and jumped to his feet, ready to defend himself. But a second blow never came.

"Ah, it is you, sir."

"How many of the hotel staff have you murdered, old man?"

Canterbury was dressed in a lavender banyan with a matching cream and lavender nightcap that now hung slightly askew on his head. "None, sir. They do not linger in a nefarious manner, sir."

"You could have killed me." Perhaps he should tell Canterbury about the reward. That way if he succeeded next time, someone would benefit.

"Then perhaps, sir, you shouldn't give me reason to worry over who might be looking for you."

This was what came of having a butler who'd known him since he wore nappies. "I'm going to bed."

"Impossible, sir. There is a girl in your bed. A child by the name of Apple. She claimed you sent her."

She'd actually come? He covered the distance to the bedroom in a few strides. His first impression was that it wasn't Apple.

She looked far too young and innocent. And clean, for that matter.

She wasn't truly asleep. Her eyes were clenched too tightly closed and her body was too stiff.

"Glad you were smart enough to come, Apple."

She peeped one eye open. "Can't sleep in this bed. The bloody thing's about to swallow me whole." But her eye closed suspiciously fast.

"I'm also glad you bathed."

This time she sighed. "And the water were clean *and* warm." But then both eyes opened. "Don't you think I'll be staying here long, though. I'll likely be gone come morning."

"Good. It will save me from having to toss you out on your skinny rump."

Canterbury glared.

But Apple grinned; the last thing she would have wanted was to be kept. If he tried to trap her, she'd be gone for good. She relaxed again. "Cor, but this pillow is suffocating." She was asleep by the time she'd finished speaking.

Ian tuned back to his butler. "Stop smirking. It bespeaks very little character to move a starving child into a room I never use."

"So you say, sir. You realize you will have to find her a governess. It wouldn't be proper to have a girl her age living in your rooms unchaperoned."

"Her age? What is she? Eight?"

"She's thirteen, sir."

Damnation. What the devil did he know about governesses? He would have sent her to Madeline, but she'd left to an undisclosed location to keep her baby safe.

The last thing he needed right now was someone else to be responsible for. He'd already picked up one headstrong woman today. He didn't need to add a headstrong girl.

But apparently it was too late.

"You're welcome to my bed, sir," Canterbury offered.

Yes. As if he was going to make his elderly butler sleep on the settee. Ian sank down on the offending piece of furniture before Canterbury could protest again. "I'll see about a governess in the morning. *If* she stays." He closed his eyes, hoping to shut out the entire day. Well, perhaps not the entire day.

Some of the moments with Juliana would be well worth reliving in his sleep. Her skin had been like silk under his fingers, and when she scooted closer to him on the bed . . . But those were memories he'd examine alone. "And I believe I mentioned smirking is very unbecoming in a butler."

"Your mother would be proud, sir."

Ian rolled over, turning his back to the interfering old biddy. "My mother is dead."

Chapter Fourteen

Leucretia sailed into Juliana's study. She was dressed in a rather scandalous crimson gown that would have raised eyebrows if worn by a younger woman, but she somehow managed to wear it with more grace and daring than Juliana would ever manage. "What is this I hear about us leaving for the house party early?"

Juliana set down the letter she was reading. She'd already practiced the lie several times. "Gregory told me he'd heard that Prince Wilhelm might be leaving early. I have no desire to go to the party only to discover my main reason for being there is gone." Hopefully, it contained enough of her normal dislike of such events and yet explained her seeming eagerness to attend this particular one.

She needed more practice with Ian's tricks because after a careful study, Leucretia narrowed her eyes. "You have no fondness for Sommet."

Juliana had never been able to hide anything from her aunt. But she could distract her. "But he has a fondness for you." At least it appeared so from the way Sommet always lingered over her aunt's hand.

Leucretia smoothed a hand down her still trim figure. "He was a rogue back in the day. Although I'll admit I question what I saw in him. I am, however, looking forward to this house party. He always does manage to assemble the most interesting guests." She perched on the chair across from Juliana's desk. "Now tell me your plans for Prince Wilhelm."

Juliana blinked. She really didn't have any. She'd been so caught up with her plans to rescue Gregory from his mess, she hadn't thought much about Wilhelm except as a convenient excuse.

"I thought as much." Leucretia frowned. Something she rarely did for fear of wrinkles. "I don't wish to pressure you, but we are growing short on time. I have heard the French have moved a garrison of troops to Lenoria's northern border."

"What? I've heard nothing of this."

"I have my . . . private sources."

"General Valmont?"

Leucretia lifted a shoulder in an elegant little shrug. Her aunt with her carefully selected lovers was as informed as a spymaster.

Whereas Juliana hadn't been able to make a half-blind prince with a lisp want to marry her.

"Your attempts to attract certain men in the past have been less than fruitful." Leucretia held up a hand. "I know you might not have given the earlier attempts your full effort, but now I am afraid your feelings need to be put aside. You need to find a husband."

True, Juliana had never been heartbroken by her lack of suitors. She'd never really wanted any of the men they'd deemed appropriate. But that didn't mean she hadn't tried.

"What should I do differently?"

Leucretia tapped a finger against her lip. "I'll admit you are at something of a disadvantage with the whole virginity issue. Men like sex, after all."

Juliana stared at her aunt.

Leucretia lifted a brow. "I thought you were ready for this discussion. Or shall I call Eustace in here to discuss how men like morality above all other things?"

No, now Juliana was quite intrigued. "What would you suggest I change?"

Leucretia scanned her as if deciding, but Juliana knew if Leucretia was here, she already had her desired outcome in mind. "You come across as quite regal, but I think you need to let a man know you are a woman under that starch."

"What am I supposed to do? Bat my eyelashes?"

Leucretia winced. "Never. Unless you want a man to think you have a fly in your eye. Instead, I want you to think about a man you're attracted to."

Ian appeared in her thoughts as stealthily as he did into her room.

No. There had to be someone else. She must have been attracted to someone else at some point.

But Ian remained in her thoughts. Smirking, no less.

Heavens, but the man had nice lips.

"Perfect," Leucretia declared. But then she narrowed her eyes. "Although I do have to wonder who you are— Never mind. When you meet Wilhelm I want you to think of this other man."

"I'm to think of another man?"

Leucretia shrugged. "It brings passion into your eyes, my dear. And if you add an occasional touch—I recommend the inside of the elbow and the thigh—you can easily fool most men that the passion is all for them."

This seemed almost as underhanded as her lessons from Ian. "Then he'll fall in love with me?"

"He will fall in lust with you, and for two unmarried royals, that amounts to the same thing."

"But it doesn't mean I will love him back."

Leucretia flicked lint from her sleeve. "Of course not. You only have to charm him until after you are married and have an heir. After that you are free to make your own choice of lovers."

Had her aunt just counseled her to have an affair?

But that might be the only way she could ever have Ian—

No. The very idea revolted her. If she married, she'd stay true to her husband. Even if that meant she could never have Ian.

Even if? There was no *if*. Even if Ian wanted

her, she couldn't have him. She couldn't give up her country for a moment of bliss.

And it would be blissful. She'd dreamed of his muscled chest until she thought she'd go mad. And those things he'd taunted her with—

"Who is this man?" Leucretia asked.

Juliana blinked. "No one. Just a man I met in passing."

The housekeeper came to the door. "You asked me to show you the details for tomorrow's departure?" She dipped a deep curtsy that Leucretia didn't bother to acknowledge as she swept out.

"Proceed, Mrs. Stuart," Juliana said.

The woman rattled off all the details that had been taken care of for their departure tomorrow. "Landro, the groom, has taken quite ill as well, Your Highness. But your secretary was able to hire a very able substitute this morning."

Juliana didn't know how she knew it, but she knew it was Ian. How odd would it be for her to ask to see the new hire personally? Quite odd, no doubt. She'd never personally welcomed any other grooms. "Very well."

But Juliana couldn't relax the rest of the afternoon. Every time a servant walked by the room she straightened. Which was ridiculous because the grooms had no reason to be in the house. Yet her spine didn't touch the back of her chair until it was time to dress for supper.

She rubbed her eyes with the heels of her hand.

How would she survive a week of this? Knowing Ian was near? Her stomach flip-flopped.

Not knowing if he was safe.

Had Sommet truly put a price on his head? It was one thing when Ian had made claims about the threats the first night in her room. Then he'd been nothing but a spy. A strange man with a quick tongue.

But now he was Ian. And the thought that someone was trying to hurt him . . . she might scratch Sommet's eyes out when she saw him.

Except she couldn't. She would have to smile and be gracious and save her brother.

She practiced smoothing the emotion from her face. She could do this. She had to.

She might never be able to have Ian, but if Sommet so much as sneezed in his direction, he would know her wrath.

It was rare that Ian was angry. He might be little more than a common criminal, but when he interrogated his targets or even slit their throats, he usually felt nothing but a vague distaste, a residual sickness that clung to his skin like an infection.

But now rage simmered in his veins, so hot and vivid he could taste it on his tongue like burning ash.

Juliana's lady's maid had just let him into the princess's room with only the flimsiest excuse. He hadn't even been in livery yet. He'd been in a simple jacket and waistcoat.

The maid hadn't questioned him once. What if he was a criminal?

Well, a criminal that wished Jules harm?

Just to be sure, he went back to Juliana's room. Again he passed the maid in the corridor on his way in and she didn't stop him.

He wouldn't tolerate this. Not if he was taking her into Sommet's lair.

"What are you doing in the princess's rooms?"

Ian turned to find a young, rather rakish man with chestnut hair. Prince Gregory. This was the fool who had forced his sister to get involved with Sommet.

And had tried to have Ian's friends murdered.

At least the prince had enough sense to question the man coming out of his sister's room.

That was the only thing that kept Ian from gutting him and ruining his rather dapper waistcoat.

Ian bowed. "Bringing trunks down to the coaches, Your Highness."

"Isn't that normally the footmen's task?"

Another point to the royal. "Aye, but there are a lot of trunks."

Gregory chuckled. "I swear the women could pave the road with the number of dresses they bring."

"I wouldn't know, Your Highness."

Gregory was already striding past. His interest

in the discussion over. "My valet has almost finished with my packing. See to my trunks as well."

Ian now had unexpected permission to enter the prince's rooms. Which he took immediate advantage of.

"Prince Gregory asked me to carry down some of his—"

Ian knew the valet. And theirs wasn't a pleasant acquaintance.

The rail-thin man's eyes had only a second to widen before Ian had his knife out. "Get down on your knees, Berkley. Hands on your head."

But of course Berkley had always been thickheaded, so the man punched. Ian blocked it and drove him to his knees, twisting his arm behind him.

Berkley struggled until Ian applied a bit more pressure. "If I have to break your arm, I will follow it up with your pretty nose."

That stilled the other spy. "What are you doing here, Wraith? I heard you were tossed out of the Foreign Office like the rubbish you are. This is my bit."

Interesting. "Come now, Berkley. You know our superiors never trusted you, not after the Madrid debacle."

"That wasn't my fault. It should have been clear that the donkeys were only meant—"

"Enough. Your reports on the prince have been pathetic."

He didn't deny his assignment. "It's hardly my

fault if he chooses not to confide in me. And the princess. What do they expect? She is like watching a puddle of mud. She never does anything of interest."

Ian tightened his hold on the man's arm. Berkley always had been an incompetent investigator.

Berkley squealed.

"Your work here is finished," Ian said. And now Ian would have to pay a visit to his old friend Glavenstroke.

"Wait, why should I believe you? You don't even—"

Ian sighed. It was probably too much to hope the man would leave quietly. He slammed the hilt of his knife into the base of Berkley's skull.

The fake valet slumped forward unconscious.

Now Ian needed a new maid and a new valet before Juliana left tomorrow. But they needed to be people he could trust. He needed to know Juliana was surrounded by people he could count on to protect her.

Where the devil could he find a valet— Ah. Perhaps he didn't know where he could find a valet, but he knew where he could find a rather competent, if impertinent, butler.

And he had a maid at the ready, too. Apple might not have the training, but surely she could tie laces as well as the next girl.

And it solved his problem of what to do with her. Lady's maid was as good a profession as any.

In an instant, he knew how he'd arrange for the switch. He hefted Berkley's body over his shoulder. He'd just need to dispose of the old valet first.

Luckily, he had all of these trunks.

Chapter Fifteen

When Glavenstroke entered his office, Ian motioned for him to take a seat.

Glavenstroke glared. "Get out from behind my desk."

Ian took a sip of the man's brandy. Truly, the man had good taste in spirits. "Now, now. I'm just enjoying your hospitality."

"Do you know how much that last bottle of brandy you stole was worth?"

"No, but it was delicious."

After a moment of indecision, Glavenstroke sat. "Why are you here?"

"What interest does the Foreign Office have in a Lenorian royal family?"

Glavenstroke frowned. "Why should I give you any information?"

"Because the information I bestowed upon you about the Jacobites last month has proven invaluable and you want to keep receiving such juicy morsels?"

"The Foreign Office has no interest in Lenorian

royals. They are, in effect, nonexistent on the po-
litical map."

"Then why assign Berkley to watch them?"

Glavenstroke tipped his head. "I haven't worked
with Berkley in years."

"Who does he normally report to?"

"Now, that information is—"

"It's Sommet, isn't it?"

After a pause, Glavenstroke nodded. "What is
your interest in the duke?"

Ian set down his glass. "Why? What is your interest?"

Glavenstroke rubbed the back of his neck, then
stood, looked out into the corridor, and shut the
door. "This doesn't leave this office."

Ian placed his hand over his heart.

Glavenstroke paced to the window and shut it
as well before speaking. "We have . . . suspicions."

"Oh no. Not *suspicions*." But despite Ian's mockery, he was rather surprised. Sommet was far more
powerful in the Foreign Office than Glavenstroke.
This was akin to mutiny.

"We have noticed some . . . abnormalities about
certain missions he has assigned. Outcomes that
may have been different from what he reported.
Missions run without following the proper proto-
cols."

"I think he might be responsible for betraying
the Trio to our enemies."

Glavenstroke nodded slowly. "I wouldn't put it past him. Why?"

"I have no idea yet, but I'll be visiting him soon to find out. Anything in particular you'd like me to bring home?"

"You aren't authorized to approach Sommet."

"You don't get to authorize me to do anything anymore, remember?"

Glavenstroke folded his arms. "I already have someone working on it. I don't need you mucking things up."

"I never muck things up. My missions are as smooth as butter on toast."

Glavenstroke remained silent.

Ian shrugged. "I'm going. I thought I'd do you the favor of letting you know. I'm not asking for permission."

"Won't Sommet recognize you?"

Ian lifted his glass of brandy. "We've never officially met. He's only ever spoken to Clayton."

"How do you plan to get to him? He lives in a castle."

Ian trusted Glavenstroke, but only so far. "That's my own business."

Glavenstroke pressed his fingertips together. "While the Foreign Office has no interest in Lenoria, the duke seems to. You know of the country, right?"

Ian paused, mid-sip. "You could say that." He had toppled it. What game was Glavenstroke playing? But Ian couldn't spot any unusual undertones in his words.

"I might be interested in any financial ties linking the duke to Lenoria."

"Done." Ian stood.

Glavenstroke hurriedly reclaimed his chair as if afraid Ian would depose him again. He moved the brandy bottle out of Ian's reach. "If anything goes wrong, you will not be able to claim any connection to the Foreign Office. I cannot rescue you from the gallows a second time."

Ian was used to being on his own. "Just for the record, Glaves, I never needed your rescue the first time."

Chapter Sixteen

"So this might be our last night together, Princess. Try not to shed too many bitter tears."

Excitement shivered down Juliana's spine. Finally. He was here. She'd invented a reason to go down into the stables earlier, but had been unable to catch a glimpse of him. "That is ridiculous. You'll be with me at the house party."

Ian walked toward her. The scar of his right cheek darkened by the shadows. She wanted to lift her hand to it. To trace it with her mouth. If this was her last night with him, couldn't she at least have a small taste to keep with her when she was married to Prince Toadface?

How did she go about arranging that? Could one ask for a kiss?

"There we'll go our own way. You'll have your mission. I will have mine. I might not find time to slip into your room late at night."

"But you might?" She stood and placed her hand on his cheek, letting her index finger trace the indentation. He felt so warm. So right.

His cheek lifted as he smiled under her hand. "Perhaps we should be very clear what you're offering here, Jules."

"I—" Her daring failed. No wonder she hadn't managed to land a husband. Here she was with the man she yearned for, and she couldn't manage anything more scandalous than touching his cheek.

"I thought as much." Ian stepped out of reach.

She glared at him. She might not be seductive, but annoyed was an expression she could do quite well. "What do you think?"

"It's one thing to fantasize about the hired help, but it's quite another to take that next step."

For an instant, she could clearly see herself rising up on tiptoe and placing her lips on his. She'd taste the shock on his mouth. Feel it in the sudden tension in his shoulders.

But she couldn't. Not when she needed to marry another man. She was a princess, and one thing she'd excelled at from birth was self-denial. She held still when she wanted to fidget. She wore a crown when it made her head hurt. She didn't go to the town festival. She didn't play with the servants' children.

And she couldn't kiss the man she desired. "It wouldn't be fair."

She thought disappointment had flashed over Ian's face, but it was probably her imagination since his grin hadn't faltered. "Exactly. Many women never recover from my kisses."

"I was thinking it wouldn't be fair to *you*."

"Had a lot of experience kissing then?"

She worked on keeping her face smooth. "Perhaps."

Ian's gaze snapped wider. "Oh very, very good delivery. But have you?"

Ha! She'd done it! And was that a hint of jealousy in his voice?

"Your gloating gives you away." Suddenly his arm wrapped around her waist, drawing her against him. Every inch of her from her breasts to thighs, nestled against his hard body. "I'll bet you've never been kissed."

"Seven times. And by dashing princes, too." Seven. Was that a high number? It had sounded high in her head, but when the number emerged, she feared he'd think it was rather small.

"How do princes kiss?"

Why did he have to smell so good? Like fresh baked bread and ginger tea this time. "Very well. Why do you think women are always falling all over themselves around them?"

His forehead wrinkled just slightly. "How many men *have* actually kissed you?"

She was careful not to crow this time and only lifted a brow.

"I can find out the truth." His hand slid down until it cupped the curve of her bottom.

"By gutting me?" she croaked.

His fingers tightened on her in a shocking manner. "Not nearly as fun."

And his mouth was on hers. His lips gently nipped. Each caress intoxicating.

The tension she'd been carrying evaporated so quickly that she swayed, or would have, if Ian hadn't been holding her so tightly.

All she knew was that she had to get closer. She shifted against him and the sensations spiraling through her heightened tenfold.

Ian's tongue traced the seam of her mouth and she gasped.

He muttered something suspiciously close to *Knew it*, before his tongue slipped past her lips and into her mouth.

Heavens, was this a normal kiss? There was something so earthy and primal and wonderful. When she'd imagined kisses, she'd never thought much past the brief pressing of lips.

No wonder the women Ian kissed never recovered.

Well, those harpies didn't have him now. Juliana threaded her fingers through his hair. He was hers. At least for this instant.

His hand dipped lower on her bottom, lifting her onto her toes and pulling her more tightly to him. She couldn't help arching against him.

She froze as her hips found the evidence of his arousal.

For a moment, his eyes met hers and she could see everything in them. Passion. Desire. Affection. Vulnerability.

But then they shuttered, only his normal amused smirk evident. "An honorable man would put you down now." He shifted his hips against her, sending a sharp stab of pleasure searing through her insides. "You'll notice I'm still holding you." He ran his thumb over her swollen lips.

Did he expect her to demand to be released? Perhaps he did. Perhaps his honor wasn't as absent as he claimed. What would he do if she didn't let him escape? "And you'll notice I'm not complaining." She flicked her tongue over the end of his thumb.

He stared at his thumb as if he'd never seen it before. "Why the devil not?"

"Because I'm not afraid of you."

He laughed and set her away. "And to think I'd given you high marks for intelligence."

He *had* pushed her away.

His eyes narrowed. "Why are you smiling?"

She shrugged. "I'm simply excited to begin the night's lesson. What did you say it was?"

"I didn't." He reached for a pot of tea that sat on her dressing table.

"It's cold," she warned.

"It's edible. I learned long ago not to pass up food. Or tea for that matter. Never know if there's going to be any later." He poured himself a cup and added three heaping scoops of sugar.

"Did you often go hungry?"

"I grew up on the streets. If I'd eaten once that day, it was a good day."

"But surely once you were spy—"

"There were days when we hunted rats to keep from starving." He sipped the tea. "Once, near Kiev, we had to pick undigested oats out of horse manure to stay alive."

He was trying to shock her again. Push her away. But it didn't work. "Once at a house party in Kent, they only served three courses at dinner."

He choked.

"So what is my mission for tonight?"

He gulped down the rest of his tea, then set down the cup. "You'll walk down to the kitchen and get a plate of biscuits."

"That's all?" True, she'd never actually set foot in the kitchen, but she knew where it was.

He shrugged. "Yes. Did you want it more difficult?"

"Are you certain this isn't just a way for you to get biscuits?"

His expression was far too innocent. "Merely an added reward."

"Fine." She pulled her wrapper more tightly around her and strode to the door.

Ian followed.

"You're coming as well?"

He nodded.

"How will I explain—ah." Perhaps this would be a trifle more difficult than she'd anticipated. "What do I say if I see someone?"

"That you cannot bring yourself to be out of my presence?"

If only she dared.

"You don't speak at all," Ian amended. "You're a princess. You don't need to explain yourself."

Right. She was a princess. This was her home. She could walk to the kitchen and pick up a plate of biscuits if she chose.

She straightened her shoulders again and stepped into the corridor. It suddenly occurred to her that she couldn't remember the last time that she'd walked out of her room dressed so informally. When she was a girl? Certainly not since she'd been in London.

What would the servants think? Or, heaven forbid, one of her aunts?

And why hadn't she checked her appearance in the mirror before she left? Did it look like she'd been engaged in carnal activities?

When she saw a shadow approaching, she scrambled into the nearby guest room. Ian thankfully followed.

"What happened to striding by, not explaining yourself?"

Her heart pounded against her ribs. This was ridiculous. She thought she could steal something from one of the most horrid men in Britain, and yet she couldn't even walk through her own house without panic. "I was surprised, that is all. It won't happen again."

Ian motioned for her to leave the room.

But she did peek at herself in the mirror before she—

"You were going to let me walk into the kitchen looking like this?"

Ian's smirk was wolfish. "I rather like that look, especially your swollen lips."

"You are a cad." But it was hard to be truly angry at him when he was looking at her like he wanted to kiss her all over again.

She struggled with her hair for several moments before Ian appeared behind her in the mirror. With a few deft twists, her hair was perfectly coiffed.

"How did you learn to do that?"

"Doing women's hair is not much different than tying a good knot."

"What do I do about my lips?"

"Don't kiss unscrupulous men in your bedroom?" But again he relented, his fingertip grazing her cheek. "The swelling is already fading. It isn't noticeable to anyone who doesn't know to look for it."

"Shall we go?" she asked. Except she was the one who was delaying, and they both knew it. "Fine." She threw open the door and stared right into the surprised face of her aunt Eustace.

Chapter Seventeen

*O*f all the aunts Juliana could have run into, it had to be Eustace.

Her aunt's eyes widened. "Whatever are you doing wandering the corridors in your night-clothes?"

This wasn't a situation where she'd be able to saunter past without speaking. "It is really quite simple. We were discussing moving the furniture about to make room for some things."

"This late at night?" Eustace's eyebrows inched toward her hairline. "Who is *we*?"

She'd kill Ian for this. "This—"

Ian was gone.

Bless him. The man was a saint. She'd get him a dozen plates of cookies.

"The housekeeper and I this morning. I simply couldn't sleep because I didn't think the bureau would fit on the north wall."

Eustace frowned slightly but seemed to accept her answer.

Juliana knew Eustace the least well of all her

aunts. She was always away at the hospital or her other charitable endeavors. And truth be told, Juliana was slightly frightened of her. She'd always been stern and solemn. "I have found out some information on Wilhelm for you. If you seem knowledgeable in his areas of interest, it will go a long way to helping you win him."

When had she become such a lost cause that all her aunts felt the need to take her under their wing? Juliana shuddered to think what Constantina's advice would be.

"Shall we meet in the morning to discuss it?"

Eustace nodded, then paused. "Is there another reason you couldn't sleep?"

Her lips must still be swollen. Juliana scrambled to invent a story that involved her lips being burned while sipping hot soup, but Eustace spoke first.

"I'm sorry you won't be given the chance to follow your heart when it comes to choosing a husband." She gripped the locket at her neck that held the picture of her husband. "Truly I am."

Juliana expected a *but* to follow. And an explanation of why she had to do her duty regardless, but Eustace gave her a quick hug, then glided away.

Juliana had to blink several times before the burning in her eyes faded. She had to get those papers back. She had to get her country back.

She turned and walked downstairs. Ian could choose to come or not. It didn't matter. She *would* do this. She passed two footmen and didn't even flinch. She asked a rather astonished scullery maid for two plates of biscuits without a single explanation.

Three minutes later she had two plates of flaky, sweet biscuits.

She'd done it.

She turned away from the kitchen to find Ian inches behind her. He wasn't smiling as she'd anticipated, instead he was watching. Slowly, she shifted the plates to one hand, then lifted one of the treats and took a large bite.

He jerked his head to indicate that she should follow.

No one had ever jerked his head at her before.

He didn't even check to see if she obeyed.

He opened a door a few minutes later and ushered her inside.

She cursed his choice of rooms. "Aren't we going back to my bedroom?"

"Not a chance in hell," he muttered. He glanced around. "I thought this was a parlor."

The smell of paint and turpentine permeated the large room. "It is temporarily a painting studio."

"For what?" Ian approached the cloth-covered canvas.

She tossed the plates on a table and grabbed his hand before he could remove the covering. "Just a silly picture."

His brows rose. Drat. Now she'd sparked his interest.

"That you don't want me to see?"

"Yes."

"Why?"

Because she couldn't stand the thought of him comparing her to it and finding her lacking. She also didn't want him to be amused by the fact that Dupre thought he had to paint her more attractive so a man would be interested in her. "It's of me."

"Are you naked? Then I definitely have to see." With a quick maneuver, he detached her hand from his and yanked the cloth free.

Juliana spun away and paced to the window. She knew what he'd be seeing. Some woman that vaguely resembled her sitting in a forest glade. Her dark hair loose from the wind. Perfect rosy skin. A bosom much more lush than reality.

Why didn't he say something already?

Finally, she turned. And jumped. He was directly behind her. His hand trailed down her cheek. "What bothers you about the painting?"

"Foolish, aren't I? I suppose I should be glad the painting looks beautiful. That it might actually be enough to interest a man."

He frowned. "I thought you were angry because the painter must be bloody blind. Where did the fool learn to paint?"

She winced. She knew she didn't look much like the woman in the painting, but it stung to have it confirmed.

He caught her chin. "No, you are genuinely upset by this. Shall I toss it into the fire?"

She exhaled. "It's too late. *You* have already seen it."

Ian was very rarely at a loss, but he was now. Why did it matter that he'd seen the ridiculous thing? A disturbing thought occurred to him. "You cannot think I'd prefer that woodland tart to you."

Juliana gave a choked snort.

"You do. Well, let me tell you. Her hair's been mussed from a tumble with some woodcutter in the woods. Her cheeks are flushed from over-imbibing on wine. And her left arm is at a completely un-natural angle."

A ghost of a smile crossed her lips, then faded.

"What happened to the woman triumphant at claiming her biscuits?"

Ian had the feeling she was weighing her re-sponse. He fully expected her to decline to answer. After all, he rarely came out ahead in these types of considerations.

"I cannot set foot in my homeland. I cannot give my people funds for seeds for planting. I cannot stop the French who are gathering on my borders. I cannot get the Spanish to listen to me. I cannot even get my own brother to listen. And apparently I cannot even look like a princess!" The words came out in an angry rush. "And now you've seen it and know what a bloody failure I am at everything. And you're the one person I thought I didn't have to impress, and yet I find I care immensely—" She set her lips in a hard line, and whirled away.

He should let this moment lengthen. He should make things awkward between them. Make her understand that her feelings were foolish.

Instead, he placed his hand on her shoulder and turned her to face him.

"You spend every moment of the day carrying the burdens of an entire nation. Yet you have never once shirked. You're willing to rob a madman to protect your brother. You're brave and stubborn and clever. You're more of a princess than any country could hope for." *Let it go there. Step away.* But his damned fool mouth kept moving. "You're far more of a woman than any man could dream of. You're witty and charming. And your kisses set me afire."

Her gaze dropped to his lips. Why the devil had he mentioned kisses? He needed to back away. If she kissed him now, things would end with him buried deep between those slender thighs. He was an expert at always finding alternatives. But he knew if he tasted her mouth again, he would not stop. Even sharing the same air with her seemed like the most erotic thing he'd ever done. To press his lips to her throat. To feel her tongue slip between his lips—

"And you pilfer a man biscuits," he managed.

Her eyes lifted to the biscuits a few feet away, and Ian retreated, drinking air into his lungs and trying to bring his anatomy back under control.

"Thank you for listening to my foolishness," Juliana said.

"Nothing you say will ever be foolish. Now shall we eat your prize?"

Amusement entered back into her gaze and she passed him a plate. "So, am I ready to rob a madman now?"

Ian found the cookies strangely unappetizing. But he put two in his pocket for later. "Yes, I think you are."

But he wouldn't let her.

She *could* steal the documents, but she shouldn't have to. She was good. Pure. While Ian was already a creature of the gutter.

He'd find out what her blasted brother had done, then steal the evidence back himself.

Chapter Eighteen

"Wait. Pardon?" Juliana asked. She must have misheard. After all, the coaching yard of the inn was incredibly noisy. "My maid eloped with Gregory's new valet? The footman that replaced his old valet?" The footman had only been elevated to the position yesterday.

"Yes!" Constantina said. "They snuck away together when we stopped in Cambry for tea." Her aunt waved her fan vigorously. "Apparently they'd been in love for ages."

"Love," Leucretia said, her tone clearly indicating her opinion of it. "Now we will be appearing at the duke's house understaffed and looking like fools. You will use my maid of course, but sharing maids . . . The couple should be found and horsewhipped."

Ian joined the group and bowed. He was dressed in black with silver trim, the livery of the Lenorian court. He'd ridden escort with three of the other grooms, but he'd been assigned to the back corner of the coach, so she'd been unable to see him without hanging her head from the window.

She couldn't drink in the sight of him now, either, since he was next to her, but she could study him from the corner of her eye. The livery fit him to perfection, his broad shoulders appearing impossibly massive. And thanks to Constantina's adaptations in the uniform a few years ago, his tight, well-muscled backside was clearly visible.

And he was close enough she could breathe him in. Horses. Sandalwood.

And biscuits?

She noticed a small lump in his livery pocket. Leftovers from tea, no doubt.

"With all due respect, Your Highnesses."

Now she could look at him. But she couldn't. She feared too much would be in her gaze.

"We have sent for a new valet and maid. The agency will send replacements directly to the duke's estate. They should arrive shortly after us tomorrow." Ian's hand brushed the back of hers slightly as he spoke.

She shifted a little to try to increase the contact, but Ian's hand moved away.

Is this what she was reduced to now, trying to sneak a single touch from him in an inn courtyard?

Apparently, because she found herself searching for an excuse to try again.

Constantina's eyes lingered on Ian's lower half. "Very good. What did you say your name was, groom?"

"Bogglesworth, Your Highness."

"Well, Bogglesworth, I can see you are quite . . . trustworthy. Would you carry my trunks to my room personally?"

Juliana had to turn her laugh into a cough. But, drat, why hadn't she thought of that?

The lead groom came to stand next to Ian and bowed. "The rooms are prepared."

Eustace finally descended from the coach to join them, and they entered the inn. A few minutes later, they were all comfortably ensconced in their rooms to freshen up before dinner.

Or at least the others were. Juliana didn't have a maid to help her out of her dress yet. So she wasn't all that comfortable. The innkeeper said he'd send one of his girls up to tend her, but she hadn't come yet. Juliana wandered over to the window and pressed it open as wide as she could, hoping to catch the evening breeze.

And a glance at Ian if she could find him.

She started to tug off her gloves and froze. There was a paper in her left glove. It definitely hadn't been there when she'd put them on.

Juliana slowly removed the thin strip and unfolded it. The writing was bold and slashing but surprisingly neat.

More training tonight.

P.S. Do you know how hot black is in this ~~damned~~ blasted weather?

Her heart hammered against her chest. He wasn't done with her then. At least not yet. She'd relish any remaining moments she had with him.

She knew she should have more pride than that. And she would. Eventually. Tonight she would enjoy herself.

There was a knock at the door. Juliana crumpled the note and jammed it in a crack under the window. "Enter."

Ian strode in carrying a huge wooden tub across his shoulders. He set the tub in the center of the room, then backed out with a wink.

Footmen tromped up the stairs carrying buckets of water. Soon the last one left, closing the door behind him.

Well, that was just cruel. Now she had to be dusty and sweaty *and* stare longingly into water she couldn't manage to get into without a maid's help.

"You need assistance, don't you?" Ian asked from behind her.

She spun about.

"Come now. The open window was an invitation."

Juliana glanced around, and motioned for him to be silent. Her aunts were in the rooms on either side of her and the walls were only wood. "A maid will be here any moment." And while she might have been able to explain Ian following her in the corridor last night, she wouldn't be able to explain him in her room with a drawn bath.

"No, she won't."

"The innkeeper said—"

"The innkeeper thinks you are sharing your aunt's maid and your aunt thinks you are being assisted by the innkeeper's daughter."

"But that leaves me without a maid to help me out of my dress."

Ian lifted a brow.

Oh.

But if he thought she'd blush, he was wrong. She turned so he could reach her buttons.

"Who said you get the first bath?" he asked.

She spun to face him. "What?" She only remembered to whisper at the last moment.

"You made me dress in black wool livery in the heat of summer. You owe me."

"I most certainly do not. The livery are of the finest quality. They are quite comfortable—"

"Your servants are dirty liars if they told you that. It's like being slowly roasted alive in an oven filled with ants."

"You do not get the first bath." Juliana knew some people often shared bathwater, but *ick*.

"Try to stop me." He had his livery jacket off before he'd finished speaking.

He wouldn't. But then his waistcoat followed.

She struggled to reach her own buttons. She could reach the top one on her own.

But by then Ian had his boots off as well.

With a bit of stretching, she could reach the second one. But blast it all, there was no way she could get the third. "Is it your goal to think of as many ways as possible for me to see you unclothed?"

He paused, shirt halfway off his head. "I had to have something to keep me occupied on the ride."

He dropped his shirt.

She'd seen him without it before, but that was in the dark, across a room, in a blind panic.

Now he was inches from her. In the rosy twilight. And what hummed inside her was far more wild.

He was glorious. Rough hewn. Smooth planes. She wanted to reach out and trace her finger over the ridges on his stomach.

"You might want to turn around now, Princess, my breeches are coming off next."

"And if I don't?"

He froze for the second time, but then reached for the button. "As you wish." He pulled his breeches off, revealing his white linen drawers.

And the state of his arousal.

"Um" was the brilliant witticism she managed to utter.

"Remember, I did try to be a gentleman—for the

first time in my life, I might add—and warn you. Here is my last attempt—you might want to look away now."

But she couldn't. That bulge fascinated her more than any other thing she'd seen in her life. "Feeling shy?" she asked.

He removed his drawers with a single tug. "*Shy* is not a word that has ever applied to me."

Sweet heavens. She did *that* to him. She should have been shocked, scandalized, but instead she felt more powerful than she ever had before.

She wanted to wrap her fingers around the length of him. She wanted to stroke him and know his texture and weight.

"Hell's teeth, woman." Ian climbed into the bath and sat, scooping up a handful of water and pouring it onto his face. "Total madness, Ian. Completely daft. Moronic—"

"Are you talking to yourself?"

He shrugged, the muscles rippling in his shoulders. "Figured I was a complete bedlamite already. Why the hell not?" He dunked his head in the water in front of him. "I have no idea what I was thinking. No, that's a lie. I did know. I was thinking that I loved to watch a blush darken your cheeks. And that adorable way your mouth gapes when I startle you. I was thinking how nice it would be to not smell like a horse." He rubbed his hand through his hair, leaving it in sharp, uneven spikes. "I wasn't thinking about that deliciously scandalous side you keep so deeply hidden. Nor did I expect you to look at me as if you wanted to lick me. Hell, Princess, there's only so much a man can take."

"Just how much is that?" Lick him. Now that inspired a whole new set of wicked images. She strolled toward him. Water droplets clung to his lashes and sparkled on his cheeks.

He sat up straight so quickly, water sluiced over the side. "With you, not much. You just have to look at me and I ache for a week."

She bent and picked up the smooth white bar of soap the footmen had left. After dipping it into the water, she rubbed it between her hands. "Hmm . . . lavender. Lean forward."

Ian's eyes narrowed. "What do you mean to do?"

Enjoy herself. She'd go to Sommet's house and save her brother. Then she would try to woo Prince Wilhelm to try to save her country.

This moment would be just for her.

"You said I owed you for making you wear that uniform," she explained. "I don't like to be in debt."

She set down the soap, and lowered her hands to his shoulders. He quivered under her fingers, so she continued. Spreading the bubbles all over the thick, corded muscles.

"How am I going to explain to the other grooms why I smell like lilacs?"

"Lavender."

"It's a bloody flower. Same difference." He was

right. The scent should have been feminine. Instead, on him, it smelled earthy and sweet.

She let her hands slide down the edges of his shoulder blades. "I think the other grooms might be jealous."

His voice was little more than a low rumble. "How can they be jealous of what they haven't dared to imagine?"

Her heart lurched. Actually skipped a beat. It was as if her entire being paused, then restarted at the twice the speed.

"Lean forward," she ordered. She created more bubbles, then slowly worked them down the hollow of his spine until she reached the edge of the water.

After only a moment's hesitation, she slipped her hands under the water to explore the rest of his back. She'd known having him touch her would feel good, but how could touching him make the heat pool between her legs? Her breathing was erratic and heaving.

Finally, her hands met the firm swell of his backside. Heavens, he was truly firm and muscled every—

His hands shot from the water and grabbed the outsides of her shoulders, pinning her arms to her sides. With a move like a bullfighter, he spun her around to the side of the tub.

Another tug had her down on her knees. His hand anchored around her neck and drew her to him. His lips were fierce. Hungry. Water dripped from his wet hand down her bodice. "You wanted to know how much I could take? That's about it." He buried his hands in her hair, tugging out pins until it spilled around them, the ends dangling into the bath. "You drive me to madness. You make me want things I shouldn't have. And I'm very bad at denying myself what I want."

His tongue flicked along the seam of her lips until she opened for him, their tongues tangled, searched.

But he wasn't the only one who'd had tension building. Ever building. Her hands swept down his chest.

"If your hands are on my chest, it seems only fair . . ." He drew her closer so he could kiss his way down her throat, then along the edge of her bodice.

She moaned.

He drew away and placed a finger on her lips. "Remember your neighbors."

She closed her eyes. He was right. Her moment of pleasure was threatening to be much, much more.

And she didn't care.

She wanted him. If he kissed her again, she'd give in. She'd let him strip the dress from her body. Trail the cooling water over her bare breasts and watch her nipples harden.

He could lay her back on the bed or even take her here straddling him in the bath.

But there in the backs of her eyes, he could see it. The knowledge that she *should* care about what she was doing. The knowledge that she'd regret it later.

And he couldn't stand the thought of her regretting him.

Ian pressed her away and doused himself with several handfuls of water. "Sorry, Jules. I make it a rule never to bed women who don't really want me."

Confusion warred with her arousal. "I do want you."

She was more far gone than he'd feared if she'd admit to that. "You have reservations."

"I . . ."

But it was true. He ignored the discomfort that lodged in the center of his chest. Damned inconvenient things, these emotions. "You may want me now, but you don't want anything more than this moment. I can't allow you to take advantage of me like that."

She wiped a droplet of water from her collarbone and narrowed her gaze. "And all those other women you've bedded? Did they *take advantage of you*? Or do you just have reservations about me?" A hint of uncertainty crossed her face.

Damnation. He dunked his head under the water until he couldn't hold his breath anymore. Those other women hadn't wanted him, either. They'd wanted the pleasure he could bring in bed. They'd wanted an illicit thrill. But they hadn't wanted *him*.

And truth be told, he hadn't really wanted them, either.

But he did want Juliana. He wanted her so much that he'd never let her have a clue how much he wanted her.

"Those other women were eminently more tuppable than you." He ignored her swift inhalation. "They came without complications, and you, Princess, are nothing but a complication."

She sighed. "It is not my intent. And just so you know, I think I'd be quite tuppable under other circumstances."

Had he just made a princess claim to be tuppable? What level of hell did that land him in? "What circumstances are those?"

She plopped back on her backside, tucking her knees to her chest and resting her chin on them. "For instance, if I was a shopgirl."

"It's rather difficult to think of you as a shopgirl when your dress costs more than they would make in an entire year."

"I could do without them, you know."

"Gowns? No, I think even shopgirls require clothing."

She gave him a weary smile. "The expensive gowns. If you think the livery is uncomfortable, you should try wearing five layers of velvet to an overcrowded ball."

He was trying to keep her away, so why was this conversation making him feel closer to her? "If you

were a shopgirl, what would you do? I don't suspect you have many marketable skills. Embroidery,
perhaps?"

"Millinery."

"You'd make bonnets?"

She glowered at him. "I do make bonnets. I am
quite good."

"*Bonnets?*"

She jumped to her feet, strode to her trunk, and
pulled out a box. After a quick glance over her
shoulder she opened it. Inside was indeed a half-
finished bonnet. A length of ribbon and a spool of
thread lay next to it.

"Don't you have a maid to do that?"

"I *like* to do it. I like to think that I'm not completely useless. That I'm more than a frivolous,
flighty thing."

He loved the challenge in her eye, daring him
to mock her secret hobby. "You're neither of those
things. I take it back. You'd make a lovely shopgirl."

He also loved the way she fought against her
smile. "Yes, I would. And you could be a bank
clerk."

"A bank clerk. You'd trust me near all that
money? And besides, can you not think of anything
more daring? I *am* a feared spy." He stood up in the
bath. "Hand me a towel, shopgirl."

But she was staring at him again, the box holding
her bonnet falling from her fingers to the ground.

But his princess wasn't shocked for long, and her expression turned minxish. "If I'm a shopgirl, then that towel will cost you."

"What?" he tried to ask. But it emerged as a rather embarrassing croak. All the blood that had never fully dissipated from his groin surged back, throbbing with each beat of his heart. He cleared his throat. "What will it cost me?"

"A touch. I get to touch you wherever I choose."

Surely, she wouldn't—

But her gaze rested on his arousal. If she caressed him, she'd get far more than a single touch.

Desperation made his words harsh. "But you aren't a shopgirl. Do you have any idea what the life of a shopgirl is even like? The days of little food. The nights without coal. The shawls too thin to keep out the winter's chill. The groping hands of customers. Old age spent scrimping every penny. You have nothing in common with a shopgirl."

She spun away, the line of her spine straight. The small V where she'd unbuttoned the top of her dress only served to make her seem more vulnerable. "I'm not a fool. It was simply a silly fantasy."

He grabbed a towel himself and wrapped it around his hips. "One best forgotten."

When she turned around, Ian had his breeches back on. "You said you had more training."

He tugged his shirt on over his head. "You need to know how to defend yourself."

She thought he muttered, "From imbeciles like me." But she couldn't be sure.

"Does this training involve hitting you?" Juliana asked.

"If you can. You last attempt was rather . . . less than damaging."

Oh, she'd damage him this time. "How do I start?"

Ian's mouth quirked. "Should we wait to do this training until you aren't planning on breaking my legs?"

"Only if you're afraid I can." She balled her hands into fists.

He frowned at her. "First of all, you are going to break your hand if you punch like that. Second of all, against most men, you probably won't be able to hurt them too much with a—"

"Show me how to make a fist."

He pulled her thumb to cover her first two knuckles and straightened her wrist. As soon as he stepped away, she swung.

He easily caught her arm, but couldn't help grinning. "You actually intended to hit me with that, didn't you?"

Yes, she had. She almost caught him with her other fist, but then he pinned both hands to her side, which brought his lips inches from hers. "As I was saying, you probably won't be able to do much damage with your fist unless you connect with a lucky spot, such as the throat. And even if you do punch correctly, you will likely break your hand, so instead I'd recommend an open palm like this."

He let go of her slowly as to ensure she wasn't going to punch him on the side of the head and showed her how to hold her fingers together and hit with the heel of her hand. "Go for the nose or the eye sockets if you are aiming for the face. If you are going for the stomach, I would aim here instead." He placed a finger in the V where her ribs came together inches below her breasts.

They both stilled. If she tilted her face up, their lips would meet, and from the way he leaned forward he knew it, too. His pupils had dilated, making his eyes deep and hungry.

Her hand connected with his chest with all the force she could muster.

The air whooshed out of his lungs and he staggered back. He held up a hand forestalling the second attack she'd planned to aim at his nose. He sucked in several breaths, his hand planted on his knees.

Her grin at besting him slowly ebbed, as did her anger at his earlier lecture when he remained doubled over. She hadn't meant to hurt him.

His gaze was rueful. "Thank goodness I haven't taught you to use your knees yet."

"My knees?"

He then spent the next little while going through

various attacks she could do with her knees, elbows, and feet.

Finally, however, sweat was dripping into her eyes and her arms had begun to shake.

Ian bowed. "We'll move on to some basics with daggers tomorrow." He tugged his livery jacket back on, then walked to the window.

"Wait," she called out. She wasn't even entirely sure what she wanted to say. She only knew that she didn't want him to leave. "Is this part of the training really necessary?"

"If Sommet is going to be anywhere near you— yes."

"What do you know of him?"

Ian hesitated. "He's a foul excuse of a man."

"I know. But you must know more specifics." She'd seen how he reacted when he learned the name.

Ian frowned. "The problem with Sommet is that no one *knows* anything about him. It's all rumor and whispered accusations."

"Such as?"

"Such as the man might have sold British army munitions to the French a few times during the war. Rumors of men sent on suicide missions who dared to question him. Accusations that he might be taking bribes from the very criminals he swore to punish."

"Then why has no one tried to stop him?"

Ian's face was stark in the twilight. "People have.

They just have all failed. The entire bloody lot of them."

She ignored the cold finger trailing down her spine.

Ian stepped toward her and caught her elbow. "What does he have on your brother? I will get it for you. You can go home. Stay safe."

It was so tempting. She hadn't wanted this added burden to begin with, but this was her task. Her responsibility. She would trust him with her life, but she couldn't trust him with her brother's. With the future of her nation. That was something she alone was accountable for. "I cannot tell you."

His fingers tightened. "Why not?"

"You have said time and time again that I'm not to trust you."

"What if I told you that you could trust me in this?"

But she shook her head. "Why would you want to help me? You have no love for my brother."

He exhaled and scrubbed his hands over his face. "Because I already have reason to confront Sommet. There's no reason for you to be in danger as well."

"Except for my entire country."

"What Sommet has is truly that damaging?"

She nodded.

"And when the papers go missing? What are the odds he'll guess it was you that took them?"

It was something she'd tried to avoid thinking

about. "Rather high. But perhaps he'll think I hired someone to do it."

"So do that. Hire me. And when he comes asking, give the bastard my name."

Chapter Nineteen

Ian was feeling rather bloodthirsty at the moment. The thought of Sommet threatening Juliana filled him with a rage hotter than he'd ever experienced.

And it was a righteous rage for once in his sorry life. He wouldn't let anyone hurt this woman.

She might not ever be his. But he'd give his very soul to see her safe.

So when she swung at him again, he barely saved himself from a black eye.

"*How dare you*," Juliana said. "I do not let others bear my risks. "

Ian pulled her against him just so he didn't have to worry about her attacking him. "I never said that you did. And how have I never suspected this violent streak you harbor?"

"No, you think I am a silly princess who doesn't understand how things truly are."

"No—"

"Yes, you do. But I'm not. I know how things are in the real world. I carried my brother over my mother's broken, dead body. Is that real enough for you?" She shoved against him, but he only held her tighter. "How about when all my advisers decided that I wasn't competent and that they should make my decisions for me? I managed to keep control, only to have to decide which village to send aid to and which had to be told they either had to lose their farms or starve to death in the winter. Or how I'll have to bed a man I care nothing about for the rest of my life just so my country will be able to exist." Her chest heaved against him. "I may be a princess, but I'm not weak or silly. And when we get to Sommet's tomorrow, you'd better stay out of my way."

Damnation, but she was magnificent. And he couldn't even kiss her.

Like hell he couldn't.

He crushed his lips to hers, drawing on her anger, her outrage. He deserved them both. "When I said those things, it was because if you'd touched me, you wouldn't have left this room a virgin."

And there it was again. The debate in her eyes. Always her blasted obligation and duty. But those two things were so central to her, he doubted she could survive without them.

But heaven help him if the desire ever won completely.

There was a knock on her door. "Juliana? Did I hear you cry out?" It was Eustace.

"No." Juliana cleared her throat and tried a bit

louder. "No, I'm fine it must have been voices from the common room below."

Ian's hand brushed the side of her breast as he moved away. Her breath caught and she glared at him.

Really, how could he resist that?

So he reached out and ran his finger purposefully over her puckered nipple.

Her teeth bit her lip and her eyes clenched shut.

"Shall we go over the information I was able to gather on Wilhelm?" her aunt asked.

She opened her eyes, and the challenge in them was unmistakable. "Absolutely, Aunt Eustace. Come in. Right now."

Juliana wasn't sure where Ian was. But even as fast as he was, he couldn't have made it outside.

Curse him for making her impulsive. The man was a terrible influence.

And yet she felt freer and happier than she'd felt in years.

Eustace sailed into the room. She frowned when she saw Juliana. "Why haven't you bathed?"

Juliana sat on the used towel on her bed before Eustace could spot it. "The water was too cold. I need warmer water." And where had Ian gone? She could hardly have a conversation about the man she was supposed to woo while Ian was in the room.

Her aunt tucked her hands neatly in front of her. "I have heard Wilhelm cares for three things. His five-year-old daughter. His musical compositions. And—"

"And making sure his next wife is enjoyable in bed."

"Leucretia!" Eustace's voice was shocked.

Leucretia glided into the room. "Sorry, I heard your first two, and I had to step in. You and Constantina have been providing her with information on all the previous princes. It obviously hasn't been working. It is time for a bit more." Leucretia gestured to her own cleavage.

Blood heated Juliana cheeks. Her eyes slowly scanned the room trying to find where Ian could be hiding. There wasn't all that much furniture in the room. "Perhaps we should move this conversation—"

"Shared interests are far more important."

"Nonsense, Eustace. You might think no one knows what you and Albert would do in the conservatory, but that isn't the case."

Eustace's mouth gaped. "We were betrothed."

"Precisely. And we want Juliana to become betrothed." She held up a finger to stall Eustace's protests. "I'm not telling her to sleep with him. I'm simply telling her that Wilhelm is rumored to be one of the few princes who didn't stray from his wedding vows. If a potential bride makes monogamy seem enticing, he won't be able to resist."

Eustace pursed her lips as if she couldn't think of an argument against it, either.

"Shouldn't Constantina be a part of this conversation?" Juliana asked.

Both of her aunts looked at her like she was mad.

Leucretia's lip curled. "Constantina's idea of romance is to pinch a footman on the arse."

"Leucretia—"

But Leucretia didn't pause. "It is the truth. Now about Wilhelm. You're pretty enough that he will at least have a slight desire to kiss you. When he does, part your lips. Don't keep them pressed tightly together like a virgin."

This whole situation was too ridiculous. "Isn't that what I'm supposed to be?"

Juliana could have sworn she heard a muffled cough somewhere to her right. The leather arm chair, perhaps?

"Yes, but the idea of bedding one isn't all that appealing to a man. You might try pressing your breasts against his chest as he kisses you."

"Why would I do that?" Juliana asked.

Leucretia waved her hand. "Men seem to enjoy it."

Eustace's red face verged on purple now.

"Very well," Juliana said. "And should I allow him to put his tongue in my mouth?"

Both aunts stared at her.

Leucretia lifted a brow. "Perhaps you need this discussion less than I thought."

Eustace finally recovered enough to speak. "Yes, you might tempt Wilhelm with such things." Her face drew into more pensive lines. "But that is not the basis for a relationship."

"And pretending to share interests is?" Leucretia asked.

Eustace's spine straightened. "No, but a marriage needs more than sex."

"Says the woman who was married to a man old enough to be her father."

Eustace spun on Leucretia, her eyes blazing, lighting her with an inner fire that Juliana had never seen in the staid, older woman. "Albert was more of a man than you would ever know compared to those fops and dandies that never stay more than a month in your bed. You'll never know what it's like to move past that first blush of passion into something far more incredible. Far deeper. Far more intense. *You're* the one who'd been cheated by love."

Leucretia lifted her chin, her red lips dark against her pale skin. "You have no idea how greatly I've been cheated." She whirled away and strode from the room.

Eustace closed her eyes briefly, but then followed her sister from the room.

"Well, your family certainly is more dramatic than I was led to believe." Ian stood. He was on the complete opposite side of the room than she'd expected. "I can throw my voice, too," he explained.

She wanted that love Eustace had spoken of. A man whom she cared more and more deeply for as time passed.

And she couldn't have that with Ian. They both knew it. It was cruel to both of them to keep this going.

She spoke past the burning in her throat. "Will you arrange for fresh water to be brought to my room? And send the innkeeper's daughter up to help me undress."

The humor faded from his face, and he gave her a smart bow. "Very well, Your Highness."

Chapter Twenty

~~~

*T*he Duke of Sommet's house wasn't a house—it was a castle. And not a castle as her parents' home in Lenoria had been—fanciful, majestic. This castle was one that had been made to dominate. To subjugate the land and the people around it.

And yet women in pastel dresses flitted around large white tents that had been set up on the lawns for a picnic. And gentlemen had arranged themselves in a game of cricket.

Even through the thick glass of the coach window, the occasional burst of laughter and the sharp crack of the bat could be heard.

One of the men playing would undoubtedly be Gregory. Her brother could never pass up an opportunity to show off his skills as a bowler. And since he'd ridden ahead on horseback this morning—accompanied by Ian—he would already likely be rested from the journey.

She wanted to watch the men playing and see if perhaps Ian was around as well, but Juliana knew better than to let her aunts catch her gawking out the window.

Although perhaps having her aunts correct her would be a relief. At least they'd agree on something. Leucretia and Eustace had bickered the entire six-hour ride and the two hours they'd spent stopped on the side of the road because Contantina said Lulu, the ferret, was ill. Juliana shuddered at the memory.

Juliana remained silent the entire time.

The weight of everything she had to do pressed on her chest until she couldn't keep enough air in her lungs.

But she ignored the fear. Did she wish she was in a position where she could pursue Ian?

Yes.

Did she want to fight an evil man to save her country?

No.

But she wasn't left with a choice. So when the coach stopped, she exited with her chin held high and a smile on her face.

They were barely inside the entry hall when the duke greeted them. He bowed. "Your Highnesses. I'm pleased you decided to accept my invitation."

There was nothing unusual about the man. He was of average weight and average height. His white hair was thinning on top but he made no embarrassing efforts to hide the fact. His nose was a trifle large, but it didn't ruin a face that would have been handsome otherwise.

And yet something about him made a chill chase all the way over her scalp. She didn't know what it was. Perhaps it was only her knowledge of his plans for her and her country—but no. She hadn't liked him before, either. Perhaps it was the way his eyes were constantly roving as if searching for something better, or the discontented lines his wrinkles had set into. Or perhaps it was his way of constantly stroking his stomach as he spoke as if it were a pet cat.

Leucretia stepped forward. "Charles."

She offered her hand and Sommet placed a kiss on the back of it. "As enchanting as you were when we met so long ago." Perhaps it was Ian's training, but Juliana noticed the quick moue of dislike on Leucretia's face that was gone as fast as it appeared. So quick that she doubted anyone else even saw it.

Leucretia pulled her hand away. "Not *so* long ago."

The duke turned to Juliana. "I hope you will enjoy the entertainments I have planned for you."

Ian's training again saved her, keeping the outrage from her face. He no doubt thought himself witty with his words and her none the wiser. And knowing what she did of the man, it was best he continued to think that. He had to think her foolish and weak.

So she smiled at him and asked in a hesitant voice, "Is Prince Wilhelm here yet?"

The duke's expression turned patronizing. "Indeed. He arrived two days ago. Perhaps after you've had a chance to refresh yourself, you can join us on the lawn. I can have the pleasure of introducing you."

Juliana bit her lip, hoping she wasn't overacting. "That would be lovely."

Leucretia eyed her a bit strangely so she must have done a touch too much, but the duke didn't seem to notice. His mouth curved into another lips-only smile before passing them off to his servants.

The room Juliana was escorted to could only be described as sumptuous. The immense room overflowed with mahogany furniture. Thick Turkish carpets warmed the stone floors. Vibrant tapestries covered the walls. The room had a massive stone fireplace that she could have walked inside of if she so chose.

"I'm to be your lady's maid while you are here, Your Highness." A young girl stepped forward. She was dressed neatly in a gray wool dress, her long brown hair braided and wrapped into a chignon at the back of her head. But the poor, thin girl couldn't be more than ten.

Where had Ian hired the servants from?

"What is your name?"

The girl flushed so red, Juliana replayed her words in her head to make sure they weren't harsher than she'd intended. But they hadn't been. And she'd even smiled.

The maid cleared her throat. "Apple, my name is Apple."

A footman knocked on the door, then entered bearing the first of several trunks.

"I think the pink gown is packed in that trunk. It will work for this afternoon." It was the least sweltering of her options.

The young maid found the pink gown and unwrapped it. "I will go see about getting this pressed for you."

She scurried through the door before Juliana could ask about a bath.

There was another knock on the door. Her heart skipped a beat for a moment, hoping it might be Ian. But the door opened to reveal her brother, Gregory. His face was sweaty and his cravat loose. "You missed a fantastic match." He pulled off his jacket and tossed it over the back of a chair, then sighed. "The duke thinks I've agreed to his plan."

"Good. Let him continue to think that. Just don't agree to sign anything. When does he plan for you to make the claim?"

"In three days." For the first time, Gregory looked older than his twenty years. "I'm so sorry for all this."

Juliana nodded. "How was your ride here?"

"Pleasant. We were able to get here before the heat of the day."

She picked at some dust on her gown. "Then the new groom seemed adequate?"

"Yes. He seemed competent."

Competent? Couldn't he give her a bit more information than that?

She wanted to ask more, but she couldn't think of a way to do so that wouldn't raise Gregory's interest.

The door opened and her maid scurried back inside. Her eyes rounded when she saw Gregory. She blushed even redder than before and backed out of the room.

Gregory raised his eyebrow.

"My new lady's maid."

Gregory straightened. "Then my new valet should be here as well. Capital. The footman who helped me dress earlier didn't know a thing about tying a proper mathematical." The dimple on his cheek flashed. "I'll just have to hope that my new valet's tall enough to reach my cravat."

A few moments after he left, Apple returned. "I'm sorry, Your Highness. I didn't mean to interrupt."

Juliana shrugged. "It was only my brother."

Apple's mouth gaped. "He was a prince?"

Juliana had to keep from smiling. "Indeed. If you would please help me with my buttons?"

The girl carefully laid the dress on the bed, then came to stand behind Juliana. Up close Apple was a bit older than Juliana had first suspected. Thirteen or perhaps fourteen. And she was quite pretty even with the hollows in her cheeks.

Apple's hands shook so badly that she struggled a bit with the buttons, but was finally able to free Juliana.

Juliana waited for her to bring over the washbasin, but the girl simply stood there. After a moment, Juliana stood and carried it over to the dressing table by herself.

Apple didn't look at all surprised. Or even aware that Juliana was doing the tasks a maid normally performed. The girl had no idea what a lady's maid did.

Yet Juliana couldn't bring herself to ask if the girl had any experience. She didn't want to crush her.

So Juliana poured her own water and washed herself, then removed her own pins from her intricately coiled hair.

But she didn't think she'd be able to do it back up again on her own. "Would you mind helping me with my hair?"

The girl stared at her in horror. "I— Curse Wraith to the darkest pit in hell." She whirled away and would have bolted for the door if Juliana hadn't caught her arm.

"Wait, you know Wraith?"

The girl blinked back tears, and folded her arms tightly in front of her. "I told him I didn't have no experience." The smooth accent she'd used before was gone.

"Is he . . . is he your father?"

The girl snorted at that. "As if I has one of those."

But it just went to show how little she knew about Ian. He could have a dozen kids, for all she knew. They hadn't spoken of those sorts of things. "Then how do you know him?"

Apple shook her head, her jaw tight. "Shouldn't have listened to him. But the man can twist near anything like a bloomin' magician. Made it sound like I were doing him a favor. But I should be old enough not to listen to tales of spun gold. The man's a nutter."

"Ian asked you to act as my maid?"

"There's no need to dismiss me. I'll go." Her small chin lifted.

"No, if Ian asked you to be my maid, I am definitely keeping you."

Apple blinked, but then crossed her arms even tighter. "I can't do them fancy hairstyles that I've seen the other ladies wearing."

"Did you do your own hair this morning?"

The girl frowned. "Yes."

"Well, I think that style is perfectly adequate for me."

Apple unfolded her arms long enough to pat the back of her head. "This is what I wore when I was a flower seller, before—" Her eyes darkened, both sad and filled with loathing.

"Well, I think it is lovely and perfect for an afternoon picnic."

The girl hesitated for several long moments, before she stepped away from the door. "Wraith said your last maid wasn't trustworthy."

"Are you?"

Apple's gaze didn't waver. And her accent suddenly regained its polish. "If Wraith asks me to be."

Juliana knew the feeling. "Then shall we figure this out together?"

Apple nodded. After they had pulled Juliana's dress over her head, Apple began to work, her teeth clamped lightly on her lower lip.

"So have you seen Ian since you arrived?" Juliana asked, keeping her gaze on the table in front of her.

Apple nodded, mumbling past the pins she held between her lips. "He stopped me when I arrived to tell me I was to keep to your rooms and gut anyone who tried to enter without permission."

She said *gut* with far too much relish. "Have you had much opportunity to gut people in the past?"

Apple's face fell slightly. "No, but I could do it. Or he said I could report anyone suspicious to him, and he'd do it." She placed the last two pins. "And he *would* do it, too. I heard that one night he snuck into a rival rookery and killed the lot of them in their sleep. Seventeen of them there were. In the morning, he held a coronation party and named himself the Gutter Rat King. He controlled the western half of London after that."

Juliana stared at Apple in the mirror. "When was this?"

Apple shrugged. "I'm not sure. Long time ago. Perhaps a dozen years?"

"How do you know of this? You would have been too young to remember."

Apple tugged a few wisps of hair loose by Juliana's face. "Well, he's a legend. There are a hundred more stories like that. Criminals we have lots of in London, but blokes with flair like that? There's just Wraith."

Juliana tapped an extra pin against the edge of the table. Then how much of this was story and how much of it was truth? "Are any of the stories more recent?"

Apple smiled slowly. "Now there are even more stories."

"Like the one you just told me?"

Apple smiled. "No. The new ones are far better."

Chapter Twenty-one

Juliana wanted nothing more than one of the triangle sandwiches from the table to her right. But she knew if she tried, Leucretia would snatch it out of her hand with the speed of a crazed nursemaid. She'd never forgiven Juliana for the time she'd dropped a raspberry tart down the front of her white lace gown at the regent's Christmas soiree.

Apparently, she couldn't be trusted with food unless she was seated.

Ian would tease her for her hesitance. In fact, if he were here, he would have already slipped an entire tray's worth into his pockets.

And found a way to pass her three or four.

No. She wouldn't think of Ian.

She freshened the smile on her face, startling Lord Neromy, who launched into another story about his hounds' propensity for getting distracted by gooseberry bushes.

Gregory moved to her side. "If I might steal my sister away for a moment?" He freed her without waiting for a response. "Wilhelm is here."

Juliana kept her gaze trained on her brother despite her sudden compulsion to whirl about and look for the other prince. She'd given up on seeing Wilhelm before dinner. Apparently, he couldn't be bothered to leave a piece of music he was composing.

"What does he look like?"

Gregory scowled at her. "Like a man? I'm about to introduce you to him. You can form your own opinion."

Juliana's legs wouldn't move. Which was foolish since Wilhelm was one of the main reasons she'd come. Yet she suddenly had no desire to see him. As soon as she turned, she'd have to pursue him. No matter his appearance. No matter nearly everything. She'd have to do her best to marry this man.

"Juliana?" Gregory asked.

Juliana cleared her throat. "My heel was stuck in the grass."

She turned.

And there was Ian. A half smile lifted his lips. Her heart hammered so fast that it took her a moment to notice the impeccably dressed man beside him. He stood several inches taller than Ian. The only hint to his true age was touch of gray at his temples. His jaw was square and his nose straight. His shoulders were broad.

The man she needed to try to convince to marry her was very handsome.

And although he tried to hide it, he was incredibly annoyed.

Ian winked at her, then disappeared back into the crowd.

Gregory led her to Wilhelm's side. "Princess Juliana, may I introduce Prince Wilhelm of Prussia?"

Juliana could feel the gazes of all three of her aunts burning between her shoulder blades. "A pleasure, Your Highness." She lowered her lashes and tried to look seductive.

The prince's pale blue eyes swept past her. He sketched her the briefest of bows. "I was told that Sir Henry wished to speak to me." He glanced around the tent. "But I do not see him." His English was excellent with only a hint of a Germanic accent.

"Do you see *me*?" Juliana asked.

Sweet heavens, what was wrong with her? That was not how she planned to woo him.

Both Gregory and Wilhelm straightened at that.

After sending her an exasperated glance, Gregory tried to fill the awkward silence she'd created. "I hear you're working on a new symphony."

But Wilhelm's gaze found Juliana's for the first time. "For my daughter's sixth birthday next month."

"She wanted a symphony?" Juliana asked.

For the barest moment, Wilhelm's stern expression softened. "A kitten, actually. I'm sorry, who are you again?"

"Princess Juliana Castanova, my sister," Gregory supplied.

She curtsied, but she kept it as quick as his bow had been.

He offered her his arm. "Would you care to accompany me while I look for Sir Henry?"

"I'd love to." She kept it simple so she didn't sound catty again.

Wilhelm's eyes narrowed as if he wasn't sure if she was being sarcastic or not. Truth be told, she wasn't entirely certain herself.

But she accepted his arm with a polite smile.

Wilhelm cleared his throat as he led her away. "Sir Henry has a violin in his possession that I'm anxious to obtain. Sommet swore he's arrived, but I have yet to see him. A groom informed me Sir Henry was ready to meet, but I must have missed him."

Ian had lured him down here? "What is so special about this violin?"

Wilhelm gave a deep sigh. "It is a Stradivarius. Crafted in 1692 by Antonio himself. The tone alone—" He cut off, his face flushing. "It is said to be a particularly fine instrument."

They circled the edge of the tent.

"So is your daughter going to get a kitten?"

Wilhelm frowned. "A symphony is a far more meaningful gift."

She was no expert on children, but she suspected a six-year-old wouldn't see it that way. "Having been a six-year-old girl once, might I suggest you give her both?"

He looked as if she'd asked him to cut off his right hand. "Do you think that is necessary?"

"No. But it would make her happy."

Wilhelm's brows drew together. "Now, I will have to get the cat."

They came to a stop by the refreshment table.

"Would you care for punch?" Wilhelm asked.

"No, but one of those sandwiches would be divine." If the prince gave her one to eat, her aunts wouldn't dare intervene.

Ian would be proud of her maneuverings.

Confound it. She wouldn't think about him now.

She made sure to brush the inside of Wilhelm's elbow as she released his arm to accept the small china plate.

Wilhelm cleared his throat again. "Princess Juliana, I must be frank with you. I fear I'm not skilled in the art of flirtation. I can barely craft a civil compliment. I find little time for anything but my music, but if you're interested, you may join me in the music room this evening. I will be working with musicians on the first movement of the symphony."

Elbow touches were apparently far more powerful than Juliana had given them credit for. "I would enjoy that."

Wilhelm bowed over her hand. "I believe I might as well."

Then he strode back toward the house.

Leucretia slid into the gap at Juliana's side. "That appeared to go well." She lifted the plate out of Juliana's grasp and handed it to a footman.

Juliana let it go without protest, her appetite suddenly gone. It *had* gone well. And that was the worst part. Wilhelm was handsome and polite. And even if he was lacking in some social graces, he cared deeply for his daughter and was passionate about his music.

The only thing wrong with Wilhelm was that he was far too *possible*.

And he wasn't Ian.

Chapter Twenty-two

He deserved to be sainted.

Yet Ian gave up that possibility in order to swear freely in every language he knew.

He should be skulking about the castle, not trying to glean every little detail he could about the prince he'd just delivered to Juliana.

And he could find nothing wrong with the man. All his servants adored him. The only complaint by some of the other aristos was that he ignored invitations to social events to stay home with his daughter.

Ian's only negative was that the prince hadn't dashed to Juliana's side as soon as she arrived. What type of red-blooded male could resist her?

Ian stopped by the stables and checked on Juliana's horses. Thankfully, his tasks as a visiting groom were minimal. The duke's grooms already saw to the basics of the stable itself, leaving Ian and three other grooms to tend to ten horses.

Later, he would be assigned to help take down

the tents and move the tables, but for the next few hours, he was free.

And now it was time to focus on the real reason he was there.

He needed to find out what Sommet's game was. He needed to know why Sommet was singling out the Trio. He needed to know any other traps the duke had lying in wait for them.

And then Ian would destroy him.

Not quickly, either. Ian would strip away everything thing the duke valued—his influence, his power, his money. Only after the man was homeless and pox-ridden in the street would Ian slit his throat.

No one was allowed to hurt his friends.

Rather than heading straight to Sommet's rooms, Ian found a small secluded space between the statues of dead dukes and the stairs and waited.

He'd learned how to wait in absolute stillness. He no longer felt the burn in his muscles or the temptation to scratch an itch. He'd gained much from this one skill.

He enjoyed the reputation for be all-knowing, but the truth was much more mundane.

After he'd run away from Canterbury the first time when he was seven, he'd made it a day on the streets before he'd been robbed of his jacket and shoes.

He'd huddled amid the rubbish, too afraid to

move. He wasn't entirely sure how long he huddled there. Two, perhaps three days. But long enough that he knew the baker opened his back door for about ten minutes every morning while he waited for his delivery of coal.

Even as shaky as he was, Ian had been able to sneak in and steal two rolls.

He'd eaten only two bites when the other boys found him again and stole the bread—until he told them he could get them more the next day.

He'd returned to his pile of rubbish. By the next day, he also knew when the fruit seller would step away from his cart for his afternoon pint.

By the end of the week, the other lads were no longer robbing Ian, but bringing him things to trade for edible food and drink.

Ian peered through the gap between the statues as a maid walked by carrying a pile of sheets. She was only the second maid to climb the stairs. The other had carried a brush to scrub the floors and a bucket of water.

Soon he knew the maids' schedules. And that one of them despised Sommet's valet.

Sommet was a suspicious bastard. He alone had rooms in the west tower. Ian had hoped with the crush of people who'd come to the party, he would have been forced to house other guests there. But the duke remained apart.

The duke would soon find that his secrecy worked against him. Fewer servants meant less chance of being discovered. All the empty space meant more places for Ian to hide. It would also be easier to tell which rooms were normally used, what drawers were opened, and what objects were moved.

Sommet finally came. The old vulture. He was accompanied by the footman Ian had seen in the tower earlier. The footman stayed guarding the foot of the stairs as Sommet ascended.

The duke walked with the slightest hesitation on his left leg. Gout apparently, rather than the two assassination attempts on his life.

And even now in his own house, for every two steps he took up the stairs, he glanced back over his shoulder.

If it weren't for the footman, Ian would have been tempted to put a knife in Sommet's back and end all his threats right here.

Instead, he watched for any other bits that would be useful when he destroyed the man later.

Sommet always glanced over his right shoulder.

And he left his rooms unguarded while he wasn't in them. Which would make for a perfect surprise later.

"Charles!"

The duke stopped on the stairs as Leucretia approached.

"You wanted to speak to me?"

"Not here."

"Are you certain of that?" Leucretia skimmed

up the stairs to stand next to him; she trailed one long finger down the duke's wrinkled cheek.

They had better not kiss. If they kissed, Ian might betray his hiding spot.

The duke caught Leucretia's elbow. "Shall we go to the library?"

"I have fond memories of a certain library."

The duke slid his arm down her back and over the boney curve of her hip. "I have learned I negotiate far better if we remain upright."

Ian hoped his gag wasn't loud enough for Sommet to hear as the duke led her back down the stairs.

The footman followed them, allowing Ian to fall in behind.

When the two disappeared into the library, the footman took up his post at the door there as well.

Damnation. There were too many guests still lingering out front for him to risk scaling to the window. And the walls of the castle were solid English stone, far too thick to hear through.

But he hadn't been named Wraith for nothing.

If he entered the adjoining parlor, there was a fair chance the windows to both rooms would be open in the humid July heat.

He would hear at least—

Juliana snuck past him down the corridor toward Sommet's rooms.

No, that wasn't giving her quite enough credit. She didn't sneak, precisely. She'd followed his instructions and kept her gait normal.

The only reason he knew she was sneaking was a rather adorable crease between her brows.

While Ian hated the thought of information being revealed without him there to partake of it, he couldn't risk Juliana getting caught in the duke's tower.

The duke's tower.

Not a bad title for a lurid novel if he ever decided to write one.

He trailed after Juliana. He would have called out, but he feared drawing the footman's attention.

At least, following her did give him ample opportunity to admire the sweet curve of her backside.

She'd made it to the top of the staircase before she glanced behind her. She jerked in surprise, then glared at him. "Are you following me?" she whispered.

"First of all, I was here before you. Second of all, are you bloody mad? Sommet is just downstairs. He could come at any moment."

"He's talking to my aunt."

"They could finish their conversation at any minute."

She strode down the corridor. "Then there is all the more reason to look about while I have the chance." She eased open the first door she came to, revealing an office of some sort.

Ian took the last three stairs in a single step. He grabbed her around the waist before she could step over the threshold. As cagey as the duke was, it wouldn't surprise Ian if he'd left a few surprises. "Did you check for traps?"

As tense as her surprise made her, she was still soft against him. So he kept her there. It made the whispering easier as well. "First, always assume there are traps. Second, I doubt the duke would keep your documents in a place this easy to access."

Her rib cage fluttered under his hand. "First, stop numbering everything. Second, wouldn't the fact that you doubt the duke would keep the documents here mean it is more likely that the duke would keep the documents here?"

An interesting point.

Damnation. He'd missed her.

And he'd only been away less than a day. This didn't bode well for him come the end of the house party. After all, she had made it clear where his place was, and it wasn't nestled against her pert backside.

Yet he couldn't bring himself to move away, not until he breathed deeply of her scent a few more times.

They both peered into the room.

"How would I precisely spot a trap?" she asked.

"I would check for any string or wire about ankle high. Or any unevenness or discoloration in the carpet or stones."

She pulled away from him to crouch down on

the ground, giving him a rather nice view down her bodice.

"I don't see any"—she looked up at him and must have caught the direction of his wayward gaze because her cheeks flushed—"strings." She stood. "What else should I check for? And I warn you, if it involves me removing my clothing I will be dubious."

"Are those lock picks in your bodice?"

"I didn't come completely unprepared."

He'd lingered far too long in this interlude already. "If we aren't gone by the time the duke finishes his conversation, we'll be trapped."

"Why?"

"Because—"

There were voices below. Ian ushered her inside and shut the door behind them. "Because he keeps a footman posted at the foot of the stairs when he is in his rooms."

Her lips formed a little O of shock. "Then how can we get down without being seen?"

"We don't."

There were footsteps on the stairs. It was definitely Sommet. One footstep was slightly louder than the other.

The office had an unused feel to it. It was perfectly clean, but there was a certain mustiness to the air that bespoke a lack of frequent air circulation.

But he wouldn't risk Juliana to a supposition.

"Get under the desk."

She blinked at him.

Probably not an order princesses normally received. He jerked his head toward the door. "Sommet."

She paled, then ran to the desk and disappeared under it.

Ian remained by the door but stood behind it. If Sommet did choose to come in, Ian would disable him before he had a chance to find Juliana.

But the footsteps passed by the room without pause. After hearing Sommet climb the next flight of stairs, Ian went to join Juliana at the desk.

"So there's no way out of here then?" she whispered as she climbed out.

"Not unless you happened to be with a genius."

"We must hurry then. Dinner's in less than an hour."

"Eager to get back to your handsome prince?" He hoped the words didn't sound as bitter as they tasted in his mouth.

"He won't be at dinner. We're meeting in the conservatory later."

"Alone? That moved rather quickly. Good job." He examined the bookcase looking for anything out of place, but the books were generic volumes that every proper Englishman pretended to have read.

"We're listening to musicians for his symphony."

He looked behind a hideous painting of a bowl of fruit. "Ah, likely story."

Her mouth gaped slightly. "He—"

He carefully replaced the painting, aligning the frame with the darker square of wallpaper behind it. "Tell me you at least considered he had other motives."

Her cheeks darkened. "He's not like that."

"If he's seen you, then he'd be a fool not to be like that." He went over to a small table and picked up a figurine of a shepherd so he didn't have to see her face.

"Thank you." The longing in her voice speared something deep in his chest.

"I'll need to speak with you afterward." No, he didn't need to. But he always had been a greedy bastard and if she was with him, she couldn't be offering her sweet lips to the prince.

Hell. Hell. Hell. He didn't need to see the way her eyes lit at the prospect.

"We need a better plan for your search. This won't be as easy as we'd hoped." He swept his hands under the desk, then around the sides.

She flipped through the blank papers on top. "Agreed."

"Are you ready to tell me what you're looking for?"

"I can't."

Ian had hesitated to push her in the past. But he no longer held any such qualms. He was protecting her safety now. He was very good at getting the information. It was time to put that to use. "I'll be looking for information on his betrayal of the Trio. If I know what you're looking for, I'll know if I happen to stumble across it."

Still she hesitated.

"You say you want what's best for your country. Then you must know that *I'm* your best option for retrieving it." He stepped forward and placed his hands on her shoulders. "Trust me."

The words were ones he'd uttered to gain information he wanted countless time, but now they were the truest plea he'd ever spoken.

"Can I?"

"Most women fall swooning at my feet and swear their trust by now." He'd done his best to convince her he was untrustworthy, but he longed for her to see past it.

She shook her head. "No. No foolishness now. I want you to tell me if I can trust my entire country in your hands."

Ian's throat suddenly felt dry. "Yes."

Juliana exhaled long. Apparently he hadn't been the only one holding his breath.

He listened with growing anger as Juliana explained about Sommet's blackmail and his plans to put Gregory on the throne.

Never. Ian would eat day-old eel pie before he let that happen.

"Your brother is lucky you already bargained for his survival. May I at least give him a fierce beating for his stupidity?"

But she frowned. "Gregory truly isn't stupid. He is young and desperate to regain what we lost. Only slightly more desperate than I."

"Why?"

Her frown deepened. "What do you mean?"

"Why is it so important to regain Lenoria? Is being a princess really that important to you?"

She shook her head, looking at him as if he'd grown a second nose. "That isn't it at all. People live happily in cottages over five hundred years old. Families in the southern mountains have farmed the same land as far back as we have written records. The crown has rested on the head on the Castanova family since before the Romans. The land is in my blood. It *is* my blood. I won't be the one to lose it." Even though her voice had never risen above a whisper, she glowed with so much pride and determination Ian feared she'd burst into flame. "Being a princess isn't important. Lenoria is."

He clenched his hands so tightly they shook, but he had to do something to keep from drawing her to him and basking in her light. He forced his voice to sound amused. "Touchy subject apparently. Perhaps we should save the monologue for a time when we're not in such a precarious position?"

She flushed and glanced at the door. Her light extinguished.

If he'd been worthy of her, he would have fallen at her feet and begged her forgiveness. Instead, he asked. "Your lock picks?"

She pulled the set of picks from her bodice. The small motion was the most erotic thing he'd ever seen.

He'd planned to make her pick the locks to the desk as long as they were here, but now he only wanted out of this study as quickly as possible. So he used the picks himself to open the drawers.

Unfortunately, Juliana chose to press up behind him to see over his shoulder, her breasts resting against his back.

He was damned lucky the drawers were empty. He didn't think he would have been able to read a word.

Her disappointed exhale stirred the hairs on the back of his neck, sending a shiver down his spine.

"So how do we get out of here?"

He had to step away from her so he could think. "The safest option would be to wait until he goes down to dinner."

"I don't have time for safe. I'll be missed before then. My aunts generally check my clothing before important events." She glared at him, daring him to comment.

So, of course, he had to. "Do they wipe your face, too?"

A slight smile ruined her glare. "So what can we do to save me from the wrath of the Fates?"

Why hadn't he realized that whispering with her would make him think of pillows and the conversations shared on them, curled together in the safety of the night.

Where? In the hovel above the brothel? In a dock-side tavern? He had no place having those dreams.

He walked to the window, peering outside at the growing twilight. The lawns had emptied of guests, the people having gone inside to change. He studied the distance to the bushes below. "How well can you climb?"

Chapter Twenty-three

Juliana ran into her room. It wasn't very regal to run, but it was even less regal to be caught with leaves and sticks in one's hair.

"Coo-ee, Your Highness," Apple said, eyes wide. "Where were you? I looked for you everywhere. Then I looked for Wraith everywhere to tell him you were missing and I couldn't find him neither."

Juliana had been dangling off the back of a madman as he climbed down the outside of the castle like some sort of monkey. He hadn't seemed bothered by her additional weight until she'd pressed a kiss to the back of his neck to thank him and he'd spooked and dropped her in the bushes. Thankfully, they'd been only a few feet off the ground at that point. "I had a private meeting that went longer than expected."

"You've only got a half an hour to dress."

Juliana nodded, turning so Apple could see to her buttons.

"I didn't know what you want to wear, so I pressed your yellow silk. It seemed like it would

the coolest dress on a night as flash as this one."
This time Apple was quick to bring her a bowl of
water and towel to freshen up, and she had the
dress ready as soon as Juliana rushed through a
quick scrubbing.

Apple picked a leaf out of her hair after she'd
settled the dress over her head. "Just what sort of
meeting was this?"

"Juliana!" Leucretia sailed into the room.

The leaf Apple held disappeared into her sleeve.

"This is the maid the agency sent?"

Apple's cheeks reddened as she brushed out Juliana's hair.

"She might be young but she comes highly rec-
ommended. I have been quite pleased with her thus
far."

Leucretia tapped her slender finger against her
leg. "This is unacceptable. Why isn't your mistress
ready?"

"She was resting and I thought to let her rest
after the journey. But she'll be ready in time for
supper."

Juliana knew even if she had to wear the same
hairstyle the entire party, she would keep this maid.
The girl was bright. And loyal.

"Dinner is in twenty minutes," Leucretia said,
the disbelief in her voice clear.

Juliana was scrambling for a reason to cast her
aunt from the room so Apple didn't have to bear
her censure, when Apple picked up a lock of her

hair and then another, and with a few deft twists had arranged Juliana's hair in a style as elegant as any Juliana had ever worn.

When had she learned that?

Leucretia face calmed. "See that she's ready earlier tomorrow."

Apple bowed her head and dropped into a credible curtsy. "Indeed, Your Highness. It won't happen again."

Apple picked up the used dress, quickly folding it to hide the dirt on the one side, and backed from the room.

"She's young," Leucretia pointed out.

"But talented." Juliana fought to keep the surprise from her voice. "I like her."

Leucretia obviously had other things distracting her. "Wilhelm won't be coming to dinner."

"I'm to meet with him afterward."

Her aunt's brows flitted upward. "Well done. Where are you to meet?"

"In the conservatory."

She nodded, but then the lines around her lips deepened. "Be on your guard around Sommet."

Which reminded Juliana of Leucretia's meeting with the man this afternoon.

"I thought he was a friend."

Leucretia smoothed a finger along one of her black braids. "We were many things to each other, but never that."

"Why should I watch for him?"

As far as she knew, Gregory had told no one else of his trouble. Had Sommet told Leucretia about his plans for Gregory?

Her aunt seemed to be picking her words carefully. "He's not one to appreciate a powerful woman."

"Has he been giving you trouble, Aunt?"

Her nostrils pinched. "No man has ever been trouble to me. Now Wilhelm wants to meet this evening? I will go as your chaperone if you like. Unlike your other aunts, I know when privacy is preferable."

That gave Juliana the perfect opening. "I was going to ask you earlier, but I couldn't find you."

Her aunt waved her hand. "I was out speaking with Lady Totherton for a bit. I must have been there."

She wasn't going to admit to being with Sommet. Were they still lovers or was there something more treacherous? As ruler of Lenoria, Juliana had the right to ask, but Leucretia was her aunt. And Juliana had to force herself to pry. "That's odd. A servant said he saw you with Sommet."

Leucretia's gaze turned calculating. "For a moment only." She clicked her tongue. "Perhaps it's best you know. It's why I warned you of him. He advised me on some business dealings long ago, and when I proved more successful, he grew angry."

"If he is threatening—"

"No, do nothing to interfere. I can take care of my own problems. Now shall we go to dinner?"

A short time later, Juliana found herself smiling intently at her turtle soup. Being the highest-ranking female in attendance, she had the rather dubious honor of sitting next to the duke.

"It must be burdensome to be tasked with so much at such a young age. I myself inherited this duchy when I was but ten."

Did he think to soften the blow of his intrigues?

She stirred the brown broth with her spoon. "Not at all. I relish the responsibility. It is what I was raised to do, after all."

The duke lifted a stringy white eyebrow, and slurped the soup off his spoon. "So pleased to hear it. I'll admit I was surprised when you accepted my invitation. You have never done so in the past."

"How could I stay away? It promises to be quite interesting."

The duke's eyes narrowed, but after searching her face, he turned to the woman at his other side.

Juliana turned as well. She'd been sandwiched between two dukes. To her right sat the dark-haired, rakish Duke of Abington.

She started when she found his gaze already trained on her.

She didn't know the man well. He'd been back in London for only about a year, having lived abroad before that. He was always surrounded by so many swooning females that Juliana had never shared more than a brief nod of acknowledgment with him.

But he had to be better than Sommet.

"How are you enjoying the house party, Your Grace?"

He lifted his cup of wine and took a sip. "Quite well. Even better now that it's provided me with the opportunity to speak to you."

"You don't find it boring to only speak to one woman at a time?"

His head rocked back and he grinned, dimples appearing on his cheeks.

"Apparently not if she is you." He leaned toward her as if to impart some great secret. Some of the tension escaped her shoulders. Perhaps she wouldn't starve to death at the house party after all. She'd simply eat when she spoke to Abington and hope she could keep the food down while she conversed with Sommet.

"So does Lenoria share this unseasonable heat in the summer?"

Juliana hated that she had to pause to think of her answer. "Quite. My family would often take trips out of the city to escape it." She also hated how everything she said about Lenoria was past tense. All her memories were old ones, or snippets and glimpses she got from the letters from the ragtag officials who held together the local government. For some reason, she felt compelled to prove that her knowledge wasn't lacking. "My aunt owns a beautiful chateau on Lake Lago. The lake is over three hundred feet deep but you can clearly see the bottom of it. Cherry trees grow along the banks and when the petals fall from the trees, they float, turning the entire lake pink."

"Lake Lago?" Abington asked, his dimple deepening. "Now I know this pink lake is fiction. Who would name the lake *Lake Lake*?"

"Apparently there was a dispute hundreds of years ago with some Spanish immigrants. That was the compromise."

"I traveled all over Europe. I'm sure I would have heard of it."

"The lake is in the mountains, and the mountains are only accessible through the Lenorian side." That was what kept the land mostly safe during the war. After her family had been dethroned, the Spanish had swooped in but the terrain had proved too difficult to be strategically useful. But their treatment at the hands of the Spanish had convinced the Lenorians that they'd prefer their own monarchy back as opposed to that of the French or Spanish. "They don't get many travelers. The few villages there keep mostly to themselves."

"Which mountains?" Abington motioned for the footman to refill his wineglass.

"The Palas."

"I've heard there is to be archery tomorrow," Abington said abruptly, grabbing for his wine glass even though it was only half full.

"What was this about the Palas?" Sommet cut off his conversation with the lady at his side and swiveled to Juliana.

"The lake there," Abington said. "The princess was regaling me with its beauty." He made it sound as if she'd been forcing him to listen to the linen inventory.

Had she been boring him? Was Abington so great an actor that she hadn't suspected?

"It is." Sommet nodded. "I was there long ago. The mountains hold many treasures."

Abington's eyes wandered, apparently he *had* lost interest. "Ah, natural beauty so fascinating."

"Have you heard anything about them recently, Your Highness? How they fared in the war?" Sommet's spoon swished back and forth in the center of his bowl.

"Nothing." But now she intended to learn everything she could. Something about them had caught Sommet's attention—

Gregory's blasted deal.

How had she forgotten? Her brother had given away the rights to the minerals in the southern mountains—the Palas.

"That is unfortunate. I find them of particular interest."

"When were you last there?" she asked. She knew she should let the matter drop, but she was a princess—a queen if she could get back to her country—and she'd only take so much of his sly comments. Over the past year and a half, she'd debated if things would have gone better for Lenoria in the treaty negotiations if she'd been more aggressive. If she'd been louder. If she'd been stronger.

"Not for years."

She wouldn't suffer those doubts again. If she lost to Sommet, it would be because she'd been torn down, fighting, clawing, screaming the entire way. "I'm pleased you have such interest in *my* mountains. I intend to see they remain undisturbed."

Sommet set down his spoon.

Abington jostled into her as he moved aside as a footman came for his bowl. "I beg your pardon." At first she thought he'd been trying to interrupt, but no, his face was flushed. He was inebriated. He motioned a footman over again to refill his glass. That had to be his fourth. Or perhaps fifth. And he'd been drinking something in the parlor before they'd been led into the dining room, "I much prefer beaches to mountains myself. Especially if there is bathing involved. There was one in Greece—"

Juliana only half listened as Abington launched into an amusing tale about becoming separated from his clothing while swimming.

Instead, she let her gaze battle with Sommet's. Let *him* worry about what she knew.

She was done being the only one who couldn't sleep at night.

Chapter Twenty-four

"*P*lease tell me this is part of your disguise." Ian had planned to spy on Juliana in the conservatory, but then he'd stumbled over Abington sprawled in the corridor. The man was nearly insensible with drink.

"What disguise?"

Ian tucked his arm around the other man and hefted him to his feet. "Glavenstroke told me he'd sent an operative to look into Sommet. As soon as I saw the guest list, I knew it must be you." He'd worked with Abington briefly a few years ago in Constantinople, where Abington had been training a group of Greek rebels.

He'd heard rumor that Abington had become somewhat unstable since his return to London. Now, Ian was normally the last person to require stability. He hardly ever slept in the same place two nights in a row, but when it was Juliana's country—her life—at risk, he found he had very little tolerance for this nonsense.

"Officially, have no idea what you're talking

about. Unofficially, what the devil are you doing here? I thought you no longer worked for the Foreign Office."

"I don't."

Abington's frown was pronounced as he tried to work that out in his mind. "Then why are you here?"

"Sommet and I have a more personal score."

Abington nodded, as they slowly stumbled toward his room. Ian waited to say any more until they were inside with the door shut behind them. "How does Sommet not know you?"

"I was one of Glavenstroke's pet projects. Since I only worked with the Greek rebels, I never had reason to interact with anyone else from the office."

"What do you know about Sommet?"

"Not much. The man's a damned tight drum. Or runs a tight ship?" He pressed his hands against the sides of his skull. "Hell, perhaps this is a conversation better held in the morning."

"I don't have time to waste. What can you tell me?"

Abington scrunched his face. "Don't know if I should."

"I'm trying to protect Juliana from Sommet. I have to keep her safe. You know how important that is." Ian felt a twinge of guilt at his words. Abington's rebel lover had been hanged in Constantinople, and he'd been helpless to stop it. Ian was a beast to play off that pain. But he was not a man given to qualms. Especially not when it might help Juliana.

"Juliana?"

"The princess," Ian supplied.

"I know she's a bloody princess. I sat by her at dinner. First-name basis, are you?"

"You know me. No decorum at all."

Abington's bleary eyes focused for a moment. "I do know you, Wraith. I may be drunk, but I'm not blind. You like her."

"She's a princess. Everybody likes her. Swallows roost on her windowsills and puppies follow her about."

"She has a death wish if she keeps provoking Sommet."

"How was she provoking him?" Really, he couldn't let that woman out of his sight.

"The Palas."

"The mountains?"

"Yes. Don't quite know Sommet's connection to them yet, but he wants them. Which means if your princess keeps laying claim to them, Sommet will find a way to get rid of her."

"So help me protect her."

Abington sighed and rubbed the back of his hand across his mouth. "All I know is that Sommet is wealthy. Very. But about a year and a half ago, there was a sudden decrease in his finances. He's still wealthy, but the money coming in was cut in half. It appears tied to undisclosed investments in the Palas."

"What type of investments?" Ian helped Abington out of his jacket and the man collapsed on his bed with a groan.

Ian was lucky the man was foxed, otherwise he doubted Abington would be so forthright. He should let Glaves know his man grew talkative when cup-shot.

"Vague. But my guess is mining. And the French. Always the damned French."

"What—" But Abington's eyes rolled back and he let out a huge snore.

Ian left. He'd finish first thing in the morning. With carefully silent feet, he crept to the conservatory. Although as he approached, it became apparent his stealth wouldn't be necessary. A violin and cello were in the process of tuning while someone picked out a few notes on the pianoforte.

When a footman walked by, Ian nodded and continued past as if he had somewhere to be, then circled back.

He could hear voices on the other side of the door. A deep voice and then a higher, sultry one. How could Wilhelm want to listen to music when he could be listening to Juliana?

Juliana laughed at something, the sound breathy and surprised. Happy.

Ian backed away from the door. Information to

him was like ale to a tavern—essential. It had been his livelihood for most of his life. Every bit, every morsel, he stored away for later use, gathering more and more details until nothing surprised him.

He hadn't been surprised since his mother had offed herself.

Except by Juliana.

Juliana surprised him every moment.

For once, he didn't want to know what was happening on the other side of the door. He told himself that he respected Juliana enough to give her privacy, but he knew that wasn't the case. He spied on everyone.

No. He had to be honest to himself and to the cold sweat on his palms.

He was scared. Terrified like a hen in a cock fight.

Of losing her to a man who actually deserved her.

Wilhelm might be a master.

She'd heard only parts of the first movement. But it managed to be both haunting yet strangely playful. It was a combination she wouldn't have thought possible if she hadn't heard it herself.

Ian needn't have worried about her virtue after all. Wilhelm was almost entirely focused on his music. Occasionally, he'd remember her presence and return to her side to ask for her opinion on a certain violinist or share some humorous commentary on his work.

She suspected this was what her evenings would be like if she married the prince.

There could be worse fates.

This could be a life she might even come to enjoy after a while.

If she didn't have another man awaiting her in her room. A man that made her heart pound and breath cease.

Wilhelm stopped the current cellist with a nod. "That will do for tonight."

The now sweaty musician lowered his arm and sagged against his instrument.

Juliana rose to her feet but kept her gaze from straying to the door again. Ian was either waiting for her in her room or he wasn't. Staring at the door did nothing but make her neck sore.

Wilhelm joined her as the other musicians began to pack up their instruments. Leucretia caught her eye, then slipped from the room.

"Thank you for humoring me," Wilhelm said.

Juliana smiled. "No, it was enjoyable. Your daughter will love it."

"Truly?"

She wasn't sure if he was asking about her enjoyment or his daughter's, so she nodded. They were both true.

"She's blind, you know. My Greta. Has been since birth." He watched intently for her reaction.

Juliana met his gaze a bit confused. What was he watching for? She'd spent the entire evening trying to ensure she said the right things. Did the right things. She second-guessed herself at every interaction. And she was exhausted. "Have you thought about getting her a puppy rather than a kitten then? She could train it to come when she called. One of my old nannies had a dog who would pick up whatever she dropped. It might be useful."

A slow smile spread over Wilhelm's face, sincere and uncertain at the same time. "Then you don't assume she's slow of thought?"

"You only said she was blind."

He caught her hand and raised it to his lips. His lips were warm and firm, his caress gentle, but her insides stayed firmly in place. Not a single flip or roll.

"I'm glad you joined me tonight."

"So am I." But as she hurried out of the conservatory a few moments later, she had to face the truth that she was far more excited to be going back to her room than she had been to go to the conservatory.

Juliana exhaled. There really was no chance she'd be able to stop the anticipation that hummed over her skin.

Was it somehow unfair to Wilhelm? Her desire for Ian?

She'd made no protestation of affection. But she'd made her intentions clear. Should she be honest with the prince? What she wanted with Wilhelm was little more than an alliance at this point. Could she explain that?

Could she marry a man in the hope that it would someday grow into something more?

After all, she'd forget what she felt for Ian.

Or at least time would lessen it.

Eventually.

She opened the door to her room and could tell immediately that Ian wasn't there. It wasn't just that she couldn't see him, but she couldn't feel him, either. Ian had a way of charging the very air in the room.

Apple sat over in the far corner of the room. When Juliana entered, she tucked a book behind her. "I washed my hands before I touched it."

"I'm fine with you reading."

Apple flushed. "I was going to put the book back."

"You can read whatever you like."

"Truly?" The girl looked disbelieving.

"Yes. Has Ian been by this evening?"

Apple frowned. "He said he wanted to find out a bit more about Sommet. Were you expecting him in to be *here*?"

It was Juliana's turn to have her cheeks heat.

"Sorry, Your Highness. I don't see anything or hear anything."

"I rather suspect you do both very well."

Apple brightened at that. "I do. Wraith said so, too. I learned how to do your hair by watching one of the other maids. She didn't even know I was there. But," she hurried to add, "whatever you do is safe with me. I won't tell anyone." Her lips pressed together. "Except Wraith. I would tell him anything he asked. But no one else."

"Thank you. When you said he wanted to find out more about Sommet, what did he intend?"

"I think more information on the man's defenses."

What was he planning? Her heart inched up her throat. She thought they were supposed to work out a plan together. This was her responsibility. "Did he say where?"

Apple shook her head. "Why? Do you think something is wrong?"

Juliana tried to smile. "Probably not." But she walked to the door. Sommet wouldn't kill someone at his own house party, would he? If he found Ian snooping, he'd probably just have him arrested.

There were too many guests about, too many servants.

Except it was late at night and most were in bed.

"What time did you see him?"

Apple hurried over to stand next to Juliana. "A hour ago. I'm coming, too."

"No. I need you to wait here in case he comes back."

Apple snorted. "Wraith would hang me if I let you go about at night on your own."

But Juliana didn't need to worry about this girl as well as Ian.

Apple must have sensed her hesitation because she planted her hands on her hips. "I've lived on my own since I were ten years old. I know more about moving about unseen than you do."

Juliana really couldn't argue with that. "Chances are he is well and he'll flay the both of use for sneaking about."

Apple shrugged. "Worth the risk."

"I think so, too." Juliana strode into the corridor.

Chapter Twenty-five

The footman obviously didn't know charm when he saw it. Ian was charming. Everyone told him he was charming. He could talk to anyone. He could hold a conversation with a three-legged dog if he so chose.

Yet Sommet's footman/guard didn't look up once from his stew when Ian sat beside him in the kitchen and tried to have a civil conversation.

The hulkish lout also ignored Ian's offer of a quick game of cards when he spotted him on the way back from the privy.

Ian swore. He couldn't approach the man again tonight without raising suspicion.

But the night hadn't been a complete waste. The footman had shared quite a bit of information even with his refusals.

He was a former boxer, his thickened knuckles said that. He was right-handed. He didn't interact with anyone except for a brief nod to Sommet's butler. The nod of an equal, not an underling, which meant he was important to the duke not just a body to guard the stairs.

Not that Ian was entirely sure how to use any of this information yet. But he was patient. He knew it would all be of use eventually.

He moved down the corridor toward Juliana's room. She should be back from the prince now.

"Groom!" A deep voice called behind him.

He knew who the voice belonged to without turning. He kept his pace steady. Once around the corner he could disappear.

"Or should I say *Wraith*?"

Ian stopped and turned to face the duke.

Sommet stood at the other end of the corridor, his hands deceptively relaxed by his sides. "My servant has orders to inform me of anyone who tries to speak to him. You really should do something about the scar on your cheek."

"I think it lends me a rakish air."

Sommet didn't react and neither did he come closer. "Why are you here?" His eyes swept over Ian's livery. "With the princess."

Ian shrugged. "Had to find a job somewhere. Why are you here? Oh, you live here. Never mind."

Sommet scowled. "You would do best to quiet your mouth."

"Why? It's not tired at all. I could talk all night." His hand was only inches from his dagger if he needed it, but he was better at stabbing than at throwing. He needed the duke to move closer.

"Why are you here?"

"The privy. The other one was occupied, so I—"

"I wouldn't play games."

"Why not? I love games. A good game of conkers never goes amiss. Although perhaps you don't like that game, you are pretty soft."

Sommet's face grew mottled. Really, the man needed to be mocked more often. He allowed himself to grow too agitated.

The duke drew a pistol.

One he couldn't fire in his own corridor.

This was almost too easy. Now Ian knew what he carried and where he carried it.

Sommet was still too angry to realize his blunder. "I know you were in my study. The doorknob was askew."

The man was that careful? But that was another important fact to tuck away.

"You were a fool to come here. Glavenstroke is too far away to save you."

"But I'm not." Juliana walked into the corridor, followed by Apple. She stepped directly into the path of the gun. For the first time in the encounter, Ian could hear his heart pounding against his eardrums. Perhaps he should gut all interfering women.

"Your Highness." Sommet licked his lips as he slowly replaced his pistol in his jacket. "I regret to inform you that you have a spy in your employ. And not just a spy. A vile killer."

She flinched only slightly. "I know. That's why I hired him as the head of my protection detail."

He wanted to shake her until her teeth rattled. Why was she binding herself to him in Sommet's eyes?

"Then why was he wandering my halls?"

Juliana strode forward, her chin tilted high. She stopped when she was inches away from the duke. Ian half expected her to spit in his face. "I sent him on a task that is none of your concern. Good night, Your Grace."

"I want him gone by morning."

"No."

"I beg your pardon, Your Highness?"

Ian inched forward until he was shoulder to shoulder with Juliana.

And within dagger's reach of the duke.

"No. Where I go, he goes," Juliana said.

"You may leave as well."

"Then my brother will leave with me. And I don't think that will work for you, will it?"

There it was. The truth of it finally out in the open.

"You *do* know." Sommet's tongue slid over his lower lip, and his nostrils flared as if scenting prey. "But your brother won't leave. He values his own neck far too dearly."

"You won't take my crown."

"As much as you bat your lashes at Wilhelm, he moves too slow to be a threat. Do you think I would have invited him otherwise? The man takes hours to pick a neck cloth."

But if Sommet thought to intimidate Juliana, he'd soon learn her spine was forged from steel. If she wasn't facing such a vindictive bastard, Ian would have sat back and enjoyed her performance.

Instead, he drew attention to himself. "We already have the letters."

Sommet laughed. "Impossible."

"I would think you heard a thing or two about me over the past ten years. I have a rather particular skill set."

Sommet's laughter faded. "You haven't touched the letters."

Ian just grinned.

Sommet stepped back. It wasn't more than half an inch, but it was a retreat. "I'd be careful with your servants, Your Highness. These old castles can be dangerous."

Juliana stiffened. "You dare threaten me?"

"Not you. It would look bad to the regent if a princess died while at my house, but a groom? Servants are so often unreliable. They go missing all the time."

Juliana's lips had gone white about the corners.

Sommet turned his back and walked down the corridor. "Go home, Your Highness. Things here are far beyond you. You cannot lose a country you never had."

Ian grabbed Juliana's elbow to keep her from

chasing after the duke and pushing him down the stairs. "Time to return to your room."

Juliana's breathing was tight in and out of her nose, her gaze distant.

He didn't want her to dwell on the things the duke just said. "Thank you for my elevation in rank."

But she wasn't distracted. "Who does he think he is?"

"Unfortunately, he is one of the few men that *is* as powerful as he pretends to be. Do not take his threats lightly."

She shook off his hand. "Then you think I should crawl home and let him win."

"Definitely not, but neither should you provoke him. What were you doing in the corridor?" He glanced back at Apple.

The girl shifted, not meeting his gaze. "We were looking for you. We were worried."

"Touching, but unnecessary. Can you make sure she stays in her room this time?"

Juliana's face whipped toward him. "Where are you going?"

"To follow the duke."

"He just threatened to murder you."

"Everyone is always planning to murder me. And I cannot waste this trap."

"Trap?" Juliana asked.

"I'll tell you a little secret about how I was so

successful as a thief. Quite simple really. I posted a sign on Bond Street warning of cutpurses."

Juliana frowned. "How would that help? Wouldn't it make people wary?"

"If you fear someone is going to steal something, what is the first thing you do?"

Juliana and Apple looked at each other, recognition on both their faces.

"You check and make sure they haven't taken it already." Juliana looked at him with such admiration, Ian's chest ached.

"So I'd know where they kept their valuables."

For half a moment, he wished she admired him for something that didn't involve duplicity and larceny.

But it was all he had to offer.

"I'm coming, too," Juliana said.

"No."

"I am."

Ian felt a smile tugging on the corners of his lips. "You can't keep up with me if I don't let you."

"Then I'll follow on my own."

He glared at her. She glared back. There was no chance he'd allow that.

She knew it, too.

"You're the one he plans to kill. Not me," she said.

"We're wasting time."

"Then let me come." She reached for him and

placed her hand on his chest. He was selfish enough to do anything to keep that hand there.

"Fine. But I'm not carrying you on my back this time."

There were footmen patrolling the perimeter of the castle. Unfortunately for Sommet, the men were walking close to the building.

While Ian was twenty yards back in an oak tree with a spyglass.

He tracked Sommet's movements through his tower. Fortunately, like most proper Englishmen, it hadn't occurred to Sommet to walk through his own rooms with the lights out.

Juliana was nestled behind him against the trunk of the ancient tree, her gown tucked securely around her legs so it didn't flap in the growing wind and catch the attention of the footmen.

Apple had been sent back to her room. They needed someone to find their dead bodies if this went poorly, after all.

Ian followed the candlelight as it flickered from window to window. Sometimes bright, sometimes no more than a flicker under a closed door or through a pulled curtain.

True, Ian had no way to know for certain that Sommet was actually checking on his documents, Ian might have missed that in the brief time it took him to locate this tree.

However, Ian was counting on the fact that

Sommet thought he was smart. He wouldn't rush to check on his letters. No, he would wait in case anyone was watching.

But he wouldn't be able to resist for long.

And anything Sommet was doing this late at night was of interest.

Juliana remained perfectly still and quiet as Ian had ordered, but he could still feel her every inhale. Each gust of air from the oncoming storm brought her scent into his lungs.

He tightened his hold on the spyglass, forcing himself to not breathe any deeper.

Sommet entered a room on the second floor. Bookcases. A desk. His real study, perhaps? He walked to the far wall.

Promising.

But then he walked to the window.

And waved.

Ian blinked, swearing under his breath. He knew better than to give the slightest movement to betray himself. With a smile, Sommet blew out the candle.

Damnation.

What were the odds that something had given Ian away? A glimmer of stray moonlight off the lens? Or was this all a calculated guess on Sommet's part?

Where had he gone?

Ian watched the surrounding windows, but no light reappeared. No misplaced shadows. No quivering curtains.

So was there a significance to the room Sommet had chosen to wave from? Was it a taunt? Or a trap?

"I've lost him," Ian told her.

She didn't speak. She simply leaned forward slightly and peered over his shoulder to help him search.

But after about half an hour, the duke hadn't re-emerged and neither had he appeared in his room.

"What time do you think it is?" Juliana finally whispered.

He checked the watch in his pocket. "Three in the morning."

"How long do we wait?"

"As long as it takes." He was tempted to point out that if it had been up to him, she would have been cozy in her own bed right now, but he showed a rather remarkable restraint and kept silent.

When a fat drop of rain plopped on his cheek, he gloried in it. Let her see that these tasks were better meant for a man like him. Princesses shouldn't be up the trees with dirty frocks and scraped hands.

He waited until the rough bark was completely soaked under him and his coat was clinging to his skin before looking back at her. She'd be cold. She'd be miserable, and she'd go back to her room where she belonged.

Juliana sat, with her back against the trunk, her knees drawn up to her chest for warmth.

But her face was turned up to the sky as droplets

sparkled on her lashes. Her mouth was curved into an expression of pure rapture.

As if she could imagine nothing better than being on this branch with him.

Her tongue darted out to lick a raindrop from her lip.

The growl came from somewhere deep in his chest. He couldn't have her forever but he was bastard enough to take as much of her as she'd give him now.

He wanted to stride purposefully to her at this point, but he was on a wet tree branch, so he stood and inched his way to her instead.

She looked up when his boots touched the edge of her gown—the damned gown that was now molded to her. She hurriedly wiped the water from her cheeks. "Did he come out?"

"No." He took hold of her arms and drew her to her feet.

"Then—"

He crushed his mouth against hers, pressing her against the trunk of the tree. Her lips were cool and wet. She tasted like summer and rain. Her hands fisted on his lapels, drawing him closer.

He cupped her head and deepened the kiss, licking the rain from her mouth as she'd just done.

When she moaned slightly, he lifted his head. "If you want me to stop, tell me now."

But her eyes were so hot with passion he knew she wouldn't.

"Just promise me we won't fall out of this tree. I'd have a hard time explaining that one to my aunts."

So he lifted her and switched places, sitting with his back against the tree and Juliana straddling his lap. "Better?"

She answered him by catching a drop of water on her finger and painting it over his lower lip.

And suddenly he just had to know. "Why are you so happy out here in the rain?"

"I've stolen away in the middle of the night. I've climbed a tree—something I've never had an opportunity to do. I've thrown expectations and conventions to the wind. And I've done it with you."

Had he been cold and miserable before? He couldn't remember. He could remember nothing but the way her wet lashes clumped together and the heat of her soft body in his lap.

His hands shook so badly he buried them in her hair, needing to hold on to some part of her as he kissed her.

He didn't know how long he sat exploring her lips. He'd planned to continue to other parts of her body. But her lips were so exquisite, so pleasurable, that he couldn't bring himself to move away.

Then Juliana took control, pressing kisses along the edge of his jaw, down his throat to the collar of his jacket.

His blood was molten in his veins, and there was no way she'd be able to doubt his continued desire for her. It was pressed between them in a rather obvious manner.

He freed one hand from her hair so he could cup her breast, testing the weight of it in his hand, tracing her already taut nipple with his thumb. She tipped her head back with a gasp and he took advantage of the easy access to the delicate skin of her throat, kissing his way down until he reached the swell of her breasts above her bodice.

He lifted his hand from her bosom to tug the wet fabric lower. She arched so quickly she wobbled and he had to grab her to keep them both from tumbling from the tree.

Her laughter against his chest was just as erotic as her kisses had been.

A gust of wind twined around them, causing her skin to pebble under his fingers.

Hell, he needed to get them out of the tree. He helped her stand, then slipped over the side of the branch, the rough bark biting into his cold fingers as he moved to the lower branch. Then he reached up and helped Juliana down.

They weren't high, only perhaps a dozen feet, so they were on the ground quickly, even with the rain.

The footmen seemed to have given up their patrol in the rain—another useful fact—so he led her back to the castle and through a window whose lock he'd broken earlier in the day.

He paused there in the parlor after lifting her

inside, his hands on the smooth curve of her waist. But he didn't kiss her again.

But he would. Perhaps he owed her a warning. "I intend to have you."

Juliana swallowed even though her throat no longer worked. How was it possible to feel both elation and despair in the same moment? In the same beating muscle? "I—"

But Ian placed his finger to her mouth. "I know what you owe to your country and your future husband. I won't take that from you. But the way I see it, we have two days left until we part and I refuse to waste either of them." The expression on his face was serious. "So unless you tell me no here and now, I plan to claim every moment from you that I can. I want to be the one who teaches you of passion. I want each and every sigh and moan I can provoke. They will have to last me a lifetime, you know."

"Ian—"

He shook his head again, his eyes almost sad. "We both go into this knowing the rules. Knowing that this is all there will ever be. You may be a princess, but I'm a man of the shadows; something more between us can never happen."

How could she think with all the blood in her body pounding in her head, echoing in her ears? But she knew even if she could think, her answer would still be the same. "Why are we wasting time talking?"

Chapter Twenty-six

*I*t should have been too early for the maids to be about, but Ian wasn't taking chances with Juliana's reputation. If a single breath of their interaction got to Sommet, Ian didn't doubt the man would use it against her. He might hesitate to kill her, but he wouldn't hesitate to ruin her. Not if he wanted to put another on her throne.

So after kissing her in the parlor briefly—well, almost briefly—he led her to her room, careful to keep his hands at his own sides in case they met one of the hearth maids.

Apple would be waiting inside Juliana's rooms, but she had been assigned a bed in the servants' quarters, which she'd probably be eager to retire to so—

Apple wasn't alone in the room.

Juliana's aunt Leucretia sat in a chair by the window, her bony back straighter than a pike. Her cool eyes swept the two of them, lingering on the muddy, snagged fabric of Juliana's skirt. "Would you care to explain this?"

Juliana's composure held. "No."

Leucretia's eyes narrowed to slits. "What have the two of you been doing?"

Juliana folded her hands in front of her.

But Ian didn't want to be the cause of a rift between them. "I am not, in fact, a groom. She has appointed me minister of security."

Juliana's eyebrow lifted slightly at the new title he'd bestowed on himself, but she nodded.

"You do not have a minister of security," Leucretia said.

"I do now."

"To what purpose? And who is this man?"

Ian was more curious how Leucretia knew Juliana hadn't been in her bed. Apple never would have given her away. "Why did you come to look for the princess?" He just stopped himself from calling Juliana by her first name.

"I do not like your tone. Juliana, who is this man?"

"Why did you come to look for me, Aunt?"

"The duke told me he'd seen you in the corridors with a—" Her lips thinned. "Whatever you choose to call him. You know how much is at stake. Don't ruin things with a dalliance with *that*."

"I do know what is at stake," Juliana said. "My crown. Sommet intends to take it from me."

From the way Juliana watched her aunt, she apparently shared some of his suspicions about the other woman.

Leucretia's face went chalky under her rouge. "What? How?"

"He intends to force Gregory to contest me for it."

Leucretia's hands shook, but there was a look of betrayal on her face. "Impossible. Gregory would never do it."

Ian stepped closer to the older woman. "You know Sommet better than that."

Her aunt's hands stilled. "I do not like your tone again."

"*I* do not like that a woman the princess trusts is holding private meetings with the man who plans to harm her."

Leucretia surged to her feet. "What are you suggesting? I have given my life to Juliana."

Or at least the last twelve years. As far as Ian could tell, Leucretia had little to do with her nephew and his family before they fled Lenoria. "Did you know about Sommet's plan?"

"Why should I answer you? I still do not know who you are, other than an ill-mannered lout."

"He is the man I have chosen. But you will answer me," Juliana said. "As your monarch. Did you know of Sommet's plan?" Her pulse fluttered at her throat.

Leucretia squared her shoulders. "No."

"Do you support his plan now that you know of it?"

Her aunt's mouth worked several times before any sound came out. "No." The word was filled with such loathing he actually believed her. Leucretia dusted off her skirt with a sharp flick. "And now since you obviously have no need of my counsel any longer, I'll bid you good night." She stalked from the room.

Juliana relaxed as a shaky sigh escaped her. "She didn't know."

"Not about Gregory." He hesitated before telling her but she deserved to know. "But she *is* hiding something about Sommet."

"She told me earlier that she'd had business dealings with him."

Interesting. "What sort? Here or in Lenoria?"

"She didn't say." Juliana grimaced. "And I should have asked now, but I allowed her to overset me. I make a lovely spy, don't I?" She sat on the edge of her bed, her earlier excitement and fire gone. Weary lines marked her face, reminding him it was almost dawn.

Ian hadn't really believed he had a noble bone in his body, but she proved him wrong. He'd find out what Leucretia was hiding on his own. Juliana carried so much on her slender shoulders. He would lighten her burden however he could.

That small task suddenly seemed far more important than anything he'd ever done for the Foreign Office.

Chapter Twenty-seven

The press of lips against hers startled Juliana awake. She glared at Ian. "What?" She was perhaps not at her best when awakened suddenly. The pale light of dawn danced across the stone walls of the room.

Ian grinned at her, his smile lifting his scar higher on his cheek. "I thought that was how I was supposed to wake a princess."

"Not one who's gotten two hours of sleep." And why did he get to look handsome and roguish on so little sleep? She knew for a fact that her eyes would be puffy and her skin dull for at least two days. "Are you always this cheerful in the morning?"

"When I'm spending it with you."

"Oh." That improved her mood.

She could have sworn he reddened slightly.

She'd reached halfway to his cheek when she remembered they might not be alone.

She whipped her head around but couldn't see Apple.

"I sent your maid down to the kitchen to find some breakfast for you."

"Thank—" Then they were *alone*.

Ian leaned forward and brushed the back of his hand over her cheek. "Do you have a preferred method of being awakened? I can be quite accommodating." His hand continued down her throat to the neckline of her shift.

She shifted on the bed, trying to escape her blankets, eager for more of him.

His hand skimmed the outside of her breasts, and the rest of her body skipped to awareness. Sparks of pleasure tingled in her tired limbs.

"This method shows promise," she said.

He frowned as if disappointed. "Only this?"

"I meant as a starting place of course. You could embellish."

"That is a far better invitation." He lifted his hand to the tie on her shift and tugged it undone. "But I warn you, if you leave it up to me, you might be shocked at the consequences."

She'd never wanted to be shocked more.

With his index finger, he lowered the shift until her breast was bare, then he leaned forward until his mouth hovered above her nipple. After a pause, he pursed his lips and blew a slow stream of air.

She arched off the bed, her muscles seizing at the unexpected sensation.

But before she could even whimper, Ian had

retied the bow, pulled the blanket up to Juliana's chin, and stepped away from the bed.

Apple's footsteps grew quite loud before she entered, enough that Juliana knew the maid was stomping to give warning. Even so, she looked warily between them before entering with a tray.

Ian bounded over to take it from her, balancing it on one hand while he opened the lids on the various dishes. "Did you know I was once a waiter in Paris?" He ate a small pastry from one of the plates in a single bite.

Juliana's heart was still beating out of control. But if Ian could act so unaffected, so could she. "Did any of your patrons' food actually arrive at the table?"

"Always. Well, some of it did. It might have been less than the cook had intended, but I was so charming the patron's never cared."

Apple rolled her eyes. "Turn around so I can help the princess dress."

Ian gave an exaggerated sigh but then went to study the mantel.

Apple assisted Juliana into a sage green morning dress. She was halfway done with the buttons when there was a frantic pounding on the door.

A dagger appeared in Ian's hand, and he moved to the space directly to the left of the door.

"Mr. Maddox, sir!"

Juliana didn't recognize the voice, but Ian tucked

his dagger back in his boot, and Apple ran to the door.

She opened it to reveal an older servant wearing a pale blue bowler hat with a yellow satin ribbon. His face was pale almost to the point of being green. "His Highness, sir." The servant sucked in a breath. "He's injured."

Ian brushed past the old man and disappeared into the corridor.

Her stomach dipped. "Who?"

"Your brother, Your Highness."

Juliana grabbed her skirts and hurried out into the hall after Ian. Apple and the other servant followed.

The old man was surprisingly spry. He easily kept pace with Juliana. "He told me not to expect him last night, so I didn't suspect anything was amiss until he arrived this morning."

Apple beat Juliana to her next question. "How bad is it, Canterbury?"

"There appears to be some sort of trauma to his torso. But he arrived in the room on his own before he collapsed."

Juliana ran the last distance to her brother's room. By the time she entered, Ian was bent over her brother. Her brother's shirt was off showing mottled purple blotches across his chest and stomach.

She rushed to his side. "Is he all right?"

Ian was pressing gently against Gregory's injuries, checking for broken bones.

"I think so. I have yet to find anything broken."

"And internally?"

Ian remained focused on his task. "We'll have to call a surgeon."

Gregory's hand suddenly latched onto Ian's. "No." He shook his head slightly as he opened his eyes, as if trying to clear it. "You're a groom. Where's my valet?"

"I'm here, Your Highness," Canterbury said, although each time Ian pressed a sore spot, he looked as if he might faint.

"I'm here, too." Juliana laid her hand to his brow.

"No. You shouldn't be here." He tried to push her hand away. "It's not safe."

She smoothed back his hair. "What happened? Where were you last night?"

"We should send for a doctor," Ian said.

Gregory groaned when Ian pressed a spot by his stomach. "No. Fetch Eustace."

Ian raised a brow at Juliana.

"She's been caring for sick soldiers since her husband died. She knows more about injuries than most doctors."

Ian nodded and Canterbury hurried out the door.

"What happened, Gregory?" Juliana asked.

He was so silent she would have thought he'd passed out if he wasn't crushing her hand.

"I'm such a fool." He blinked his eyes open again, focusing on Ian. "You're dismissed."

But Juliana needed Ian to stay. "He's not actually a groom, he's my minister of security." What would Ian say if she actually offered him that position? But it would be unbearable. They couldn't be near each other without going up in flames.

"Since when?" Gregory asked.

"Since Sommet became involved. Ian is a former spy."

Gregory let out a shuddered breath. "Fair enough. But even he can't find a way out of this one." He groaned again.

She was about to add a few bruises. They only had a few moments before Eustace arrived and they very well couldn't have this conversation with Eustace present. "What happened?"

"Canterbury told us that you didn't return last night. Were you spreading your princely charm about?" Ian asked.

Gregory's cheeked reddened. "No. At least not all night." He turned crimson. "Confound it. I was trying to do the right thing. I tried to leave."

Juliana frowned. "The woman?"

"No! The manor. I thought if I left the house party all together and disappeared for a while, it would solve everything. If I wasn't here at Sommet's party, he couldn't force me to contest your throne. It might ruin me, but I can't do that to you."

Juliana stared at her brother, her eyes suddenly prickling.

Gregory's jaw set. "I'm not as horrible as you think me."

Ian glanced between them and rolled his eyes. "I'm not convinced of that yet. Who did you tell that you were planning to leave?"

Gregory's fingers twisted in the blankets and he shifted on the pillow. "I'm not entirely sure. As I was leaving, I met some friends in the billiards room and had a few drinks." His hands switched to plucking at the quilt. "What? It was starting to rain. I *may* have said something about leaving."

"What happened after you left the billiards room?" Ian prompted.

"I went to get my horse. And suddenly the lamps I'd lit went out and a couple men grabbed my arms and began pummeling me. They said that it wasn't polite to leave the duke's hospitality. I awoke in the hay a short while ago and returned here."

"The duke was counting on you doing that. That's why he left your pretty face untouched."

Gregory stiffened, then winced. "What was I supposed to do? I can hardly stand let alone mount a horse."

Ian's face was hard. "You could have trusted that your sister was doing the best she could from the onset and never gone to Sommet in the first place. Failing that, you should have never gotten drunk and ruined the only good plan you've had in your entire life."

"But I—"

"And you should have thought twice before trying to play God and arrange murders." A muscle pulsed along Ian's jaw. "Do you know what happened to the woman you tried to have murdered? Do you want to know how she was stabbed and thrown into a river? How her house was set on fire?" A darkness filled Ian's eyes. Rage. Sorrow. Revenge. "Or Clayton? How an innocent woman he knew was kidnapped and scarred because of you?"

Gregory was shaking. "Who are you?"

"Wraith. The third member of the Trio."

Ian was a *member* of the Trio? Juliana's gut dropped to her shoes and a strange buzzing filled her ears.

She placed her hands on the table so she'd have something to hold on to. Ian had been one of the ones responsible?

Ian?

Her mother—

Her father—

If he'd gutted her with a rusty blade, it would have been less painful. And why hadn't he told her? No, that was a foolish question; she knew why he hadn't told her.

Despite her hold on the table, her knees buckled and she slumped against the table, shaking.

Ian glanced at her and she could feel the exact moment he reined in his wrath. Realized what he'd admitted in his anger. His rage vanished as if he'd drawn a curtain over it. He walked to the window and leaned against it.

Gregory swallowed and looked at her. "Did you know he was—"

No. But she couldn't admit to that. "Of course."

Gregory's brows lowered. "How could you consort with the man who murdered our parents? Do you remember nothing of that night? Perhaps Sommet was right about—"

Ian glanced over his shoulder. And Juliana could see that although his emotions were banked they were far from gone. "Your sister is the only reason you're still alive. I would think carefully about your next words."

The crack splintering through her slowed. How old had Ian been? He couldn't have been much older than she had been. A child. A child following orders.

But her hands couldn't quite relax at her sides.

At least he had never lied to her about it. She had just been too gullible and foolish to ask what his interest in the Trio had been.

This time it was Gregory whose jaw tensed. "What precisely is between you?"

"Nothing," Juliana hastened to say.

It was the truth, so why did it taste so vile in her mouth? And how could that *nothing* consume every fiber of her heart? "We both have plans to destroy Sommet. We are combining our efforts."

Gregory sank into his pillow, but he still studied her as if he'd never seen her before.

Ian prowled back over, but he kept a wide distance from Juliana. "As much as I'm loath to admit it, his plan is still a good one."

But Gregory shuddered. "No."

"I can get you away without another beating if that is what you fear."

"No!" Gregory wiped his palms on the sheets. "One of the men beating me said, 'If you leave, we'll visit your sister.'"

Chapter Twenty-eight

$\mathcal{I}$an had never been so grateful when Juliana's aunt bustled in a few moments later. He needed space, a distraction. Time to think.

To castigate himself more viciously.

He hadn't intended to let Juliana find out that way. Hell, he wasn't even certain if he ever would have told her at all. They had only two days left.

Now those would be lost.

Juliana stepped aside as her aunt approached. The older woman didn't blanch at all when she saw Gregory's injuries.

"What happened?" Eustace asked.

Gregory had enough wits to guard his answer. "I was in a foolish, drunken brawl."

Rather than berate him, Eustace bent over the prince. Ian had known enough to check for cracked ribs. But Eustace was slow and methodical, tracing the outlines of organs, listening to his heart, and gauging swelling. "My bag," she said to Canterbury.

Canterbury handed her a small black bag. "Certainly, *Your Highness*." That had sounded down-right worshipful.

For a moment, Ian was distracted from the rage and anguish eating his insides like starving rats.

Had Eustace's cheeks pinkened?

Eustace reached in the bag and pulled out a small vial of ink, which she used to mark the contours of one bruise over Gregory's liver.

"I think his organs were spared, but I'll keep an eye on this particular swelling for the next few hours."

"I'm most desirous to lend assistance if you wish it, Your Highness," Canterbury said, no longer appearing as if he was going to pass out. Which was unusual. Canterbury was as squeamish as they came about injuries of any sort. Once when Ian's mother pricked herself while sewing, Canterbury had fainted—

No. Ian was not going to start thinking of the past.

This was why he avoided his former butler.

Eustace turned to Ian. "You may go now. Thank you for your assistance." This was the second time he'd been dismissed by Juliana's family.

Perhaps Juliana would want him to obey this time.

But as long as there was a threat to her, she was stuck with him.

"He's my minister of security," Juliana said.

Ian wondered if she was just remaining true to her story.

And the rather depressing thing was that the title he invented for himself changed nothing in Eustace's eyes. Oh, he had no doubt she'd question Juliana later, but it provided no reason for Ian to stay with the family in this room.

He wasn't important enough for that. He never was.

Ian bowed and strode into the corridor. He would listen from the darkness as he always did. Apple was waiting outside the room. She was staring straight ahead, rocking back and forth from foot to foot. He put a hand on her shoulder.

Apple shrieked, flailing and stumbling back. "*Don't touch me.*" But then she buried her face in her hands, rubbing her eyes so hard Ian feared she'd damage them. But he also knew better than to try to touch her again right now.

Juliana ran out of her brother's room.

Of course she did. She heard someone screaming, and rather than cowering like any sane woman would, she went to investigate.

"What happened?" she asked.

Apple hugged her arms tightly around herself, her body trembling.

"What—"

But Apple needed time to recover. "Let's get her to your room," Ian said.

Thankfully, Apple allowed Juliana to guide her. And Juliana remained silent until they were in her room.

She settled Apple on the edge of the bed and tucked the blanket around the trembling girl.

"Are you all right?"

Apple seemed to struggle to breathe, still trapped by short, rapid pants.

Ian knelt before her, careful to keep his distance but moving into her line of sight. "Listen to me, Apple. I need you to slow your breathing."

Apple's eyes grew even more panicked.

"I know your body seems out of control but you can do this. Breathe with me. In . . . two . . . three . . . Out . . . two . . . three."

After about a dozen breaths, she finally clawed her way back to control. "It was just— I saw his chest— I was back there—and stupid. I'm not—not scared of him."

Juliana wrapped her arms around the girl. "Bad memories?"

Apple nodded.

"I don't know what yours are and I will not pry. But can I tell you what I do when I fight my own?"

"You are a princess." The disbelief and despair were evident in Apple's tone.

"When I was twelve, a mob stormed my family's home."

A mob that Ian had helped to spur. A mob that was carefully controlled by a few hired mercenaries who'd been positioned to keep the townspeople out of control.

Did Juliana truly realize the implications of who he was? How much of it he had personally done?

"What did you do?" Apple asked, eyes shocked.

"I was playing with my brother in the nursery when we heard the shouts. I came down to see what was amiss." Juliana's voice was calm, no doubt for Apple's benefit. Then she shook her head. "You don't want to know the details."

But Apple did. "Was it terrible? Were you frightened?" There was a plea in her voice. A plea to know that she wasn't alone in her fear. That she wasn't weak for being afraid.

"Yes. To both. As I watched over the balcony, one of the men grabbed my mother by the hair while another man pushed a rifle into her mouth and pulled the trigger." She spoke to Apple but her eyes burned into his, forcing him to know the full extent of the horror he'd inflicted.

Ian's gut rearranged itself into something unrecognizable. He'd been in enough battles to hear the screams that must have echoed. To smell the gunpowder.

His hands curled at his sides as he imagined young Juliana peering through the balustrades on the balcony.

Her parents were going to side with the French. He'd seen the proof with his own eyes. He'd give anything to have spared Juliana from that horror.

But he'd saved countless British soldiers. If the French had gained access to the iron in those mountains, the war could have ended far differently.

"One of the men set a torch to the drapes. That is when I ran back for my brother and escaped."

"But you still have those memories?" Apple asked. "They don't go away?"

Ian eased away; both females had forgotten his existence for the moment.

"No, but when they come back, I remind myself that I have already survived them. That I could have died with my parents, but I was stronger than that. And I suspect if you're here, then you were stronger than something and someone, too."

Apple's lips firmed as she latched on to the thought.

Hell, Juliana needed to be more than the queen of Lenoria, she needed to be in charge of the entire world.

Apple smiled up at her, her body now quivering only slightly. When Juliana covered the girl's hands with her own, his heart flopped like a fish just pulled from the barrel.

Damn it all to bloody, blasted, bedeviled hell.

He loved her.

Ian walked to the door, catching Juliana's eye and nodding before fleeing outside.

He was a bloody, bloody halfwit to fall in love with a woman who didn't want him. How could she?

But as worthless as he might be, he was more than a match for Sommet. And he'd keep Juliana safe from him.

Gregory had reminded him just how dangerous the duke could be. Even to Juliana. Time for a slow revenge was over. He needed Sommet obliterated.

Ian would get Juliana as far away from this mess as possible so she wouldn't be contaminated by his actions.

And then Ian would deal with Sommet in the best way he knew how.

Chapter Twenty-nine

Juliana finally calmed Apple. She'd tried to get her to agree to rest for the remainder of the day, but Apple had refused.

So Juliana sat while Apple arranged her hair.

Leucretia. Juliana held on to that thought as a million thoughts buffeted about her mind. She refused to give in to the despair that whirled about her, tugging at her, shoving, pulling.

Ian.

She didn't know how to feel. Part of her was shattered in small fragments too fragile to examine.

Yet part of her understood. She knew what it was to make decisions that ended in death.

She exhaled and focused again on her aunt. Leucretia was the key to this puzzle or at least part of it.

Her aunt was hiding something, and while Juliana had no power over the duke, she did have some power over her aunt.

Her tumult over what Ian had revealed only reinforced her original thoughts—this was something she had to do on her own. She couldn't rely on anyone else. She had to be strong enough to manage. After all, if she couldn't keep her country, then she wasn't fit to rule it.

Besides, Leucretia was her responsibility and if she was involved, Juliana wanted to take care of it privately. The situation with Lenoria was precarious. She didn't want to show her enemies just how divided the royal house might be.

So when Constantina burst into the room, her cheeks flushed, to tell Juliana that Wilhelm was in the breakfast room, Juliana coaxed her to sit down for a moment before returning.

Juliana did her best to smile conspiratorially— Constantina loved a good intrigue. "I saw Sommet heading toward Leucretia's room last night." Juliana disliked being duplicitous to gain information about her own aunt.

But for Lenoria she'd do anything.

Constantina sucked in a heaving breath, her ample bosoms threatening to jiggle out of her gown. "Was she? I thought she was finished with him."

"So she did have a relationship with him before?"

"Yes, but long ago. Back in Lenoria."

"Why was the duke in Lenoria?"

Constantina shrugged. "The war with Napoleon was getting nasty. Lenoria would have provided a fine ore for the French."

"But my father planned to side with the British. We discussed it many times."

Constantina frowned, confused, and Juliana was reminded that this aunt might not prove the most useful. "Then I don't know what else happened. The duke was angry about something when he left. Or was that the French ambassador? Although Leucretia already seemed to know the duke when he arrived. So perhaps earlier than that? Well, either way you had better hurry if you want to catch Wilhelm." Constantina stood and held out her hand. "Did he kiss you last night?"

"No." But another man had. A man who was responsible for what happened to her parents. A man who'd calmed a terrified girl without hesitation. A man who'd rushed to tend the injuries of a man he hated.

She'd thought this new revelation about Ian would allow her to free herself from him. How could she care for the man who'd been behind all the horrible things that had happened to her?

But she still did.

Apparently her heart did not know the meaning of a lost cause.

Juliana smoothed a hand down her blue silk frock. A dress she'd changed into because Apple had reported that *Wilhelm*—the man she should wed—was going to wear blue.

She gripped Constantina's hand, and her aunt patted her on her arm. "He'll come around soon. If not, your brother could always become king."

"What?" Juliana froze.

"Gregory would make a dashing king, wouldn't he?"

Juliana advanced a step. "Why do you think my brother might become king?"

"Brothers have done it before. And I heard Leucretia arguing with the duke about it this morning."

Leucretia had been arguing over it? A small weight lifted from her heart. Then perhaps her loyalties weren't as divided as Juliana had feared.

"Come, come. As I said, you must hurry if you are going to catch Wilhelm before he leaves."

"Wait, *leaves*? The breakfast parlor?"

"No, the castle. He said something about a violin."

Juliana let go of Constantina's hand and hurried ahead. She reached the breakfast parlor just as the prince was exiting.

He stopped and bowed. "Juliana. I was about to come request an audience. I'm afraid I must take my leave. Sir Henry informed me that I'd be able to purchase the violin, but that he'd neglected to bring it with him as I'd thought. We ride to his estate this morning. We'll return on Friday evening."

"Can't the violin wait?" Juliana kept her voice light.

Wilhelm's expression turned a bit sheepish. "I've tried to purchase this violin from Sir Henry before, only to have him change his mind. I won't risk that again."

Another idea snaked into her thoughts. "When did Sir Henry tell you of his decision?"

"Only this morning. It was rather sudden or I would have warned you of my departure last night."

Most likely Sommet had decided not to take chances with Juliana's marital options.

"But may I be so bold as to ask you to save me a dance at the ball on Friday?" Wilhelm asked, a hint of uncertainty on his face.

Might she be so bold as to beg him to stay? To propose now and end all this? What if she explained the situation to him? Would he agree to marry her to help her?

But to do so would place him in danger of Sommet's wrath, and she couldn't do that to him. Not when he had a daughter to care for.

And as soon as she committed herself to Wilhelm, she'd have to sever her ties with Ian completely. And she wasn't ready for that. Not yet. She had two days with him.

And despite everything, she wasn't going to waste them.

Those two days were going to last her a lifetime.

So she nodded. "I look forward to it." She bid good-bye to Prince Wilhelm, then entered the breakfast room.

Sommet was there, sitting at the head of the table speaking to some young girl who couldn't have been more than seventeen. Sommet looked up at Juliana as she entered, his smile like a dagger digging under her ribs.

So she smiled back and helped herself to a plate of food she'd never be able to eat. Abington appeared at her side. He looked a trifle poorly, his eyes bloodshot. And when someone replaced a lid with too much force, he winced.

"I'm surprised to see you this early." That was tactful at least.

"I wouldn't be here if our mutual friend hadn't ordered me to move my blooming arse down to the breakfast room to watch over the only person who kept him from burning down the house. In a rather foul mood this morning, he is."

Abington knew Ian? How?

But Sommet stood and tapped his spoon on the side of his cup. "My dearest guests, I'm pleased to inform you of an exciting addition to our ball tomorrow night. The ambassadors of Spain and France have agreed to join us. You can thank Princess Juliana for their willingness to attend."

The countries that wanted rip to hers in two.

The ten or so other guests in the room applauded politely and smiled at her.

Juliana debated whether she could throw her fork hard enough to stab Sommet in the eye. He lifted his glass to her in the slightest of mock toasts.

"Don't give him anything," Abington murmured. "And your friend wants to meet with us in my rooms as soon as we leave here."

Juliana nodded, but laughed as if Abington had said something witty. "I look forward to it."

A hint of admiration entered Abington's eyes before he wandered over to chat with the Marchioness of Lionsbury.

"What do you look forward to?" Sommet asked. He took her plate from her and led her to the table.

"The hunt later today."

"You are a bloodthirsty type of female then?"

"When necessary. It's strange that the ambassadors will be making the trip solely for a ball."

Sommet lifted his brows. "Ah, but they have told me how eager they are to have things resolved."

"Then tell them to leave my country alone."

"They're willing to."

"What?" She was too shocked to hide her reaction.

"They have told me they're willing to support a strong *king*."

Oh, the bastard. Gregory had said Sommet had some way to force the other countries to comply, but she'd thought it was another one of the duke's lies.

Was it the truth then?

Uncertainty clawed at her thoughts. If this was true, perhaps it *was* better to let Gregory have the crown. If Lenoria could be free, even if she wasn't the one on the throne, she could return and help the people.

"It's better this way, little princess. Isn't having

your country free of foreign influence more important than your desire for power? Think of it. By Friday night, Lenoria could be free and independent once again. No bloodshed. No lost territory."

She wanted to press her hands over her ears and stop his words entering her mind. From tempting her.

But the man was far too good at this. And he knew it.

"You can still help your people even if you were not their sovereign. Your brother would need your counsel."

But what would Sommet ask in return? What had he already bargained for? "Would my brother also have *your* counsel?"

"I have no interest in running your country. I only need my contracts. Contracts that will enrich the country and the royal coffers."

The man had a gilded tongue and the subtlety of a snake in the garden. She had a new sympathy for her brother. Perhaps she should have had a little more understanding for his weakness.

The brother who was lying upstairs because this duke had arranged his beating.

She would not let the duke sway her.

Sommet leaned closer. "You carry too many burdens on your shoulders. Imagine if you could let them all go."

"What do you want in those mountains? The gold?"

He chuckled. "Hardly. Gold is near worthless compared to the mountain's other riches."

She stared at his smug expression. "The iron."

He shrugged.

"People have lived there for centuries. I won't let them be displaced for the sake of your mines."

He had the audacity to reach over and cut the ham on her plate like she was an infant in the nursery. "Sorry, my dear. But there haven't been people in those mountains in over a decade."

"But there are a dozen villages . . ." Her voice trailed off at his expression. "What have you done?"

"Nothing. The war had its casualties, that is all. You cannot expect your country to have escaped unscathed."

"One of my agents would have reported it to me."

"Would they? Even when money is scarce and they have many mouths to feed?"

Only the duke would be dastardly enough to have this conversation in the breakfast room where she could do nothing but smile politely and reply in pleasant tones.

"You'll never mine those mountains."

He straightened her knife and fork. "Just keep in mind that the ambassadors will either leave with a new king for Lenoria or the country carved up between them. They grow tired of waiting. After all, what is a signature on a treaty? Just ink on paper. What is the absence of a few strokes of a pen?"

Juliana called on every lesson Ian had given her and chuckled.

For the first time, Sommet appeared slightly taken aback. "What?"

She kept her laugh going on a second longer and shook her head.

Sommet's eye twitched but before he could answer, Abington strolled over. He was tucking a silver flask into his waistcoat as he approached. She wanted to think his loose gait and broad smile were an act, but the smell of brandy on his breath was real enough. "Your laughter lights up the room." He caught her hand and brought it to his lips. "Like a candle or something . . . brighter."

She had to hope this was the rescue she thought it was. Even if it wasn't, she'd take advantage of it. She withdrew her hand. "Thank you."

"Don't you think so, Sommet?" He rested his hand on the other man's shoulder. "Is that why you're monopolizing her? Shame, shame."

Sommet stood and bowed, the disdain on his face clear as he looked at his fellow duke. "I leave her to you."

Abington caught her hand again as Sommet walked away, but this time his eyes were focused. "You leave first. I'll follow shortly." He told her where to find his room, then turned to flirt with Lady Plimpington.

She hurried to the south tower where Abington was housed. She kept her pace steady and her head straight forward. And as Ian had predicted, none of the servants or guests she passed dared question her.

She circled past Abington's rooms twice before going inside.

"I was afraid Abington had passed out before he could deliver my message." Ian stepped out of the shadows, a bag slung over his shoulder. A servant's dress was laid out over the bed.

Excitement charged in her blood. "Do you know where the papers are? Are we going to get them? But if I recall, you mocked the idea of me dressing like a maid."

"You aren't coming with me."

"What? Oh, did you want me to keep watch? Or distract the footman with my"—she rose up on tiptoe and pressed a kiss to his jaw—"feminine wiles?" The muscles under her lips were tight.

"What the devil are you doing? You hate me."

She lowered down. "No, I considered it, but I don't."

But he remained tense. "It doesn't matter. You're leaving."

She stepped back. "What?"

"Now. It's arranged. There's a farmer waiting outside to take you. He thinks you a maid fleeing Sommet's advances. You will hide under the flour sacks in the back of the cart."

"No."

Ian gripped her shoulders. "Your brother was

right. Neither of you should be at Sommet's mercy. I will get you both out and then deal with Sommet."

"On your own? Without consulting me?"

"I have issues of my own to resolve with Sommet. I know you wanted to be the one to bring Sommet down, but there are more important—"

She shoved at his chest before he could finish. Did everyone truly think that of her? "You pompous fool. I don't care about receiving the credit."

"No, but you do always have to be the one in control."

"No, I don't."

"Then assign me to do this instead of you."

"I—I can't." This was her responsibility. If she gave it someone else, it would be the same as saying she couldn't do it.

"Then we do this my way." He picked her up around the waist and carried her to the bed.

She struggled but he still wouldn't release her. "If you want me to leave, you'll have to bash me over the head and carry me from the room."

He tossed her on the dress on top of the bed and glared at her. "If I must."

"Then do it."

His hand clenched and unclenched at his sides, but he made no move to touch her.

She pushed herself on her elbows, trying to be rational. "Why don't you ask me why I don't want to leave?"

"I give you my word Sommet will be dealt—"

When she huffed, he was suddenly on top of her, his hands braced on either side of the bed.

And she realized she was seeing just a fraction of what her brother had seen earlier, the intensity, the darkness that Ian kept so deeply hidden.

His voice was rough, like it scraped from his throat. "Don't you see, I *cannot* let anything happen to you. It was selfish to let you come here in the first place. If anything were to happen to you, it would rip out my entrails."

The outrage slowly seeped from her body. She cupped his cheek. "That is why you need to trust me enough to be a useful part of this, not some poor princess who needs to be coddled."

"I don't think of you like that."

"But you do. Otherwise you would have asked if I got any information from Sommet in the breakfast room."

The tendons stood out against Ian's neck. "You got information from Sommet?"

She knew it was impolite to point out when she was right, but she did pause to let him figure that out on his own.

With a sigh, he rolled off her onto the bed and lay next to her. "I take it I'm missing some pertinent fact that will change my mind and make me look like a buffoon."

She told him about the ambassadors and Sommet's plan.

"So either you let him win or your country is

carved to pieces. You could have started with that bit of information when you entered."

"Well, you could have thought twice before picking me up and tossing me around like a rag doll."

"A valid point." He propped himself up on one elbow, his cheek resting on his fist. "So if you and Gregory were to disappear—"

"The other countries will move."

"Curse Sommet. I knew he was good, but the man is a master." He flicked her nose. "Thankfully, I'm even better."

She loved his cocksure attitude, but she had to know. "Do we stand a chance against him? He's had months if not years to plan all this."

Ian's brow wrinkled. "That's a good point."

Her heart stuttered. "Then we don't have a chance?"

"Don't be ridiculous. Of course we have a chance. Sommet might be clever but I'm a devious bastard. No, the interesting point is, when did Sommet become involved with your brother?"

Juliana frowned. "I'm not sure. I think perhaps at the Congress of Vienna."

"So why then? What changed?"

"The war was finally over."

"Yes, but why was it important to gain control of your brother? Sommet obviously has some power in Spain, why not get them to give him the mountains after Lenoria is chopped to bits?"

It was a good question, one she hadn't considered before.

Ian traced the shell of her ear with a slow sweep of his finger. "But you'll find out, won't you?"

She turned so she could rest her hand on his chest. "Yes. And despite your high-handedness—which you had better never try again if you value your life—thank you for trying to protect me."

"I warn you, if it comes down to it, I will pick keeping you safe over protecting your country." He grasped her hand and brought it to his mouth, catching her index finger lightly with his teeth and flicking his tongue over the tip. "Each and every time."

"And I warn you I won't ever let you." But she thrilled at his words, at the knowledge that he found her more important than anything else. Than an entire country.

"Why are you lying in this bed with me?" he asked. "Why don't you loathe me?"

The heat from his mouth traveled up her arm and down into her core. She undid the buttons on his coat.

"Why did you do it?" Neither of them needed to clarify what they were discussing.

"We were following orders."

"Did you hate my parents?"

He glared at the ceiling. "I never even met them."

"Then did you hate me?"

"No!" He draped his arm across his forehead. "I see where you are going with this."

"Why are you so eager for my anger?"

"Because then one of us would have the strength to push me away."

She nudged his arm away from his eyes, and peered down into them. "I don't want to."

"You should."

"I don't."

"I thought princesses were supposed be sweet and biddable."

"Princesses, perhaps. But remember, I'm nearly a queen."

He groaned. "Bloody, bloody hell. I hadn't made that leap in logic yet."

She grinned at him. "Oh, in that case, just to warn you, puppies grow up to become dogs."

With a quick movement, he caught her hands and pinned them over her head, poising himself over her. "Then I'd better have my way with you before you get even further out of my reach."

His words carved gashes in her heart, but not as deep as the knowledge that she couldn't contradict them. So she rubbed her hips against his. "Distance doesn't seem to be a problem right now."

His lips quirked for a brief second before descending onto hers. His lips were fierce. And thorough. Oh so thorough.

After exploring her mouth, his lips moved onto her neck, then downward to the neckline of her gown—which was blessedly low this morning.

He released her arms so that his hand could caress her breast. She moaned at the sensations inspired by his fingers.

"Tell me." His voice was low and hoarse. "Tell me how you feel."

"You make me forget about being a princess. You make me care only about being a woman. I've never had that before."

Ian's breath was hot against her neck, and he tightened as if fighting for control.

"More. I need more to take with me." His intensity only fed her arousal.

How could she put this in words? "Like pleasure has replaced my blood. Like I'm being strung tighter and tighter until I might splinter."

He skimmed his lips along her collarbone, wandering to explore the hollows above and below it. "Greedy, greedy woman. You already had a country, did you have to take my soul, too?"

She pressed his jacket off his shoulders. It tangled around his elbows until he paused to remove it. "Do I have it?"

"Completely."

Her hands clenched in the sheets next to her—or not the sheets—the dress. The fact only registered because one of the buttons dug into her hand.

She closed her eyes tightly trying to regain control of herself. "We're in Abington's room. He will be here at any moment."

Ian swore and scooted off her. He stood, but then sat back down on the bed with a thump. His head in his hands. "I'm so far past sanity that I cannot even stand."

That's how she felt, too, but she sat up and placed her hand on his shoulder. He covered her fingers with his own and just held her there until their breathing returned to normal.

"Remind me why I invited Abington to his room?" he finally asked.

"Because you thought you'd need help carrying me kicking and screaming from the castle?" She lifted a hand to her hair, but luckily, Apple's pins had held fast.

She stood so that they wouldn't be found together in bed. Ian apparently trusted the other man, but some gossip might just be too good to withhold.

"He would have done it, too. The man is overprotective of females to a fault. Too bad he is jugbit so much of the time."

"I prefer to say that I bit the jug, not that the jug bit me. Or better yet—foxed. That has a rather proper aristocratic ring to it." Abington strolled into the room. "And I don't protect all women." He grinned at Juliana. "Just the pretty ones."

Ian snorted. "And the ugly ones and the old ones."

Abington raised a brow. "I'm flattered that you pay so much attention to me."

"Your strutting makes you rather hard to avoid."

Abington shrugged. "I *am* a duke." He spoke to Juliana in an exaggerated whisper. "Commoners just don't understand these things.

Ian's face grew pensive. "Indeed. Now we should focus on how to catch the other duke in residence."

"We still need the papers," Juliana said.

Ian nodded. "When does the hunt return?"

Abington shook his head. "Before luncheon, but Sommet didn't depart with the other men. He claimed his leg was paining him."

"Nice to know we're making him too nervous to leave the house," Ian said.

"But if he's missed the hunt, he'll need to make an appearance at archery later this afternoon," said Juliana.

Ian rose and folded the servant's dress from the bed. "Which is when we'll move." He paused. "And when I say *we*, I mean me."

Juliana stilled. "I thought we agreed to work together."

"We will. You'll pray most earnestly on my behalf. And Abington will distract the duke with his stellar wit."

"Pray?" Juliana asked through clenched teeth.

"Unless you prefer something else. You could meditate, perhaps?"

Abington pulled a silver flask from his coat but

then put it away when Ian glared at him. "I'm coming with you. Glavenstroke did give me the mission, after all."

Ian shrugged. "Suit yourself. Just keep in mind that Sommet *is* actively trying to kill me."

"*He* can go?" Juliana protested, but she could hear the tremble in her voice and hated that her fear for Ian was so near the surface.

"*He* is a spy."

Abington frowned. "That's not meant to be common knowledge."

Ian grinned, but it didn't quite reach his eyes. "Sorry, chap. I'm about as common as they come."

"If Abington is with you," Juliana said. "You'll need someone to distract Sommet."

Ian's grin disappeared. "Not you."

"You are going into the lair of a man who you admit wants you dead. I'll do whatever I can to remove as much danger as possible."

"By putting yourself in it?"

"You're doing the same thing."

"But I am expendable." Ian's words were harsh. He spun away from her, tension tight in his shoulders.

Was that truly what he thought?

She wanted to go to him and catch him by the shoulders. She wanted to look him in the eye and tell him just how much of a lie that was.

Yet as carefree as he pretended to be, she knew he wouldn't care for her drawing attention to his weakness in front of Abington.

"You will hate me forever," Abington said. "But I must point out La Petit bore that role many times."

"Juliana is not La Petit."

Juliana was fairly sure that wasn't a point in her favor.

"There are three footmen guarding the stairs," Abington reported when he returned to his rooms.

"That is a rather insultingly low number." But it matched what Ian had glimpsed in passing. "I checked with the butler. He's shorthanded because Sommet assigned seven of his footmen elsewhere. That leaves us with four elsewhere in the tower, including Sommet's pet pugilist."

"He has a pet pugilist?"

Ian explained about the man Sommet normally had guarding the stairs. "But he's not there now, so I can only assume—"

"He's guarding something more important."

"Exactly," Ian said. He resisted the urge to check the clock again. Juliana wouldn't be with the duke yet. She was going to check on her brother.

"So how do you plan to get past the footmen?"

"Quite easily."

Abington grimaced. "And people think *I* am arrogant."

Ian shrugged. A supply of swagger hid many shortcomings. Far too many. Gads. He'd thought more about his failings in the past week than he had since he was seven years old. And he had no one to blame but himself and the foolish dreams he should know better than to have.

"So why does Sommet want the Trio dead?" Abington asked.

Ian checked his daggers and secured a length of rope around his waist. "We know too much. We're a liability."

"To whom? What knowledge do you have that he wants to protect? You never ran any missions for him."

"We ran several, including our first."

Abington looked at him oddly. "No. Glavenstroke was the only one to give you orders. No one else wanted to be associated with you in case you failed miserably."

"We were ordered to topple a country." Juliana's. "I think I remember it rather clearly."

Abington frowned. "I read your files. Your first mission was Salamanca."

"You read our files?"

Abington shrugged. "Several times. Haven't you?"

Ian felt like a chub. He'd assumed he knew what was in them. And he knew better than to assume anything. "They must have decided to leave it out of the records."

"Glavenstroke?" Abington's disbelief was clear. "You were his favorite creation. He probably wrote down when you pissed."

An unsettled cold began to form in Ian's stomach. "Then perhaps Sommet ordered him not to record it."

"Perhaps," Abington said, but his gaze was clearly disbelieving.

Ian tried to recall every detail he could about his first mission. They'd received the orders from one of the approved couriers. They'd never thought to question it.

Twelve years and he still had never thought to question it.

Ian wanted to brain himself with the chamber pot. Glaves hadn't been sarcastic when he'd asked about Lenoria earlier; he'd had no clue what Ian was speaking of.

Ian braced his fist against the wall.

Sweet mercy, what had he done? He wasn't one to believe in higher powers but he was tempted to pray now. Juliana had forgiven him his role because he'd been following orders. How would she feel knowing he'd been tricked?

He had saved Lenoria from falling to the French, but what the devil did that matter?

He slammed his fist hard against the wall, relishing the pain that seared up his arm.

Gregory had agreed to kill the Trio for what they'd done to his country. Ian had thought Sommet had simply used Gregory because he was a convenient enemy to take the blame.

But what if Sommet wanted to kill the Trio not

just because they were a general liability but because they knew—even if they didn't realize it—his interest in Lenoria? What if Sommet's conspiracy was tidier than Ian had thought?

But what the devil did he think they knew? The Trio had been too green to gain anything useful. They had followed their orders, then left. There had been no time for additional reconnaissance.

"So what is the plan?" Abington asked.

"The plan's simple. I go exactly where everyone can see me. And no one will."

Chapter Thirty

*H*er aunt's cheeks were flushed a rosy pink as Juliana entered her brother's room. She couldn't remember ever seeing her aunt's cheeks rosy with anything other than outrage, and Eustace didn't look at all outraged now.

Eustace was focused on Gregory's valet. "And the entire group was saved thanks to the liberal application of the salve."

Was her aunt boasting?

"Amazing, Your Highness," Canterbury said. He stood on the other side of the room, brushing stains from one of Gregory's coats. He was intent on his task, but Juliana didn't miss the quick glances he cast in her aunt's direction.

"How is Gregory?" Juliana asked.

Both of the other occupants started and her aunt's cheeks darkened further.

But her tone was as brisk and businesslike as always. "He appears well. I gave him some of my sleeping draught to help with pain."

"Are his injuries that severe then?"

Her aunt smiled slightly. "He is sore, no doubt. But you must remember even a simple headache sends your brother to bed for days."

Clearly wanting to give them privacy, Canterbury bowed and left the room with the jacket over his arm.

Eustace's eyes followed the servant, then she hurriedly glanced away when she noticed Juliana watching. "He reminds me of my Albert. They have the same sense of fashion."

Juliana had only ever seen the small portrait Eustace wore about her neck. Albert had always seemed like such a stern man, but now that Juliana thought about it, he was wearing a bright yellow cravat in the painting.

Some of her surprise must have showed on her face because Eustace smiled. "Did you picture him dour and dressed in black?"

Juliana searched for the right words.

Eustace laughed, staring down at her black dress almost in surprise. "I can see why you would think that. But this was my reaction to his death not a reflection of him. Leucretia always called him something of popinjay."

If she hadn't been so well-trained, her jaw would have been hanging open. Her aunt had never spoken of Albert with anything but hushed reverence.

And, Juliana realized with a prick of guilt, she'd never bothered to inquire.

"How did you know you loved him?" Juliana

asked, the words tumbling out of her mouth too quickly.

But Eustace was too lost in her memories of Albert—or perhaps a certain valet—to take note.

"I shouldn't have been. He was too old for me. And even before we married, we had suspicions he might be ill. But I knew any moment I had with him was worth the pain that would come."

That was the conclusion that Juliana faced. "Was it?"

Eustace smiled sadly. "Yes. I think one of the reasons I had trouble moving on was that I was content with my memories, and I feared diluting them."

She'd spoken of her trouble in past tense. That had to be a good thing.

Eustace sighed. "I should have spent more time with you rather than leaving you to Leucretia and Constantina and heaven knows how many governesses and tutors. But I feared you pushing Albert out of my thoughts and I couldn't risk that."

Juliana's chest throbbed and her eyes burned.

"Now," Eustace said, her eyes returning to the rather stern focus Juliana was used to. "What precisely is going on here?" She pointed to Gregory's sleeping form. "If he'd gotten into a fight over a woman, he'd likely have at least some bruising on his face and certainly have swelling and abrasions on his knuckles."

Juliana wasn't sure what she was ready to tell, but

she did know what she needed to find out. "What can you tell me about Leucretia and Sommet?"

Eustace frowned. "Do they have something to do with this?"

Juliana remained silent.

Her aunt debated a moment before speaking. "They were lovers several decades ago. They met on one of Leucretia's many trips around Europe. Then when iron was found on Leucretia's estate, I believe she contacted Sommet, who had connections to several mining companies. They approached your father for permission to mine. He refused."

That explained what the duke had been doing in Lenoria all those years ago.

"Is Leucretia in some sort of trouble with the duke?" Eustace asked.

"I don't know." But it was an angle she hadn't considered. What if Sommet was holding something over Leucretia? "But she did say Sommet had cheated her. Do you know what business they were in together?"

Eustace's brow wrinkled. "I don't know. She was always vague about which of Sommet's ventures she was involved in. All I know is that it has made her extremely wealthy."

"Wealthy?"

"Where do you think all her jewels come from?"

Juliana's cheeks heated. "I thought from her . . . cicisbeos."

Despite all the day's revelations, Eustace was still somewhat herself because she frowned at Juliana's use of the word. "She may have gotten some from those men. But most, she purchased on her own."

"How did I not know this?"

"Leucretia has always been secretive about her investments. Once I asked if we should put some of your money in the same investments since she seemed to be doing so well and she panicked."

"She gave no explanation why?"

"She said Sommet didn't wish to bother with more investors. Oddly enough, all her extravagant purchases ceased a little over a year ago."

About the same time Sommet had begun to befriend Gregory. Had investments gone wrong? That would explain the sudden interest in the ore again. Perhaps he was counting on her mountains to make up for some bad investments? She'd have to tell Ian her theory. All the pieces fit. Perhaps if Sommet himself owed money to investors, they'd have something to hold over *him*.

She glanced at the clock on the mantel. It was time for archery. She stood and walked to the window. The targets had been set out on the lawn, and already, several ladies and gentlemen had emerged to test the bows and boast.

But there was no Sommet yet.

"Is Leucretia or Constantina chaperoning you this afternoon?" Eustace asked.

"Leucretia." At least that had been the plan; she

didn't know if Leucretia would appear after the events of last night.

"Ah yes, I forgot that Constantina has a fear of flying things. Perhaps you can get Leucretia to tell you of her investments. She might resist, but I cannot think she would lie to you if you pressed her on it."

Juliana stiffened her spine. She *would* get the information.

She hurried to her room and retrieved her bonnet from Apple. She hurried out into the corridor as she tied the bow. The blue satin ribbon popped free. Drat. She'd only tacked it on. She'd forgotten she hadn't yet done the final stitching.

She glanced back to her room. This was the only bonnet she had that matched this dress. So she would either have to take the time to change her dress or the time to fix her bonnet. Leucretia wouldn't let her outside without one.

"Might I be of assistance, Your Highness?"

She turned to find Canterbury. He pulled a needle and thread from his pocket.

"I . . ." She was in a hurry and hats weren't the simplest thing to mend.

He seemed to sense her hesitance and pointed to the creation on his own head. "I do have some experience, Your Majesty."

She handed him the bonnet. As he stitched, she found herself leaning over to watch.

"I never thought to attach it that way," she said.

"I find it puts less stress on the ribbon. Did you design this one?"

Why not admit it? "Yes."

"It is quite fine, if I might be so bold."

"Thank you." If he was being bold, perhaps she could be, too. "I notice you seem to love hats as well."

A ghost of a smile crossed the old man's face. "When Mr. Maddox came to me and asked me to serve as a butler to one of his friends, I was a bit hesitant as I was already enjoying my retirement. But Mr. Maddox claimed I could still have as much freedom as I wanted. I could wear a peacock on my head if I so desired."

Juliana grinned at the man. "So you took him at his word."

"Indeed, Your Majesty. It irks him to no end."

"So you know Ian well?"

Canterbury's face stilled and he handed her the mended bonnet. "Better than he knows himself. As I think you do."

Did she? "I—"

Leucretia sail past with little more than a nod in Juliana's direction. Juliana had to rush after her. She needed her answers and she didn't want to waste this opportunity to be alone with her aunt. "We must talk."

Leucretia didn't respond. She kept gliding forward, her chin lifted.

A short time later, Juliana found herself at the

stairs, all her questions still unanswered. Juliana hadn't been able get a single word from her. What should she do next? Shake them out of her?

She'd felt rather like a silly child trailing after her mother's skirts. No, Leucretia had never been a mother to her, but she had been a mentor, an adviser.

As soon as they walked outside, her aunt had stalked off to chat with some other women under the shade of a large tree. Quickly enough to earn a few whispers.

And the fascinated attention of the newly arrived French ambassador, Monsieur Gallant, who eyed her like a hungry crow.

Perfect. Now he'd carry tales of a rift in the royal house of Lenoria.

Juliana took her time at the bow table. She fully intended to shoot in the contest—the idea of causing potentially lethal damage to something appealed right now—but the table provided the best view of the assembled group.

And Sommet had yet to arrive.

She picked up a bow, then put it down as if she was dissatisfied. No one would comment on her being picky; she was a princess after all.

Where was the duke? What if he didn't attend this entertainment after all? She'd have to trust that Ian was monitoring that before he made his attempt.

As she picked up the final lady's bow, the duke joined the guests. He immediately went to speak to the ambassador. After several seconds, Sommet lifted his eyes to hers, the taunt in his face clear.

But that taunt meant he thought he'd already won. And a prideful man made mistakes.

So she slung a bow over her shoulder and strolled to the other intrepid women gathered to shoot at the ladies' targets.

A footman handed her an arrow and she set it to the string. With a slow exhale, she let the arrow fly. It buried in the outside ring with a solid thunk.

A bull's-eye would have been more dramatic, but her hands were shaking so badly that she was glad she hit the target at all.

She shot three more arrows, keeping Sommet in her peripheral vision the entire time. He spoke to an earl and then to Lady Plimpington, who latched herself on to his arm.

Juliana's shoulders relaxed slightly. Lady Plimpington was immensely talented at trapping people into long-winded conversations about the untouched potential of her daughters.

Now that Sommet's back was to her, she allowed herself one quick glance at the duke's section of the castle.

And her heart stopped.

Ian was scaling the side of the castle tower.

Outside. In front of everyone.

She whipped her head back to the targets.

Was he mad? She knew he could climb it. He'd done it before with her on his back, but now there were thirty people who could spot him. True, he was wearing a gray shirt the same color as the stone. And he was already past the second floor so they'd have to look up to spot him.

But if she'd seen him, Sommet could as well.

Where was Abington? And why hadn't he dissuaded Ian from this insanity?

She didn't attempt to shoot another arrow. She feared she'd drop it entirely. She risked another glance back. He was already to the third floor. Her terror mixed with pure raw admiration. The gaps between the stone couldn't have been more than an inch deep and yet he managed to climb as easily as if he'd set up a ladder. His toes found grooves to cling to that she wouldn't have guessed existed.

He appeared to be working on a window with something. His dagger, perhaps?

A footman strolled directly underneath where he was perched. She forced her gaze to the grass at her feet.

Air refused to enter her lungs.

But after a moment, when no alarm had been sounded, she allowed herself to look up.

But where had Sommet gone? He was no longer with Lady Plimpington.

Her gaze darted around the guests. *There.* How had he gotten close to the door so quickly? She handed a footman her bow and strolled toward the duke. She didn't dare risk another glance at Ian in case Sommet followed her gaze.

And she realized after all her time planning for Leucretia, she didn't know what she was going to say to distract the duke.

Even if she had some of Leucretia's flirtation, trying it on Sommet would only serve to make him suspicious. In fact, if she approached him at all, Ian would be in trouble.

She could faint from the heat. It was rather unbearable.

But she suspected he'd see through her ruse and rush inside.

What could she do that would bring the duke to her? She forced her thoughts to calm. She could do this. She had told Ian she would, and she would.

Monsieur Gallant.

Planting a large, seductive smile on her face, she strolled toward the French ambassador. "Monsieur Gallant!" She made certain to call a touch louder than normal.

The man's eyes never lifted above her bodice. And under normal circumstances, she ensured she never spoke to him alone. But desperate times . . .

She offered him her hand for his customary molestation, but after he'd finished salivating over it, rather than wiping it on her skirts, she placed it on his arm and leaned closer.

Monsieur Gallant's rat eyes widened under his thin brows. She never had been able to tell if he plucked them, but he was vain enough it was a possibility.

"I had not thought to see you here, monsieur. You mentioned nothing of it when we met a few days ago."

His tongue polished his front teeth. She'd met with him in enough failed negotiations to know that meant he was nervous.

Perhaps she could do more than distract Sommet with this conversation.

And she had distracted him. The duke had ceased his movement to the door. In fact, he turned back to speak to Lord Bentersly, who was distinctly closer to her.

"So, Ambassador. I've been thinking of the proposal you suggested when we last met."

His tongue probed his teeth again. "You have?" Gallant was too skilled at his profession to betray more than that.

"Yes. I don't agree with it. But I'm thinking we might be able to come to a more favorable solution than the one you have with Sommet."

Sommet glanced at her then and she made sure to jerk her head quickly away as if she was hiding something.

"France wins either way," Gallant said.

"You believe Sommet has France's best interests at heart?"

Gallant hesitated. "He is interested in his own pocketbook, and France is interested in continuing to get her ore."

Continuing? But she couldn't ask without revealing how little she knew about Sommet's actual activities.

"I might be interested in providing ore." If *might* meant never in her lifetime. "After all, the royal coffers will need to be filled after all the neglect."

Gallant tipped his head slightly. "Sommet said you'd refuse."

"Of course Sommet would say that." Had she worked the duke's name into the conversation enough to draw his interest yet?

"It is essential that the shipments not be stopped."

Her whole body went cold. Somehow Sommet was already mining. But what about the villages— *Casualties of war.* The duke's earlier words now resonated with new meaning. "Why would they stop?"

"Sommet assured me that you'd follow your father's decrees."

"And you listened?"

"A rather indifferent day at archery, was it not, Your Highness?" Sommet stepped into the space between her and the ambassador, his eyes glittering. "I fear you might not have enough experience at the game. Gallant, perhaps you'd care to join me inside for the brandy I spoke to you of earlier."

Juliana rested her hand lightly on the ambassador's arm. "But the ambassador and I still have much to discuss."

Gallant bowed at her but backed away. "We can continue this discussion later."

But if he was about to sequester himself with Sommet, she could wager how productive her future meeting would be.

She couldn't risk letting Sommet go into the house, either.

How long had Ian been in? Ten minutes, perhaps? Surely even a man as skilled as Ian needed longer than that.

She tried to use Leucretia's trick and let passion enter her eyes. "Perhaps I do not want to wait."

From the way the ambassador's mouth gaped she must have come close to accomplishing it, but it wasn't good enough. "Sorry, Your Highness, I must go with my best option."

None of them pretended he was speaking of the brandy.

A footman came and murmured to the duke, then hurried away.

What was it? Had Ian been discovered? Were they out of lemonade?

The duke's expression betrayed nothing.

But the duke began to walk away and the ambassador followed. He strode across the grass with only brief nods and greetings to the guests seeking his attention.

She couldn't let the duke reach the castle.

She was out of options.

She hurried after them a few steps, then fell to the grass with a cry.

Sommet and the ambassador both glanced back.

"My ankle. I think I've twisted it."

She was close enough that the duke was forced to come to her side. To walk away from her would have been too callous for a man who claimed to be a gentleman.

He loomed over her. "What happened?"

She winced. "I stepped on my ankle poorly."

Several other gentlemen and ladies had surrounded her.

"I'll fetch your aunt," Sommet said.

"No." She turned to one of the other men. "Sir Thomas, can you find her?"

A muscle in Sommet's cheek twitched. "Then I will find a footman to bear you inside."

"No, not yet. I need a moment to compose myself. I would appreciate your assistance."

The duke's eyes narrowed, and his lip curled slightly. He dropped to his knee beside her and rested his hand on her shoulder as if giving comfort. But his words were for her ears alone. "Your diversion is naught but wasted effort. Your spy is already dead."

Chapter Thirty-one

"*I* could have found my own way in," Abington murmured as they crept along the corridor. "I was a competent spy."

He probably still was competent.

When he was sober.

"I arranged a distraction for you, nothing more." The maid bringing supper fifteen minutes early to the guards at the bottom of the stair, to be precise. Not too early so as to raise suspicions, but enough to allow Abington past if he was paying attention. "You were smart enough to use it, good for you."

And now Ian knew that Abington wasn't drunk enough to be a liability.

They walked past the office he and Juliana had hidden in before. He would have liked to examine it again, but they didn't have time.

The next room was a parlor. Again, Ian doubted it held anything. His years as a thief and his eons as a spy had given him a nearly unfailing sense about these things.

The next three rooms were equally pointless.

But then Ian had expected them to be. There were no extra guards on this level. And Sommet wouldn't have placed anything valuable this close to the ground where a smashed window would have allowed access.

People always thought they were hiding their valuables in places no one would think to look. They never realized it usually came down to the same three or four places.

Sommet would like to think he was more clever than everyone else, but Ian had found many men who thought the same thing.

That tavern keeper in Cheapside, for instance, had been paranoid as a pig in a butcher's shop. But at the end of it, his valuables had been hidden under a floorboard beneath the chamber pot.

Rich people just didn't understand that men of Ian's ilk didn't have the same squeamishness that plagued everyone else.

The next floor proved no more fruitful.

Sommet would be the type to have a secret something. A secret safe. A secret compartment. Perhaps even a secret room.

That might explain how Sommet had disappeared so thoroughly last night.

Ian held up his hand to halt Abington as they climbed the stone stairs that spiraled to the next level. There was someone at the top of them. Ian could smell the footman—yet another skill neglected by noble spies like Abington. The servants always smelled of ale and wig powder.

With silent steps, Ian closed the distance, peering around the curve of the stairs. He could see black leather shoes—the toes. The footman was facing the stairs.

So Ian sprung toward him. He took advantage of the split second of shock and moved behind the servant, clamping one hand over his mouth and his arm around the man's throat.

Thirty seconds later, Ian dragged the unconscious man down the stairs. Abington's eyes widened but he simply moved into position behind Ian.

The final corridor contained six doors. The sixth footman was guarding the door at the end. It was the room Sommet had taunted him from last night.

Which mean Ian was definitely going inside.

If he had a fatal flaw—like that Greek fellow in the play who'd gouged out his eyes—it was curiosity. He just couldn't *not* know what Sommet intended him to find.

Besides, they were down to two servants. Ian could handle two servants if need be.

Make that one. Ian dispatched the servant at the door with a quick blow to the side of the head.

Ian would need to talk to Sommet about the quality of his guards. This was rather embarrassing for all of them.

The final footman must be inside. And it would

be Sommet's boxer, which meant he would be more skilled than the rest.

After checking the handle, Ian eased the door open. It was Sommet's other office. There was no sign of the last footman. So Ian walked to the desk. The locks on the drawers were slightly more sophisticated than he expected.

But it opened easily under his picks. Abington reached past him to open the drawer.

There was a faint click. Ian jerked Abington's hand out of the way as a blade popped out of the edge of the drawer.

They both stared at it. It would have slit open his wrist.

But that meant there was something worthwhile inside the desk. Inside the first drawer were financial records. Ian withdrew the most recent and tucked them away to examine later. But there were no incriminating letters from Gregory.

And where was that missing footman? It was possible Sommet had sent him on some sort of mission, but Ian doubted it. Sommet would want him close where he could be useful.

They searched the other hiding places in the room, finding nothing.

"I suspect Sommet has some sort of hidden room."

Abington took off his jacket and shoved it in the crack under the door to the corridor, then he gathered some blank papers from the desk and lit them in the fireplace. He motioned for Ian to remain still and after a moment, he fanned the smoke into the room.

Perhaps Abington was competent even drunk.

Ian held his shirt over his nose as the smoke dispersed evenly through the room.

Except by the base of the bookcase. Small eddies swirled in the smoke, clearly highlighting the unexpected location of the draft.

Abington nodded and they both slowly approached. There was no obvious secret door, the bookcase appeared solid, but then Sommet would only have paid for the best.

Ian reached up and ran his fingers around the shelves searching for some sort of latch. Abington did the same. The wide mahogany bookcases reached to the ceiling, and when they couldn't find anything, they began removing books. But after they'd cleared all the shelves they still had nothing.

They were out of time. They should have left five minutes ago. This was far longer than Ian usually spent at the scene of any of his other investigations.

They had one last option. Ian lifted his hand and knocked loudly on the bookcase. "Hello. Just so you know, we are robbing your master blind."

After a second, there was a click. The space in the bookcase slid open, revealing the taciturn footman; he had one hand over his mouth, coughing in the smoke.

In the other, hand he had a pistol. He pulled the trigger.

Chapter Thirty-two

Sir Willowby had insisted on carrying Juliana back to her room when no footmen had been available. Juliana was grateful. She wasn't certain if she could have managed to walk with the shock that had drained her ability to move. And she wouldn't give Sommet the satisfaction of seeing her falter, especially now.

If what he'd claimed was true.

Her aunt walked silently beside them. Other than a single inquiry as to Juliana's current state, she hadn't spoken.

Sir Willowby stopped by her room and gingerly set her on her feet. "I wish you the best, Your Highness."

"You're too kind." She smiled, even as she was already peering into her room, searching for Apple. Perhaps the girl had heard something. Or Ian might be waiting.

Sommet could have been lying. He was always lying. He must have been lying about this.

But neither of them was there.

He couldn't be dead.

He was practically omnipotent. An old, ferret-faced duke didn't stand a chance.

She didn't have to feign the instability in her step as she walked to her bed. She couldn't breathe and yet she was breathing too fast. Her chest burned, yet was as cold as ice.

How could she look for him? Where did she go?

She would have to storm the duke's tower. But what if Sommet was merely looking for Ian and she led Sommet straight to him?

She pressed her knuckles against her mouth until her wrists trembled from the pressure.

Leucretia stepped into the room, observing. "I warned you about Sommet."

Rage seared across Juliana's thoughts. Ian might be dead. And her aunt and her prevarications were at least partially to blame. Juliana embraced the anger. This was at least something she could resolve. "You've been mining in the Palas."

Leucretia stepped back. "How did you—"

"No." Juliana cut her off and stalked toward her. "How long has it been going on?"

Leucretia seemed to deflate on herself. "Since we came to England. The duke came to me with the proposal. The ore was there just waiting to be sold." Her aunt's back stiffened. "And it was my land. It was my right."

"And the people living there?"

Leucretia shrugged. "The war forced many

people to move. Ourselves, for instance. We survived."

Had she ever known this woman? "What changed at the end of the war?"

Her aunt's fingers turned into claws. "After Versailles, the duke told me the mining had been suspended. The mountains were in the part of the country that was to go to the Spanish."

"Why would that matter?"

Her aunt sighed. "He'd been selling iron to the French."

"But Spain controlled Lenoria during the war."

"Spain had no time to keep watch on the mountains. Not when they were fighting for their survival. That is why he needs Gregory. If the Spanish get the mountains and they find out just how much Sommet was aiding the French? Sommet loses everything."

Juliana stared sat her.

She finally had her leverage.

If the duke had been selling ore to the French during the war, that was treason. And it was something she could prove. "But Sommet told me if Gregory doesn't challenge me tomorrow, the ambassadors have agreed to ignore the treaty and move forward with the division. Why would he want that? "

Leucretia's kohled eyes narrowed. "He doesn't."

He'd lied. Again.

And she'd gobbled up every word.

She glanced at the door again. Still no Apple. Still no Ian.

Enough.

She'd demand to see him. If he was dead—Juliana's chest tore open at thought—the duke should be able to present a body. If he could not, that meant he was lying about this, too.

She flung open the door to reveal a startled Abington. He was missing his jacket but other than that appeared unscathed.

He shook his head slightly, then held up his hand to motion for her to stay inside her room, then he continued down the corridor.

What was that supposed to mean? Was it a condolence? Was she too late? Was Ian well and would come for her?

And why was she obeying his command to stay in her room rather than finding out?

"Your Grace?" She took a step toward him.

Abington turned around, surprised. He must have read the same panic on her face that Leucretia had because he returned. But he cast a long glance at one of the duke's maids who was lingering nearby. "Don't worry, Your Highness. I heard the news as well, but the duke can in no way think this reflects on you."

She played along. "Of course not."

"How were you to know that your groom would

attack one of Sommet's servants? Or that he'd flee afterward."

"My servant fled?"

"The duke is hunting him now. His injured servant is ready to swear out a warrant against him."

Ian was alive. She would have swayed if Abington hadn't grabbed her elbow. "I'm sorry your servant's perfidy has overset you."

"Do they know his motive? Did he steal anything?" Did he have the papers they needed?

"Nothing, Your Highness," Abington's expression was grim. "Nothing of value. But do not worry. The groom is far away now. You have nothing to fear from him." Abington bowed to a deep courtly level. "I must dress for dinner."

Juliana stepped back inside her room.

Ian was gone. And if the duke was hunting him, she hoped he stayed that way.

She wouldn't be so selfish as to wish for a final day with him. Another word of advice. Another taunt.

Another kiss.

His safety came first. To wish for him to be here would be the same as wishing for his death.

The void in her chest at his absence was just early, not unexpected.

She turned back to her aunt. "Where do your loyalties lie? With your money or with Lenoria?"

Her aunt's chin lifted. "With Lenoria."

Juliana nodded. She now had the tools she

needed to bring about the destruction of the duke. And she would use them. "Well then, I will need your help to bring down the duke. Hand me some paper."

Chapter Thirty-three

People could be so gullible. They always assumed Ian fled when he was chased. No one ever saw him slip into another room, then simply hide inches from where he'd started.

As fearful as the duke was, he still thought himself safe in his own room.

Ian watched Sommet prepare himself for bed. He must have been fearful of a knife to the back indeed if he'd forgone a valet.

When the old weasel had his breeches around his ankles, Ian stepped into the light.

"Going to bed early? Tired, perhaps? Getting old?" Ian drew his dagger.

The duke scrambled back, tripping over his clothing. "Mullins!"

"Mullins has stepped away to use the chamber pot. And since you're inconsiderate with the facilities you allow him to use, that means you and I have seven minutes. Do you know what I can do with seven minutes?" He twirled his dagger around his fingers. A silly alley trick but one that made men quake.

Sommet struggled to pull up his breeches. "He'll kill you when he returns."

"Yes, because he was so successful last time. He's still recovering from the blow to the head I gave him." Which he'd even managed before the other man had seen Abington through the smoke.

Sommet's eyes probed him. "He said he injured you."

He had. His bullet had caught Ian in the shoulder. Ian had bound it with one of Sommet's cravats while he was waiting. Thankfully, he'd managed to claim Abington's jacket to hide his bloodstained shirt.

Ian shrugged despite the pain. "Of course he claimed that. He wouldn't want to look as ineffectual as he truly is."

The duke wasn't the only one who could sow doubt and suspicion.

But neither was the duke fond of appearing vulnerable. "You think you're so clever. But you have always been easy to manipulate."

"With false missions?"

The duke paused. "With everything. The right information planted in the right place is all I need to convince you of anything."

Ian very much feared this interrogation was

about to spiral out of his control. So he stepped closer and pressed the tip of this knife to Sommet's throat, enough to draw a bead of blood.

But the duke met his eyes with pure malice. "For instance, a letter to Napoleon hidden in a Lenorian king's study. That was all it took to convince you that he was going to side with the French." Sommet pressed his finger against the blade of the knife, moving it away from his throat, showing no sign of pain as the well-honed blade sliced into his finger. "He wasn't, you know. He'd decided to help the British."

Ian didn't move. But everything inside him shriveled, coiling in on itself in cold, hard agony in his chest. The hand holding the knife felt numb, so numb that he feared dropping it if he tried to return it to Sommet's neck.

"What, no witty response?" The duke smiled. "Have I shocked the all-knowing Wraith? I didn't know that was possible. What will your princess think when I tell her?"

Ian knew he had to speak. "She already knows."

"That you were a member of the Trio, perhaps. But does she know that if you were smarter, you might have been able to stop it all? You might have been able to save her parents? Does she know the rest of the Trio waited on your final order to proceed?"

He felt vile, like something that had been dragged through the filth of the gutters.

"Does she know that I have always outclassed you? That she never stood a chance against me, especially once she had your help?"

Ian was too empty to feel the blow to his pride.

Juliana's parents had been murdered in front of her at his instigation. Because he'd been too blind to look past the information he'd been set up to find.

Hell, he'd always known he wasn't worthy, but this?

Ian was suddenly sick of the game. Of Sommet and his cruelty and deception. "I should kill you."

"But you won't because your princess would know it was you. Then she'd never be able to look at you again."

And he was right. Not only because it would horrify her, but because it would prove him no better than the thug he feared himself to be.

For the first time in his life, Ian wasn't happy with that title. He didn't want to be a common criminal. He wanted to be the man who could walk at Juliana's side. Claim her for all the world to see.

Not that she'd ever have him.

Sommet tipped his head. "And that will be Mullins returning."

Damnation. He'd been played like a two-penny marionette. Ian scrambled to the window like a common thief, grateful he'd at least been smart enough to prepare for a quick exit. He grabbed the rope and slid down, breaking into a run as soon as his feet touched the ground.

"After him!" Sommet shouted to the startled footman below the window.

But while Ian's thoughts were muddled, his instincts still served him well.

He dodged the younger man's awkward grab, then easily outran him.

He could hear sounds of a search behind him as other footmen joined the first. But Ian circled and backtracked through gravel, brush, even a fountain or two until he was certain they could no longer track him.

He finally settled in the branches of an oak. The castle was only a collection of glowing dots in the distance. But even from here, he knew which window was Juliana's.

He watched that window long past when his legs had begun to cramp and his shoulder burned like a red-hot poker had been jammed all the way to the bone.

If he was smart, he'd continue on. He'd just keep walking. Minimize his losses.

Be the one to leave first.

Never let Juliana hear of any of this.

Not be there to see Juliana's face when she learned the truth.

But then he'd never been that smart.

And he'd bloody well never been in love before, either.

Sommet had posted guards under Juliana's window. Devious man.

So Ian made his way around, searching for another open window.

Gregory's was open, so after waiting for the footman to pass, he let himself in.

"I had suspicions you might return, sir." Canterbury rose from a chair by the fireplace, where he sat mending stockings, and offered Ian a plate of bread and cheese.

"You left the window open for me, old man?"

"If you chose to use it, sir."

"Barring the window would have been wiser."

"I thought you might not need the challenge tonight, sir."

"A locked window isn't a challenge."

"As you say, sir."

Gregory was still asleep, but other than that, Canterbury was alone. The stockings and a half-finished hat were his only company.

"Where is the fair Eustace, Canterbury?"

"It is eleven, sir. I said I would watch Prince Gregory while she slept."

"Considerate as always. But I was hoping to ask her to bind my shoulder."

Canterbury frowned. "What is wrong with your shoulder?"

"A bullet passed through it."

Canterbury sat back down. "Ah, how bad is it, sir?"

"Not mortal. The bullet just grazed the flesh on the outside of my shoulder. It is in the devil of a place to bind properly on my own."

Canterbury stood. "I will help you, sir."

"You would be at my feet unconscious before I removed my shirt."

His brows drew down. "No, sir." He retrieved a bag over by Gregory's bed. "Princess Eustace has bandaging material, I believe." He pulled out several neatly rolled bundles of linen. "Remove your jacket, sir."

His butler was insane if he thought he could do this. "I appreciate your desire to help, but I can manage."

"No, sir, I will help."

Ian removed his jacket, and as he expected, Canterbury's skin paled as white as the prince's sheet. "You can't even stand the blood on my shirt."

"I am determined, sir."

"What does being determined get you, old man?"

"I cleaned the room after your mother's death, sir."

Ian froze. He'd never considered who'd been left with that task. They hadn't had any maids left by then.

Only Canterbury.

"You saw to her burial, too, didn't you?" And all the other details that Ian had never considered as a child.

"Yes, sir."

"Did you know why she—" Ian could barely form the words. They seemed to belong to a seven-year-old boy. "Why did she do it? Did she leave a note? Did you have suspicions?"

Canterbury walked to Ian's side. He motioned for Ian to sit, then helped him remove his shirt.

Canterbury's lips were in a tight line, but he remained conscious. "It wasn't the first time she attempted it, sir."

"What?" That wasn't what Ian had anticipated. "I don't remember that."

"You were a child. Your parents kept the truth from you."

It seemed like a sick topic of discussion but he suddenly had to know. "When? When did she try?"

"Several years before your father passed away."

"She tried to commit suicide while my father was still alive? While she still had the house? The servants?"

Canterbury's hands were clammy but steady. "Yes, sir."

Ian stared at the toes of Canterbury's impeccably polished shoes as the implications crashed over him. It wasn't that he hadn't been enough. His father. Wealth. Security. Those hadn't been enough for her, either. The guilt he'd carried slowly crumbled. He hadn't been lacking.

She'd been ill.

He winced as Canterbury secured the bandage.

"Why did you come after me all those years

ago? Why did you leave the window open for me tonight?"

Canterbury picked up Ian's bloody shirt and threw it into the fireplace. Only after he had disposed of it did he sink into his chair as if his legs could no longer support him. "Because you were a good lad, sir."

"Too bad that didn't last."

"No, sir, now you are the finest of men."

That might be stretching things, but from now on, he'd do his best to ensure Juliana and Canterbury thought so.

Chapter Thirty-four

When a man loomed over her bed, Juliana attacked. She wouldn't be murdered in her bed by one of Sommet's goons. And she screamed at the same time, too. Like a madwoman.

She'd been feeling the fool after she'd failed to scream when Ian had appeared that first night. She wouldn't make that mistake again.

Her palm connected with a man's nose. He stumbled back, clutching his face. "Bloody hell, Jules. Good thing I didn't teach you to fire a pistol."

"*Ian.*" She scrambled out from under the covers. "Did I break your nose?"

He gingerly pressed the sides. "I don't think so, but I'm about to start dripping blood all over the duke's fine carpet." He swore and then dropped flat on the floor behind her bed as the door to her dressing room opened.

Apple ran in, a candle flickering in one hand and a heavy brass candlestick in the other. "What is wrong, Your Highness?"

Ian stood, cursing again.

Apple stared at him in shock. "Why'd you come back?"

Juliana wanted to know the same thing.

Ian shrugged. "The job isn't done."

Her maid scowled. "But the duke—"

There was a knock. "Juliana? Are you well? I thought I heard a scream."

Apple hurried to the door. She opened it as Ian again dropped to the floor. "It was simply a bad dream, Your Highness."

Eustace peered in, relaxing when she saw Juliana. "Would you like one of my tinctures?"

Apple tried to block her view. "As you can see, all is well."

Juliana didn't want her aunt to find Ian, either. "No, I'm fine," she called out.

But now Eustace was suspicious and she brushed past Apple in true royal style. She circled the room.

An excuse was on Juliana's tongue, but Eustace walked right past the bed without pause. Finally, she stopped by Juliana. "Will you tell me what is truly going on?"

Juliana shook her head. "I have taken care of it." It felt amazing to say that. Now she just had to hope that the letter she'd sent with the courier reached the prince regent in time.

Eustace looked as if she was going to speak, but then sighed. "Good." She bid Juliana good night and then left the room.

Apple turned to Juliana. "I'll go check on the

linens I asked to be laundered. And make sure no one else heard your scream." She paused before leaving. "He's under the bed, you know."

"What?" Juliana asked.

"You looked confused about where he'd gone. It's the only logical place."

"Must you kill all the magic in my life?" Ian crawled out from under the bed. He was holding a handkerchief to his nose. "There is something to be said for mystery."

Juliana rushed to his side as Apple shut the door. "Why did you come back?" She ran her fingers along his jaw, unable to resist touching him any longer.

He drew back slightly. "Hoped to be rid of me?"

"*No.*" She shoved him, and he stumbled back with a grimace.

She caught his arm before he could fall. "How hard did I hit you?"

"Like a rampaging bull. But I was also shot this morning."

She dropped his arm. "What? Where?"

"Just grazed my shoulder, but I'm in less than ideal condition."

"Has anyone tended it? Take off your jacket." Her heart was hammering against her ribs. Both from fear for his injury and knowledge that it hadn't stopped him from returning to her.

One side of his mouth lifted higher than the other. "If only I'd known all it took for you to undress me was a gunshot wound."

She scoffed. "All it takes is for you to come into my room and give me five minutes."

His hands stalled on the buttons of his jacket. "Why, you naughty princess."

A warm tingle eased down her spine at his husky whisper. "No distractions. I need to see to your shoulder."

He lifted his shirt over his head. "It's been tended. Canterbury saw to it."

"Canterbury?"

"Yes, I'm afraid it will take him longer to recover than me."

Juliana studied the bandage. It appeared secure and there was no blood that she could see. "You cleaned it?"

"With fine French brandy."

"And the bandage seems secure."

"Indeed. He might not like wounds, but he is an expert at folding."

"Oh."

"Why, Princess, I do believe you are disappointed."

She wasn't. Not truly. But she'd liked the idea of being able to tend him, of being able to repay him for all he risked for her.

"Did you want to be my nurse?" His words were low and wicked.

The sight of the clean white bandage around his muscular shoulder did something to her insides.

He was her warrior. He'd been wounded in her service.

And she had one night to repay him.

"Do you have something you'd like me to tend?" she asked.

His good arm snaked out and wrapped around her waist. He pulled her to him with a quick tug. "Would you like the list in alphabetical order?"

"Perhaps I should just examine you to see what I can find." She drew her fingertip over his brow, then down along his cheek to the point of his chin. "All seems in order so far." She stood on tiptoe and replaced her finger with her lips.

The anticipation singing in her veins was shadowed with a touch of bittersweetness. This would be their moment together.

Then it would be over.

But she refused to think on that yet. A few minutes earlier, she'd thought she'd never have this time with Ian at all.

Regrets would have to wait. She'd have time enough for that grief later.

She twined her hands around his neck and pulled him down to her. His lips were hungry. As if he were starving for her touch.

So she let him feast, her hands caressing every inch of skin she could find.

"Eager?" Ian asked. The word was half laugh, half groan. But the light in his eye was pure pleasure.

"I didn't think you were coming back." She kissed her way down the column of his throat. "But I should have trusted you more than that. I should have known you'd never fall prey to Sommet's scheming."

His exhale was harsh. "Bloody, bloody hell."

That did not sound like a happy exclamation. "What?"

"Look what you've done. This is your fault." He stepped back. "You had to go and make me grow morals. Damned inconvenient things. That's why I always avoided them in the past." He rubbed at his bandage, his face almost haggard.

Her heart skipped uncertainly. "If you're worried about my virtue—"

For a moment, his expression lightened. "I've spent the past weeks thinking of a dozen ways around that issue. That isn't my problem." But then that glimmer of humor disappeared.

"If you're in pain, we don't have to—"

"That's not it, I could be choking on my dying breath and still want you."

Perhaps not the most romantic of phrasings, but it was pure, wonderful Ian.

"But I cannot proceed until I tell you something." He cleared his throat, then began pacing. "Damn Sommet. May his corpse rot in the Thames. But I refuse to let the man have anything over me."

Her earlier excitement was dissolved under a

slow stream of dread. "If you mean the mishap this afternoon, it doesn't matter. I don't believe Sommet's version of the story." She realized in her excitement she hadn't told him of her day's actions yet. "I was able to—"

"Who was your father going to side with during the war?"

She frowned at the change in topic, the air in the room suddenly chilly. "The British." Bands of iron wrapped around her lungs, squeezing.

Ian's head bowed until his chin almost touched his chest. "I had hoped— But it was a foolish wish. Sommet played me. Like a deck of cheap pasteboard. He used me to murder your parents."

Juliana sat on the edge of her bed before she fell. But while his words were harsh they were nothing new. "You were a member of the Trio. You followed orders."

"That's just it. There weren't any orders. As least not real ones. I thought we were acting on behalf of the British government. But it was a lie. Sommet told everyone that Lenoria planned to side with the French. That's what he told us. He even staged false documents for me to find. I am the one who confirmed the erroneous information Sommet gave us. I'm the one who stirred up the people with stories of the horrors that would be inflicted on them when your father joined with the French."

Juliana had to take slow breaths to block out the images his words summoned. Her mother's screams. The smoke. The angry shouts of the mob.

"I—" He cleared his throat again. "I cannot even begin to apologize for my role in this, but I am sorry." He clenched his eyes shut. "So very, very sorry."

Juliana counted her breaths, the task soothing her. By the time she reached twenty, she realized something.

She wasn't angry at Ian.

She opened her eyes. "You didn't know the orders weren't from your government."

"We were too green—"

It was her turn to cut him off. "That was a statement. Not a question."

His head slowly lifted.

"Why did Sommet think this was effective blackmail?"

"Because the only thing I fear in my whole worthless life is the loss of your regard." His gaze seared hers. "Sorry, my heart seems to be on my sleeve this evening." But then his eyes shifted to the window. "So have I lost it?" His back was stiff, the muscles on his forearms corded into tight ropes. "I'll leave if you wish it."

She went to his side. "I don't wish it."

Ian's brows drew together. "Why not? I'm little better than a fraud. I told you I could deal with

Sommet when he'd already duped me so thoroughly I hadn't a clue."

"Gregory was duped, too, and I haven't ordered his execution yet."

Ian grimaced at the comparison. "And the rest? Even if I haven't lost your regard, I have lost my own."

"You really think you should have known, don't you? But you can't. No one can know everything."

"Then what worth do I have to you?" He spun away from her.

How could she answer him? What could she say? What pieces of her heart did she reveal? But he'd taken a risk in telling her the truth. She could do not less.

"Everything. You're worth everything to me." The words were so silly. Trite almost. They did nothing to capture the depth of emotion that threatened to spill out of her. But how could she express that? Her true feelings were so bright. So glorious.

So forbidden.

She caught his face between her hands and forced his eyes to meet hers. Let him see what her words could never say.

"Jules." He turned his face slightly and kissed the palm of her hand. "How am I going to survive when you leave me tomorrow?"

Her eyes stung. And part of her wished he'd plead with her to stay with him.

But then, she hadn't begged him to stay with her, either. She could hardly change their deal just because her heart had become involved.

"With memories of this." She pressed her lips to his chest, right above his heart. Then again, a butterfly's caress on the edge of his bandage.

Then finally to his lips.

Although she'd started the kiss, Ian claimed it, his mouth possessing hers. He pressed her backward until her thighs collided with the bed.

She'd been so wrong. So wrong to think that her heart could recover after this.

How could she go back to a life of being bowed and scraped to? Where people treated her as if she were a throne and not a woman?

Ian's lips made her skin hum with sensation. With pleasure.

She ran her hands over his chest, then down his back. Smooth. Hard. Hers.

His hands found her breast and she moaned at the sensation, arching against his hand. "There may be some things I cannot change, but I can do something about this blasted wrapper." He moved his hands to the buttons down the front, freeing one after the other, stripping the dress from her shoulders and letting it slide to the ground. "If we don't have much time, then I don't want to waste any moment you could be gloriously naked."

She stilled as he removed her shift. And so did he. His gaze traveled down her naked body. "Hell's bells, Jules. You're perfection." He caught her up and carried her over to the bed with three swift strides.

He dropped her in the center with a grunt. "Sorry, that was supposed to be more romantic but my arm stings like the devil."

When he started to lower himself next to her, she caught him and rolled him onto his back. "Then why don't you lie here and rest?"

When she pressed a row of kisses down the center of his chest he groaned. He tucked his hand behind his head, a grin on his face. "So I can just lie here and do nothing?"

Oh, he thought to taunt her, did he? She could play his game. "Yes." She leaned over him, pinning his arms over his head and bringing her breasts inches from his lips. "You are not allowed to do anything."

He lifted his head to kiss her breast but she pulled back. "Ah-ah. Still."

His already hooded gaze narrowed until his eyes were mere slits. "Sorry, Your Highness. I'm afraid you have no authority in this room."

She squealed in a rather embarrassing manner as he suddenly flipped her onto her back. "Your shoulder," she protested.

"To hell with my shoulder. I plan to enjoy every inch of you before the morning comes." His lips ruled hers, teasing and tasting. And his hands skimmed over her hips.

•

She bucked against him. "Hurry." There was a pressure growing inside her that she wasn't sure she could bear.

But again he ignored her plea and listened to her body, seeming to know exactly where to touch. Which area needed more pressure. The warmth of his mouth. The gentle rasp of his teeth.

And he proved as apt a teacher in this as he had in spy work. She was able to quickly return the pleasure, learning his body's reactions. She loved the tension along his spine. The thick shudder that rumbled through him when she did something he particularly liked. The way he briefly clenched his eyes shut.

But when his hand slipped between her legs, the bliss was unlike anything she'd ever experienced. And so for the first time in her life, she let go. All the responsibility. The duty. The burdens.

Nothing mattered but being in this bed with Ian.

The humming in her body increased until it danced on her skin. Blurred her vision. She could do nothing but try to keep breathing.

Ian's grin had disappeared and he watched her with raw possession. "Tell me you'll remember this. When you are being bedded by your prince, tell me that this will be in your thoughts."

"Yes." It was nearly impossible to speak yet she managed to force the words out. "My heart has chosen you even if I never can." She never wanted him to think that she had parted from him by choice.

His fingers increased their tempo.

Her hands clenched in his hair, needing an anchor to keep her in once piece. She needed something to hold on to so she didn't fly apart. She tried his shoulder. His waist. But none of them were enough. The wildness tossing within her only grew.

Then it was too late.

Ecstasy slammed though her body, pouring through her veins, robbing her of her thoughts.

When her brain could function again, Ian was still there. His hands tracing slow caresses over her skin.

"That was glorious," he said.

She followed the curve of his smile with her finger. "For me. I don't think it was nearly as pleasurable for you." She ran her hand up the front of his thigh. "And fairness is a virtue in a queen, is it not?"

He thought he managed to nod his head. She was wrong. It had been pleasurable for him. Watching her as she'd come apart in his arms had been the most exquisite thing he'd ever experienced. He'd damned near cried. But that might have been awkward to explain so he'd refrained. Instead, he poured his adoration into his hands.

She might not need him after this mission was over, but she needed him in that moment.

Now her hands were on him. He'd thought to gently lead her along the paths of passion, but she was more than able to find her own way, stripping him of the rest of his clothing. Exploring his body with the same determination with which she did everything.

Ian bit back a groan as her hand finally found his arousal. She ran her finger along his length, then swirled her finger over the top. And when her hand wrapped around him and she gave a tentative stroke, he barely held on to his control.

And she looked damnably thrilled by that, too. Her eyes glittered as she pleasured him with her renewed arousal, but with something deeper as well.

She needed him. She needed this. She took as much pleasure pleasing him as he had her.

It was that emotion that made him lose control; he bucked under her hand and she gripped him tighter as his body exploded with bliss, spilling on the soft skin of her stomach. The room spun, tilting everything about to and fro until he finally collapsed on top of her.

When his heart stopped trying to escape his chest, he rolled off her and retrieved a wet cloth. He slid it over her skin, fascinated by the way her skin pebbled under his ministrations.

"Is it always as good as this?" she asked.

"No." She was unlike anything he'd ever experienced.

She dropped her head back, her soft sigh spilling over his skin. "Oh."

There would be no sadness in her voice, not while he had the power to banish it. So he lowered his head to her breast. "The rest is even better. Shall I show you?"

Chapter Thirty-five

*J*uliana didn't think she could move. Every fiber in her muscles had been dissolved and replaced by strands of pure pleasure.

She burrowed as close as she could to Ian until, if she held very still, they seemed like one being.

She didn't want to speak, didn't want to do anything that would signal an end to this. That would make them remember this couldn't last.

Because nothing would ever be more important. More perfect.

There was a loud knock on the door. "Your Highness?"

It was Apple.

"May I come in, Your Highness?"

After a quick kiss to her neck, Ian rolled out of bed and yanked on his trousers and tossed her shift at her.

"You may enter," Juliana called out as she slipped the garment over her head.

Apple waited another half a minute before opening the door. By then, Ian had his shirt on and was sitting by the window.

He'd even smoothed out his section of the bed with a quick tug so there was no evidence he'd just taught her of passion beyond imagining.

Apple kept her gaze straight ahead as she entered.

Juliana remained silent. She didn't trust herself to speak, afraid she would sound aggravated at the situation and Apple would think it was directed at her instead.

Luckily, Ian seemed to have maintained his normal charm. "Did you drag a laundress out of bed to ask about the linen?"

Apple's shoulders relaxed when she saw him clothed, but then she seemed to find her toes of great interest. "I only had a short time to invent an excuse." She dug the toe of her slipper into the carpet. "I didn't intend to come back, of course, but Princess Leucretia insisted I inform you that Prince Wilhelm has returned."

Juliana's stomach dipped at the mention of the other man. As if reality had suddenly descended onto her insides. "He is not supposed to return until tomorrow night."

"Apparently, he had a change of heart. He is most desirous to speak with you."

"Now?" The room was dark so she had to squint to see the clock.

"It is only just past midnight, Your Highness. Many of the men are still lingering over their cigars."

Even Ian's residual warmth was gone from the bed now. "Did my aunt say why?"

"No, Your Highness. Shall I fetch you a gown?"

Juliana looked to Ian, needing something from him, some sign. Anger. Jealousy. But he was watching Apple, his face carefully blank.

"Yes, the cream silk. It will be the quickest."

Apple hurried into the dressing room.

Ian didn't look at her. He didn't wrap her in his arms and demand that she stay by his side. He didn't consign Wilhelm to the devil. He remained by the window, one hand resting on the frame, the other on his hip.

Neither of them spoke.

Finally, Juliana kicked off her blankets. "I can stay if—"

"Go." He dragged his hand through his hair in a rough motion that left it sticking out in uneven spikes. "We both knew this would happen."

She wanted to smooth his hair. She wanted to pull him back into bed. But the key to her county's future might be awaiting her downstairs.

The only problem was that the key to *her* happiness was here.

She reached out and laid her hand on his back. "I—"

He surged to his feet, eyes blazing. His hands

gripped her shoulders, squeezing tightly. "Damnation, Juliana, only the slimmest of self-control is keeping me from tying you to that bed and ruining you so completely you would have no choice but to choose me. *Go.*"

She fled like a coward.

Apple helped her into the gown, then tucked her hair into the simple knot from the first day.

Wilhelm could be her solution. With each breath, she tried to steel herself to do what she must. She'd never thought herself selfish, but now she had to admit that it might be one of her most fatal flaws because she didn't want to do this.

She wanted her heart to remain whole. She wanted to be happy. She wanted Ian.

But she had to chose Wilhelm. Her country, her people's lives were at stake.

She could do this.

Her parents had sacrificed their lives. She would sacrifice her choice of marriages.

She would do this.

The litany kept her feet progressing until she found Wilhelm and her aunt in the library. When Juliana entered, they stood. Wilhelm bowed deep, his face creasing into a smile.

Leucretia nodded. "I'll just leave you two alone for a few minutes."

Then she slipped out.

Wilhelm bowed again. "I know you had retired for the evening I hope I didn't wake you."

At least she could be truthful in this. "No, I was still awake." Gasping, moaning, and screaming, to be precise.

Wilhelm reached for her hand. His hands were warm and strong, callused on the fingertips from his music, but Juliana wanted to yank hers away. Even holding his hand seemed disloyal to Ian.

Which should have been backward. Why didn't everything she'd done with Ian make her feel like she'd betrayed Wilhelm?

Because she loved Ian.

The words twisted and roiled in her brain, gaining strength like approaching thunder.

No. Ian was simply a man she admired. A man she fancied. A man she lusted after. A man she cared for.

Even as she fought the realization, she also had to accept that some part of her had known for a long, long time.

But now, she had to forget she'd ever labeled that emotion. It had to be set aside.

Wilhelm led her to a settee, and when they sat he still held her hand.

He studied her closely. "I found the violin was suddenly less important than other things."

She begged her heart to skip. Just once. She would have accepted the slightest bump.

Nothing.

"I'm not a man to waste time when I decide on

a course. I believe we are both in need of a spouse. I find you in tune with myself. I think we could be compatible."

Compatible?

"You know the situation with Lenoria?"

"Yes. I can guarantee five thousand soldiers to aid your cause once we are wed."

Compatible?

"Why do you wish to wed me?"

He looked a bit baffled. She suspected he hadn't planned beyond his declaration of compatibility. "It is expedient."

"Why?"

"That blasted Miss Scott says it is."

"Wait, who?"

"My daughter's tutor. The one who claims she can help my daughter learn to move about in the world unaided. Did you know she took her away from my house to a public inn of all places? Can you believe it? My daughter has never left that house in her entire life. It isn't wrong to shelter her. I'm protecting her—" He tapped his fingers against his knee in a rhythmic pattern, like he was playing the pianoforte in his head. He probably was.

Whether he realized it or not, he had more passion for this governess than he did for the woman he was about to propose to.

"I cannot do this." Not to Wilhelm. Not to Ian. Not to herself.

The words should have been agonizing. Damning. Instead, they floated off her tongue, lightened her soul.

"What?" Wilhelm asked as if he genuinely thought he'd misheard her.

"I cannot marry you. I'm sorry for misleading you, but I'm afraid my affections are engaged elsewhere." True, she hadn't said where, but she'd spoken of them aloud.

Finally.

And it had felt wonderful.

"Ah." Wilhelm leaned back on the settee slightly. "Then it isn't because you find me a pompous and overbearing block of stone?"

Juliana was a bit confused at his phrasing but she shook her head. "No."

"Ah, good. Then she was wrong."

"How old is this Miss Scott?"

"That's the thing. She's barely out the schoolroom herself. She is hardly an authority on men. Then she has the gall to try to drag my daughter to this house party to harangue—" Wilhelm's fingers pinched, silencing his words. "I'd ask you reconsider my offer."

She should ask him to reconsider his governess, but she remained silent on that. "I'm sorry. I cannot accept."

Wilhelm was somber, but hardly seemed destroyed by her refusal. "Will this man bring the military alliance you need?"

"No."

"Then what will you do about Lenoria?"

If Sommet could find a way to get both nations to agree to accept Gregory, that meant that there was space for negotiation despite what they'd been telling her this past year. "I'll stop waiting for a prince and save my country myself."

He could hang the man by his bollocks from the chandelier. He could use his entrails to . . . to . . . but the tortures Ian concocted for Juliana's prince did nothing to calm him.

Next, he tried reminding himself that Juliana had never been his.

But that didn't work, either.

She *had* been his this evening. She'd given herself to him. And now he'd thrust her into the arms of another man.

A bloody rich, handsome, noble prince.

"You are proving to be a blooming disappointment," Apple said. She handed him a slice of bread she'd pilfered from the kitchen.

"Sorry, I'm too bloody bitter to care."

Apple snatched back the bread. "Lawks, but you're hopeless."

"Again, my skin is like leather. And mind your accent, it's slipping." But that was because she was comfortable with him. And he found a tickle of pleasure at the thought. He reached for the bread, only to have her neatly dodge him.

"All them stories about how the Wraith took whatever he wanted. A bunch of rubbish."

He might be feeling sorry for himself but he wasn't about to let her impugn his reputation as a thief. "Those stories are true." As were many more she had never heard.

"Then why don't you get the princess?"

"It's not that simple."

"Then you only get things that are easy? Your reputation's falling to bits here."

He stared at her. "I'm trying to be noble."

"You aren't noble. You're clever. That's a right touch better."

"I don't deserve her."

"Not even close. But she likes you. Are you really going to give up a woman who's that batty?"

A slow smile grew on Ian's face.

No. He was not.

And he wasn't going to leave her in the arms of another man a single moment longer. While he couldn't stride through the corridors to retrieve her, he could skulk very rapidly.

But as he reached for the handle on the door, it opened.

Juliana strode in. Her face was bright. Her cheeks glowing.

He couldn't be too late. He refused to believe he was too late. "That was quick."

"I refused him."

"You what?"

"He proposed. Well, almost. And I told him no. I told him my affections were engaged elsewhere."

Apple winked and darted from the room, shutting the door behind her.

Ian strode over to Juliana. "Where precisely are these feelings engaged?"

She hooked a finger in the waistband of his trousers. "My moaning didn't give it away earlier?"

He slid his hands up her arms. "There was quite a lot of it. Perhaps I missed that specific moan."

"Do you want to try to find it again?"

More than he wanted food. He tucked his finger under her chin. "Jesting aside, what do you want?" He wasn't sure he could manage the same restraint this time, not when his heart was racing, ready to burst like a sack of week-old wine.

The smile on her face was radiant. "You."

"Then you've got me." She didn't seem to be bothered by the eagerness in his kiss. She tilted her face instead, deepening it.

"I'm a scoundrel and a reprobate," he reminded her as he worked his way down her throat.

"On your good days." Her hand dipped into his trousers. "On my good days, I'm much worse."

His fingers found her breast. "Then why did you pick me?"

Her breath gasped against his neck. "Because I cannot survive without you."

They were the words he needed to hear. Had needed to hear his entire life.

But he forced himself to pull back and look in her eyes. And finally their amber depths were free of reservations. Completely free of doubt.

She truly wanted all of him.

His shoulder was too sore to lift her again so instead he pointed to the bed. He'd meant to accompany it with a witty quip, but her teeth grazed his earlobe and all he managed was a deep groan.

She'd rendered Ian speechless. His inarticulation told her more than his words ever could have. So she took pity on him, leading him to the bed and pulling him down on top of her.

His hands made quick work of her dress and shift, and soon she was scrambling to free them from under her.

He pressed kisses down the valley between her breasts, across her navel, and then lower. She writhed under him.

Making love to him earlier had been indescribable, but strangely, she could describe this.

This was pure joy.

Each touch was more pleasurable because there would be more. The frantic desperation from earlier was gone, too, leaving them free to relish. Savor.

And Ian took even more time with her pleasure, drawing out each sensation. Reveling in the ease between them.

Juliana dug her fingers into Ian's shoulders as his fingers slipped between her legs, but again, he made no move to rush things. She'd cried out his name twice over before he positioned himself at her very core.

"Juliana, there is no going back for you after this."

But she lifted her hips, eager for him. "I never want to go back. Just forward. With you by my side."

He pressed forward, she gasped at the sensation. Part pain. Part completion.

Ian was poised above her, waiting for her to adjust, protecting her as he always did. She cupped his cheek, tracing her finger across his scar, his slightly crooked nose, his firm lips.

"I will always be there." He moved slowly; this time the pleasure outweighed the discomfort.

So she shifted her hips, bringing him deeper. Closer. "More," she whispered.

And he gave it to her, rocking and moving within her until she writhed, until she begged him a thousand times. Until she promised him everything she possessed. Her kingdom. Her crown.

Her heart.

Only then did he lose control, flying with her over the edge as they clutched each other, bliss consuming their bodies, binding them together.

Chapter Thirty-six

$\mathcal{I}$an knew he should be sleeping like Juliana, but he just couldn't give up one moment with her to oblivion. Instead, he held her tightly nestled against him. Counting each of her breaths. Memorizing the tilt of her nose.

But they would need to make plans if they were going to stop Sommet. He let her sleep as long as possible before gently kissing her awake.

She scowled at him with bleary eyes. "What?"

"We need plans."

She snuggled back tighter against him and pulled the blanket closer around the two of them. "No, we don't. I already solved the problem."

He knew better than to antagonize her when she first awoke. So he humored her. "How did you do that?"

"Sommet was mining on my land and selling the ore to the French. I sent word to Prinny. I finally have something I can use to discredit him in everyone's eyes."

Perhaps he should have asked her about her day before seducing her.

"What precisely did you discover?"

She recounted all her discoveries about Sommet and her aunt.

"So you wrote the regent a letter." She was brilliant.

She nodded. "I sent it with my groom. It should reach the prince this morning. It explains the duke's lies and his current plans. Anything Sommet tries to claim now about my brother, I can say are a desperate attempt to save his own skin."

"You are brilliant." He kissed her lips as he'd hesitated to do for the past few hours for fear of waking her. "Someone should assign you to run a country or something."

She nipped his lip before snuggling against him and falling back asleep.

All his plotting and she'd managed to solve the problem all on her own.

He wanted to crow with pride, but at the same time his heart suddenly felt like lead in his chest.

He was now worthless to her. Last night he'd been essential. Now what was he? A former—well, occasionally current—criminal?

He carefully slid from the bed. Juliana made a sleepy grab for his arm, but settled for hugging a pillow when she couldn't find him.

No. He wasn't useless. He could still get her

brother's letters back. It would be better if those papers no longer existed.

Feeling slightly better, he donned his breeches. Canterbury had loaned him one of his shirts last night. But Ian barely fit in it. The man was a rail. So he rang for Apple.

He held up a hand to hush her as she came through the door and gave her whispered orders to fetch him another set of clothes from the servants' quarters.

He returned to Abington's jacket and pulled out the file he'd liberated from Sommet's office.

He flipped through the first few pages.

They were mining records.

Iron mines. The mines appeared to have been dug ten years ago. They must be details on the Lenorian mines.

No wonder Sommet was desperate to land Gregory on the throne. The things were worth a bloody fortune.

Although if he was reading these correctly, mining didn't stop at the end of the war as Juliana had just told him. At the bottom, scribbled in a hasty hand, were entries up to a month ago.

The past two years were the most profitable ones in the ledger.

He was tempted to let Juliana sleep and figure this out on his own, but she'd proved herself quite clever at solving problems.

"Juliana."

She rolled over in the bed and pulled the pillow over her. Gracefully sleeping enchanted princess she was not. And he wouldn't want her to be.

"The mining didn't stop at the end of the war."

The pillow was flung off her head. "What?"

"I have Sommet's records from the mine."

She climbed out of bed, wrapping the sheet around her as she stood. He was such a selfish bastard. He'd just spent a night any man would have cut off his arm to experience and already he wanted more.

What would she say if he confessed his feelings for her right now? Would she admit to the same or would she look away, embarrassed at his sentimentality? Despite everything they'd shared, they'd been rather vague on the details of how things would work afterward.

Would she accept his proposal? Or was she hoping for a more informal relationship? Something she could keep hidden?

He set his jaw and showed her the paper.

"*This* must be what Leucretia meant. She said he'd cheated her. I wasn't sure what he'd done. But this must be it." She studied the paper a bit longer, her face growing pensive. "Do you have any idea what I could have done for my people with this much money?"

"What will you do with the mines now?" he asked.

"I don't know. I need to find out what happened to the people who lived there. If they want to return."

"If they don't?" Or can't. There was a good chance they'd been killed, after all.

She sighed. "I don't know. What would you do?"

"I am thankfully not one of your advisers."

"You are more than that."

"I'm lacking all your necessary qualifications."

"Not *all*." She waited a moment before speaking, her amber eyes gleaming.

She was going to say it. She was going to say she loved him, and if she said it, then the rest of the world, and her country, be damned. He'd have her as his wife.

So he hurried on before she specified. "I don't have an army." He gestured to his bare chest, loving the way her eyes roved it hungrily. "Well, I can see how you might think I am about equivalent to an entire—"

What he'd been about to say next was suddenly lost.

He *was* about equivalent to an army.

Oh, certainly not physically, but the Trio had wreaked as much damage on Europe as Wellington had. The only thing that stood between their marriage now was reclaiming her kingdom. What if he found a way to ensure she kept her kingdom on her own terms?

Sommet had been making deals with the French and the Spanish all along.

And anything Sommet could do, Ian could do as well.

At least with Juliana's help.

Excitement buzzed through him. He did have something to offer her after all.

A place to belong in her life.

"An entire what?" Juliana asked, her mouth quirked.

Ian stared at her, amazed she hadn't just felt the whole world shift. He had to struggle to remember what he was about to say. "Army," he finished.

She grinned and straddled his lap. "You do seem to have the stamina of one."

He pressed a kiss to where her neck joined her shoulder and tugged the sheet down to bare her breasts. She could be his.

If she chose him.

His constant fear still hadn't completely abated. But now, for the first time, he thought he might be worth taking a risk on.

There was a rap on the door. Juliana scrambled off as Eustace walked in.

The older woman froze, her eyes sweeping back and forth between the two of them. "Juliana? What is this?"

Juliana's cheeks heated, but she didn't try to move further away from him. She did however pull the sheet up over herself. "I think you know."

"Is he truly your minister of security?"

Juliana's hand tightened on the sheet. She was tired of hiding Ian like he was something to be ashamed of. "Yes. He is also the man I love."

That wasn't how she'd meant to reveal that fact.

Ian's brows drew together and his gaze flew to meet hers. He gave her a slight shake of the head.

She didn't know if he was denying her proclamation or telling her not to say it in front of her aunt, but it was too late for both. She wouldn't tuck him out of sight any longer.

Eustace's mouth opened, then closed. "You're a grown woman." Her aunt studied her wrinkled hands with interest. "There is a matter about which you've never been informed." Juliana worried at the gravity in her aunt's tone.

"Perhaps it would be better to discuss this alone," her aunt continued.

"No. Ian is involved. He can hear whatever it is you say."

After another penetrating glance, Eustace seemed to accept that. "I debated telling you. But Canterbury pointed out the foolishness of hiding the truth."

Canterbury? No wonder her aunt had let the topic of consorting with Ian drop.

"Especially now that I know Leucretia is involved in all of this somehow."

Juliana waited as Eustace steeled herself. Juliana was glad she hadn't moved too far from Ian. While she wasn't touching him, she liked knowing he'd be close enough to catch her if she collapsed from whatever Eustace was about to reveal.

"You know Leucretia was your grandfather's twin."

"Yes." This wasn't where she'd expected this conversation to go.

"There were—are rumors surrounding the births."

Juliana still had no idea what Eustace intended to reveal.

"Although I suppose at this point it doesn't matter what the truth is. It only matters what she thinks." Eustace shook her head. "Sorry, I didn't intend to turn into a blathering biddy." She exhaled. "Before she died, our nurse told Leucretia that she was actually the firstborn twin. That my father had decided a king would be stronger for Lenoria than a queen."

Juliana reached out and grabbed Ian's shoulder, grateful for his solid, silent support as she tried to digest this. "Leucretia should have inherited the crown? How old was she when you found out?"

Eustace frowned. "In her twenties. It was several years after your grandfather inherited the crown. It was too late to do anything. She had no proof. Our mother denied it. So she had no grounds to contend with her brother."

"And a king is always seen as stronger than a queen." Hence the laws Juliana was struggling with now.

"Exactly. I think much of Leucretia's wildness stemmed from that anger. She's always felt as if she's been robbed." Eustace shrugged, her lips tight. "Perhaps she has been."

"But she is loyal to Lenoria, isn't she?" Or had she been resenting Juliana her entire life? What about Sommet's plan to kill Juliana's father? Had Leucretia known about that? Helped plan it?

Eustace hesitated. Hesitated long enough that Juliana had her answer. "I don't know. I think so. I watched her train you and thought she had finally come to terms with it all. That perhaps she even saw you as her chance to have influence on the throne. But if she has paired with Sommet for some scheme, that might be her motivation."

There was another knock at the door and Apple hurried inside. Her face was pale. She glanced at Eustace but then decided to speak anyway. "Your messenger, Your Highness. The one you sent out yesterday. He was found dead a few miles from here."

"What? How?" She knew it was naive to hope it had been an accident, but she couldn't help it.

"He was shot."

Ian stood, his body tense. "Who knew he carried a message to the regent?"

Juliana stared at him, then at her aunt. "Only Leucretia."

Chapter Thirty-seven

Juliana couldn't feel the tips of her fingers. It was as if parts of her had simply gone numb from the chaos in her mind. "Perhaps I'm not fit to rule a country. I betrayed my one chance out of this disaster to the very person who caused it."

Ian pulled her to him without even a second glance at Eustace. "She's your aunt. It's not your fault for trusting her."

"Isn't it, though? I knew she'd conspired with Sommet. I knew she'd lied to me once before. And yet when she said she would do what she could for Lenoria, I believed her." Juliana clutched her sheet more tightly around her, the hard wall of his chest secure and stable under her fingers. The weight she thought she'd freed herself from yesterday came crashing down onto her shoulders, making her lungs fight for air. "I asked her to help me word the letter." But Juliana didn't have time to waste on self-recrimination. If the groom had been killed, that meant the documents still needed to be retrieved.

Today.

Before the ball.

She straightened, determined not to let Ian or her aunt know of the darkness encroaching at the edges of her thoughts. The desperation. She had to be strong. "Apple, bring me my clothing. The blue silk. I have business to attend to."

Apple bowed and hurried into the dressing room.

"We will wait in the corridor for you to dress," Eustace said.

"I'll remain here," Ian said, holding her more tightly. He ignored her aunt's glare. "Sorry, I'm a wanted criminal. I can't be seen in the corridor."

Eustace didn't leave until she met Juliana's eye, but then with a twitch of her brow, she left.

Juliana sat heavily in the chair Ian offered her. She'd thought she had all of this under control.

But it never had been.

She closed her eyes tightly, until dots swam behind her eyes. She needed to keep Ian safe. Her country. Her brother.

"You should leave," she told Ian. She regretted nothing about last night, but in the light of day it was impossible for her to ignore just how much danger he was in. Now not only from Sommet but from the law, which the duke undoubtedly controlled as well.

"I'm not clothed, as you many have noticed."

"I don't want you to get hurt."

He shrugged with his damaged arm. "Too late."

Only Ian could have said that in a way to make her feel slightly better. "I have to deal with Sommet on my own."

"Why?"

She stared at him. *Why?* "Because it's my responsibility."

"Why? What does facing him alone prove?"

"I can't be seen as weak." She had struggled her entire life to be seen as a strong leader. She'd had both her gender and her age against her.

"So you'll ignore help that might make you stronger?"

Was that what she was doing?

She asked for help when she needed it. She'd asked for his help, hadn't she? And unfortunately, Leucretia's. "You're the one who always tries to do things on your own."

Ian's smile was rueful. "We are a lovely, misguided pair."

"But what does it say about me if I can't handle this alone?" That she had been a failure all along.

His face grew serious. "I have come to the rather lowering conclusion that Sommet may be smarter than I am." He rubbed a strand of her hair between his fingers. "But he isn't smarter than the two of us together. He's alone. That is *his* great weakness."

She stood and began to pace. "It's not that simple. What if I can't handle this?"

"Then you are normal. You try again."

"But I am not normal, I am a *princess*." Her voice didn't break so much on that last word as it shattered. Loud, awkward, anguished. "I have to be perfect. It is my duty."

Ian caught her sheet and reeled her to him. "You don't have to be perfect. Just look at the prince regent. The man's a buffoon and somehow he manages to rule the most powerful nation in the world."

Juliana choked on her anguish, but at some point halfway through it evolved into a laugh. "The regent?" She had never even considered it.

"You'd never thought of that before, had you?"

"No." He was right. And this was why she couldn't do without him.

Ian stepped back, turning to the clothing that Apple had brought. He pulled the shirt over his head. "A queen is valued for more than the burdens she bears. She also needs wisdom. Kindness. Dedication. You have all that." He tossed his waistcoat down and spun back to her. He knelt by the edge of her chair.

"Stand up," she ordered. "I don't need you to kneel to me. I don't need your fealty. I need you at my side."

"I am fairly certain a man is supposed to kneel when he is proposing to the woman he loves. But I can swear fealty first if you prefer."

Her mouth gaped open in an unprincesslike manner but she couldn't seem to find the power to close it. "Proposing?" She might have stuttered as well.

He loved her?

A hint of vulnerability punctured his roguish swagger. "If you say yes, I was proposing marriage. If you say no, I was proposing salmon for supper."

"Yes."

He caught her hand and pressed a kiss to it. "Then you're stuck with my fealty as well." Thank heavens his actions were a trifle exaggerated or she might have begun to tear up.

But then he leaped to his feet with a whoop and swept her into his arms, raining kisses all over her face. The light caresses sent pleasure bursting through her. And if her maid wasn't going to return at any moment, she would have thrown off the sheet and let him continue to the bed.

"So what is the next step?" she asked.

"I think we find a priest. Or Scotland. I've always been fond of Scotland."

"I meant with Sommet."

"Ah." He set her back down. "An all-out assault. Sommet knows everything about us now. And he knows we know about him. Secrecy avails us nothing. We go at him with all we have."

"What *do* we have?"

He held up his hand and ticked off fingers. "An old lady and an even older butler. A drunk duke. An injured princeling. A devilishly handsome spy.

And the world's most courageous and brilliant princess."

"And me. You have me, too." Apple said from the doorway to the dressing room, the blue gown over her arm.

"She *is* worth all the others put together," Ian said.

Her maid stood straight, her eyes wide, pride lighting her face.

But could she ask Apple to put herself at risk? "You don't have to help if you're at all uncertain. You'll remain my lady's maid no matter—"

"You plan to allow me to stay on?" Apple squeaked. "Even back in London?"

Juliana felt an immediate pang that she'd left the girl uncertain. "Whether you help me or not." She needed that to be clear.

Apple suddenly grinned and spun in a circle, making her appear even younger. "A lady's maid! Cor, no one will ever believe it."

"It will be dangerous to face Sommet," Juliana warned again.

Apple nodded, her back straight. "I want to help."

"Trust me," Ian said. "Sommet will be the one in danger."

Juliana gripped Ian's hand. "How can you remain so certain about all of this?"

He lifted her hand to his lips, but this time his caress was one of a lover rather than a vassal. "Because you agreed to marry me. I am as sure as hell going to live to see that."

Ian's princess was dressed in a navy blue dress with buttons and epaulettes. She was ready to go to war.

If they weren't about to face an evil madman, he would have carried her off and made wild and passionate love to her.

On second thought, he still might. He wasn't entirely sure what was involved in a betrothal, but he was fairly certain frequent passionate lovemaking should be a large part.

She loved him. She was going to marry him. His heart still hadn't resumed its normal cadence. It might never. Gads, would he be forever floating about happy like a giddy butterfly?

There were worse fates.

Gregory was upright in his bed, a huge breakfast spread out in front of him. Far too much for any one man. Ian helped himself to one of the spare rolls, earning him a stern look from Canterbury and a confused one from the prince.

Abington was the only one in their merry band that wasn't there. But Ian hadn't wanted to raise Sommet's suspicions by having him come. He was best as a hidden weapon.

Juliana came to stand at Ian's side. Her eyes briefly met his as if seeking strength. He gave her everything he could.

She explained the entire situation to the others

in a clear, concise manner that would have made an army general proud. He suspected he was the only one who saw the way her hands clenched and unclenched at her side.

Revealing her troubles to others was still torture for her. Yet she didn't flinch.

When she was finished, the other occupants of the room stared with shock. But if she feared they'd see her as weak, she was mistaken. They all watched her with clear awe.

"Juliana." Eustace's voice was strangled. "I knew something was wrong, but I had no idea."

"Perhaps I should let Sommet shoot me. I'm so sorry." Her brother pushed away the tray.

"Sommet's a master," Juliana said. "That's why I'll need your help to face him."

"You need my help?" Gregory asked. He sounded hopeful, eager.

Juliana nodded. "Yes. I should have asked for it long ago."

Even though it must have pained him, Gregory sat up straighter.

"The duke will be expecting us to act." Ian stepped forward. This was his area of expertise. "We've lost the element of surprise, but we will have to find a way to get back into the tower."

"Why the tower?" Apple asked.

"It's where the duke has the documents," Ian explained.

Apple frowned. "Maybe."

"What?" Ian asked.

"Well, I suppose they could be there." But then she shook her head. "But there's a parlor on the first floor that the maids aren't allowed to clean. Sommet has that footman of his tend it." Apple quieted when she realized she had everyone's attention. "I'm sorry. I thought you knew. You know everything."

Ian cursed his cocksure attitude. "Not as much as you do, apparently."

Apple dipped head to hide her blush.

"Which parlor?" Juliana asked.

"It's two doors down from the library. I don't even think that it's locked. But it is watched."

Only a genius like Sommet would have put his most valuable documents in an unlocked room close to the library.

The man was fiendish.

"Well, then that changes my plan," Ian said.

"If we try to sneak in we'll be spotted," Gregory pointed out. "Sommet will stop us."

Ian felt a slow smile growing on his face. "Perfect."

Chapter Thirty-eight

Juliana played another card. Abington groaned. Juliana couldn't blame him, she hadn't been able to keep her thoughts on the game the entire hand.

"Mind on other things?" Sommet asked next to her. "I hope you realize it will be best for everyone if you bow out gracefully. I would hate to have you embarrass yourself."

"I am sure Her Highness isn't going to throw a fit over a card game," Abington protested, taking a sip of his claret.

Sommet wasn't talking about the cards.

But Juliana had been raised a princess, barbs and innuendo were an integral part of every court she'd ever attended. "How is your injured footman this morning? Is it true that one of my grooms managed to disable seven of your men?"

The duke's eyes glittered. "That reminds me, how is your brother? I heard he was feeling poorly yesterday."

"How could he be with your fine hospitality?"

"He is a wise man to accept it. You would be wise to accept it as well."

Abington played his card, then held up his empty glass. "I'll take a little more hospitality."

Eustace sailed into the room. She glanced about, her expression growing dour. "Gambling? Highly inappropriate, Your Grace. Come, Juliana. Princesses do not engage in such activities. Come with me." Her black dress lent the perfect credence to her sanctimonious words.

Constantina glanced up from the dwindling pile of chips. "It is naught but a few games of whist, Sister." Constantina couldn't have played her role any better if she'd known she was playing it.

Abington was quick to throw down his hand on the small pile of coins left in front of him. "I grow weary of cards. Perhaps another parlor game? A game of hide-and-seek?" A rakish gleam entered his eyes as he surveyed the women in the room. When his gaze lingered on the desperately marriageable Miss Rutop, her mother was quick to take up the cause.

The entire female half of the room was quickly clamoring for the game. Constantina perhaps loudest of all. Perhaps Juliana should warn him to watch his backside.

"That isn't better," Eustace protested, but Constantina took her elbow and pulled her from the room.

"I have an idea," Abington drawled. "Why don't the gentlemen hide and the ladies seek us out? Then whomever they find will lead them out in the first dance at the ball tonight?"

Soon the young men had scurried out, while the young ladies giggled and watched the clock. After five minutes, they fluttered out in pursuit of the men, mamas and chaperones following behind.

A few of the older guests remained playing cards, but the room was now nearly empty.

The duke picked up the deck of cards and began to shuffle. "You choose to stay with me? I am flattered, Your Highness. And suspicious."

"Wraith hasn't returned."

Sommet's brows lowered. "Did I ask if he had?"

She didn't have to stretch too far to appear flustered. "Well, you were wondering, weren't you?"

"Now I am." The duke dealt her one card facedown and another one in front of himself. He reached out and turned hers over. It was a two of hearts.

She picked up his card, a hand-painted depiction of an old, bearded king. "Subtle."

"Just a simple reminder that the deck is stacked against you."

"Or that you cheat?"

Sommet retrieved the card and tucked it back into the deck. "I win."

A young footman entered, clearing his throat. His eyes were wide with panic.

Sommet surged to his feet. "I suppose I should go check on the game." He strode into the corridor without awaiting Juliana's reply.

The door to the parlor two doors down from the library stood open. Flustered female voices could be heard from within.

"*I* found him first. I saw him duck in here."

". . . saw him at the same time."

"*I* looked behind the settee . . ."

Abington had been pressed into a corner by a group of young women like a fox cornered by hounds. A very inebriated fox. "Perhaps I shall defer to my fellow duke. What do you think, Sommet? Who won?"

"Why not make the decision over lunch? I believe my footmen are setting out food on the south lawn as we speak."

"Capital. It's getting rather difficult to breathe in here." He offered his arm to Constantina who had somehow managed to crowd out the younger women. "Shall we?" The women followed after him like obedient ducklings.

"Once again you appear at my side." The duke's eyes swept the room, and he seemed to calm. "But once again you have lost."

"I don't know what you are speaking of," Juliana answered.

"Perhaps you should go warn your spy that his diversion to gain access to this room is over."

"Again, I don't know what you're talking about."

"Again, I don't believe you."

Juliana lifted up her skirts and hurried from the room.

After a minute, the duke began following her.

Chapter Thirty-nine

"*H*ow far?" Ian whispered. He wrapped an arm around her waist.

Juliana glanced behind her in the corridor. "He's on the stairs now. He has the documents?"

"Indeed." Ian had watched from the window when Sommet had retrieved the papers—from inside a vase. Yes, a vase—and tucked them in his jacket. "Now keep walking."

He didn't want her anywhere near an enraged Sommet.

"I will return for you." She dragged her hand across his chest as she passed.

"I know, in about one minute."

"Fine, take the drama out of it." She then cried loudly, "You must hide. The duke knows you're here, my plum cake."

Plum cake? Ian mouthed at her. They'd need to work on pet names. "Don't give up your crown for a life on the stage," he murmured. When she stuck out her tongue at him, he knew he would love her until long past his dying day.

She lifted a brow and hurried out of sight as Sommet, three footmen, and the constable rounded the corner.

Ian launched himself at the duke, grabbing his jacket. "Where are the papers, you bastard? I won't let you do this to her." This was only supposed to be for show, but suddenly all his rage at the man poured into his arms. The duke's head knocked into the wall twice before the others pried him off.

But it had been long enough.

Two of the footmen grabbed his arms, yanking him off the duke. The third slammed his fist into his gut.

Ian grunted, the pain doubling him over. The punch had been anticipated, but the man hit like a produce cart.

"Let him go!" Juliana's face was ashen as she ran toward them.

He perhaps should have told her he expected to be rather savagely beaten during this part of the plan. Perhaps tortured.

He wrenched one arm free to hold her as she threw herself against his chest. Her eyes were so wide he could see the whites around the amber. He hated that his breath was still wheezing but it was proving impossible for him to control.

The humor and daring that had lit her face a moment before had vanished. "He's my—servant."

That small pause was the first mistake he'd seen her make all day. "You cannot touch him."

Apple appeared on cue and pulled Juliana away from him. "Come away, Your Highness. He is a criminal."

The constable—a Mr. Brandt, Ian had learned—wiped his nose on his dirty brown sleeve. "I am sorry but we all witnessed this man attack the duke. That's a hanging offense, miss."

Juliana drew herself straight, a cold hauteur that he'd never seen icing her expression. "You may address me as Your Highness."

Brandt hastily bowed, but his squinty eyes kept flitting to Sommet.

"Where are you taking him?" Juliana asked.

"There's a jail in town, miss—Yer Highness. We'll keep him there until the justice of the peace sends him on to stand trial."

Ian let a broad grin spread over his face briefly before erasing it.

"No." Sommet corrected. He smoothed his hair. "I'll keep him here until then."

"But Your Grace, he attacked you. Surely you want—"

"The man is a master criminal. I do not trust him out of my sight."

Speaking of out of his sight, Canterbury passed by Apple in that invisible way skilled servants had and continued up the corridor.

"Where will you put him then?" Brandt asked.

Sommet slowly tilted his head from side to side, stretching his neck. "This is a castle. It has a dungeon."

The constable gnawed on his lips. "I suppose that would do. But you'd be responsible for him."

Sommet nodded to the two men holding Ian, who dug their fingers into his arms. "Take him to the dungeon." His lips twisted upward. "Such an underused phrase."

"I want him remanded to my care," Juliana said.

The duke laughed. "Hardly. Do not fear. I am more than happy to let the hangman do the dirty work for me. So much more public and humiliating." He ran his hand across his stomach, then smoothed his lapels. He froze. "Where are they?"

Ian snorted. "Your courage and honor?"

"Constable, this man has stolen papers from me. I want him searched."

Ian stood still while the man ran his dirty hands over him. "He doesn't have any papers on him."

"Of course he does." The duke repeated the search, his hand growing rougher as he couldn't find them. The duke spun toward Juliana." He must have passed them to the princess."

Brandt looked uncomfortable. "I didn't see him give her any papers."

"He's a pickpocket. Of course you didn't see him."

"But where would she have them?" Brandt asked, eyeing Juliana's light cotton dress.

In a special fold Ian had prepared in the skirt earlier. But no longer. Really the duke was too slow at this game.

"It wouldn't be proper for me to search—"

"I'll do it then." The duke grabbed her shoulders and ran his hands down her sides.

Ian had considered the possibility that Sommet would have the gall to try that, but he hadn't counted on the fury that tunneled his vision. For the first time he struggled in earnest against the men holding him, his shoulder burning with tearing, ripping pain.

But Sommet stepped back from her and whirled on Apple. "Then the maid must have it."

"But the maid never touched him," Brandt protested, his voice slightly squeaky. Bless Brandt and his poor, slow brain.

"But she had contact with the princess."

"Are you saying the princess is a pickpocket?" Brandt scratched his temple.

She was. After a rather pleasant training session that involved her hands roaming his clothing. Or she was at least enough of one to pick the pocket of a man who allowed for his pocket to be picked.

"If you want to leave, Brandt, leave," Sommet said.

Brandt scuttled away without a backward glance.

Apple had gone rigid next to Juliana. Ian cursed himself. He hadn't figured in Apple's reaction to the thought of being pawed by a man like Sommet.

She should have switched Apple and Canterbury's roles. He should have—

Juliana stepped in front of her before Ian could think of the best way to react. "Enough. You touch her and I'll scream loudly enough for the entire castle to hear. I have no idea what papers you lost, but we do not have them. Apple, shake your skirts to show to the duke that you don't have any papers."

The corridor was completely silent but for the rustle of wool. There was no crinkle of paper.

Of course not, she'd passed them to Canterbury, who was now in the process of burning them.

The duke whirled around and slammed his fist into Ian's jaw. Pain exploded in sharp pointed stars inside his head and he could taste blood on the inside of his cheek.

"Stop!" Juliana cried as the duke raised his hand to strike again. She ran forward and caught his arm with both of her hands.

The duke shook her off so roughly she stumbled and landed on her backside on the floor.

Sommet's next punch to the other side of Ian's face was purely to prove he could. It sure felt an awful lot like the first one, however. The castle tilted around him and Ian spat a mouthful of blood onto the duke's rug. He'd take petty revenge when he could get it.

The duke stalked toward Juliana. "Don't think the loss of the papers changes anything. I may not have the papers, but you have given me something far better." Sommet motioned and the footman connected with Ian's ribs. "If you do anything to stop me tonight, I will spare the hangman his length of rope."

Chapter Forty

$\mathcal{I}$an had been in less humiliating positions before. "I had no idea you had such a great desire to see me naked. Now be a good fellow and return my trousers."

Sommet had him stripped and chained to the wall. Next to a crate of onions. And some radishes. The dungeon apparently also doubled as a cold cellar.

"And have you gain access to the picks you have hidden in the seams of your clothing? No."

The problem was that *had* been Ian's plan.

The stone was cold at his back and under his feet. And although the dungeon wasn't frequently used, the manacles were new and securely fastened into the wall.

"Dispose of those far away," Sommet ordered the footman, pointing to Ian's mutilated clothing on the ground. "Now, I will ask you civilly one time. Where is Leucretia?"

"Did you have a lovers' quarrel? I don't know where she is."

Or why Sommet was asking about her. Although that was the truth, it didn't stop the guard's fist.

"While you are chained to my wall, perhaps it would be a good time to inform you that I didn't kill the princess's messenger." He let those words rattle around in Ian's head. "Leucretia ordered that all on her own. And did you notice the final entries on the papers you stole? I stopped mining at the end of the war. I couldn't risk it. But she didn't. She continued all on her own."

Those entries on the financial documents weren't the money Sommet had made without Leucretia. It was the money the old woman had hidden from Sommet?

"So if you're protecting her, perhaps you should think about the danger she poses to your little tart of a princess."

Ian strained against the chains, until his shoulders threatened to pop from their sockets. The heavy iron links rattling and clanking to no avail. "I don't know where Leucretia is."

"That's unfortunate because I don't know where she is, either. And as you might suspect, she isn't very happy at the prospect of losing her property to me."

"Let me find her for you."

Sommet laughed. "To see you afraid is beyond priceless. Oh, and for the record, she came to me with the plan to use British spies to overthrow her nephew."

Ian knew his first moment of true panic. Sommet

was a liar and master manipulator, but if there was any truth to this, he had to warn Juliana. "Let me go and you might just live to see the morning. If I have to waste time escaping you will not see another breakfast."

"Unlike you, I know who my enemies are. I intend to find Leucretia because if Princess Juliana were to die at her aunt's hand, that would make things slightly more complicated for me."

"Sommet—"

Sommet's smile was cold. "Just think, I have you chained in my dungeon and yet you'll be praying for my success."

"I'm sure he's fine," Apple said as she finished Juliana's curls.

Juliana remained silent. She didn't trust Ian in Sommet's care.

They might need Sommet to think he'd won, but she loathed the way Ian had been forced to stand there as the duke had abused him. Although she might injure Ian herself next time she saw him. He'd said he'd be captured. He never said anything about the beatings, yet he had to have known.

If Juliana had felt any remorse for the public way they were going to destroy the duke tonight, it was now gone.

"They say when he escaped Newgate for the

second time, he walked back in to collect his breakfast, then escaped again."

Juliana did smile slightly at that. "I'll need the formal tiara. That's the one with the diamonds."

"And if it makes you feel better, the other servants said it isn't much of a dungeon anymore. It's mostly used for storage," Apple said as she went to the other room.

Juliana smoothed the emerald green satin of her dress, tracing a golden vine along her thigh as she tried to readjust her mental image of Ian. From iron manacles and red-hot pokers to cabbages and moldy tapestries.

But even that couldn't free her from remembering the gleam of pure hatred that had smoldered in Sommet's eyes.

Juliana was pacing by the window—it stood wide open just in case—when there was a knock at the door.

Eustace stood outside. In place of her normal tight bun, she wore an artfully elegant lavender turban.

"That is lovely."

Her aunt's blush confirmed its source. "Thank you. I—well—it was a gift."

"Did you find Leucretia?"

Eustace shook her head. "She hasn't been to her rooms all day. I keep watching for her, but so far nothing. Constantina hasn't seen her either."

More unease added to her already roiling stomach. She didn't know whether to fear Leucretia or fear for her.

"Are you ready?" Eustace asked.

She had to be. She nodded.

"Where's Gregory?" Juliana had hoped he'd walk with them to the ball so that she could go over his instructions one more time.

"Sommet came to escort him personally."

She would have to trust he'd do what he needed to do. That when the time came, rather than claim her crown, he'd announce their new treaty with Prince Wilhelm.

Strangely, she found that she did trust Gregory. There had been a purposefulness in him this afternoon that she'd never seen before.

And she was forced to admit, her hoarding of the responsibilities might have played a large part in his foolish adventures. From what she'd seen during the negotiations, he could be quite shrewd and exacting.

There was another knock at the door.

It was Leucretia. She slowed when she saw Eustace, but then continued in and locked the door behind her. Leucretia clutched some sort of bundle in front of her.

"Aunt." Juliana watched the older woman. "I'm amazed you dare approach me. You betrayed my confidence to Sommet."

Juliana had never dared reprimand Leucretia for

anything before. But she felt no remorse for doing it now.

She'd be queen. And perfect or not, she would be obeyed.

For less than an instant, resentment curled the other woman's lip. Had that always been there? Had Juliana just somehow missed it?

"Sommet is torturing your friend as we speak. I doubt your spy will survive much longer."

A quiver passed through Juliana, icy and slippery down her spine. Torture? Sommet said he was going to lock Ian away. Her eyes flew to the clock. Three hours. Ian had been in Sommet's control for three hours.

Eustace put her hand on Juliana's shoulder. "How do you know?"

Leucretia rocked back a step. "Sommet and I are old enemies. I have people in his employ. I know everything that goes on in this house."

Juliana fought to keep her voice steady. "Why should I believe you? You have given me nothing but lies my entire life."

Leucretia held out a jacket. It had been sliced to pieces. "This is the jacket he was wearing earlier, is it not?"

Juliana did not want to take it. She didn't want to confirm what her eyes could already see. Blood. The jacket was covered in blood.

Her lungs suddenly burned like they'd been pierced by a thousand needles.

"I can take you to him," Leucretia said.

But Juliana wasn't about to trust Leucretia again. "I know where the dungeon is."

"But can you get inside in time to save his life? Without tipping off the guards and causing his death?"

"What is your price, Leucretia?" Juliana asked, her hands shaking.

"Your signature on this treaty." She held up the paper. "A bit of ink and I can have you into that dungeon in time to rescue what is left of him."

It was the treaty that would divide her country. Juliana had stared at it enough to know it even from across the room.

"What good will this do you?" Eustace asked.

"I'm tired of being robbed of what should be mine. I knew you could stop Gregory from becoming king. What I didn't count on was you being clever enough to make a deal with Wilhelm for use of his troops to stop the treaty."

The deal had been mainly Gregory's work. A very favorable new trade agreement, giving the Prussians access to some of her iron ore in exchange for access to Wilhelm's troops.

"Do you know how hard I worked at Versailles to ensure those mountains went to the Spanish? They might not be happy to know they were duped during the war, but if the Spanish value one thing it is a landowner's rights—and that land belongs to me. I have a foolish Spanish king's signature to prove it."

Leucretia had wanted the treaty to go through all along. She wanted the country divided.

"Now." She held out the paper. "Do you know how easily red-hot metal can sear through flesh? How it makes grown men scream like frightened babes?"

Juliana feared she might vomit, the fear was so writhing and viscous in her stomach. Ian's screams echoed in her thoughts. The smell of smoke. Burning flesh.

Sommet would suffer if he'd dared to lay a hand on Ian. Even if she had to build a dungeon of her own.

"Leucretia—" Eustace began.

"Silence, sister. Or I'll let the world know I saw you kissing your great-nephew's valet. At least Juliana's lover isn't truly a servant."

But Juliana wouldn't be distracted. "I won't sign the treaty." It's what she'd risked all this to avoid.

"What is your plan? To try to rescue him? Sommet will kill him as soon as he suspects an attempt. On the other hand, all you have to do is sign this paper. Something you thought was inevitable just two weeks ago." She held out the treaty. "Even if you have Wilhelm's troops, what makes you think that the French and Spanish will fear them? Are you ready to cast Lenoria into war simply because you want your throne?"

The thought had terrified her since she'd made the deal with Wilhelm this afternoon. But if there was one thing she'd learned the past few days, it was that rulers had to make hard decisions. "I am ready to rule my country. Not to be ruled by you."

Leucretia's outraged retort was cut short when the lock rattled and Sommet and his footmen stormed in. "You think you are so clever, Leucretia. So much more clever than everyone else."

Leucretia whirled around. "Sommet, you've already been beaten by everyone in this room. Why don't you slink off and hide. That's all you are concerned about now, isn't it?"

Sommet pulled his pistol and pointed it at Leucretia. "I have no desire for the Spanish to gain the mines. There is far too much chance of word getting back to the British of my role in selling ore to the French. And that I will not allow."

Juliana supposed this wasn't the time to mention that she'd already sent a second messenger with a letter to the regent this afternoon.

"You're going to hold a pistol on me? You are so utterly predictable," Leucretia sneered, snatched a gun of her own from the reticule at her wrist, and pointed it at him.

"What are you planning?" Juliana asked. She might despise her aunt, but she wouldn't let Sommet shoot her.

Sommet shrugged. "I plan to kill all of you now. You damned interfering women. I already know you won't hesitate to share what you know." He paused, seemingly waiting for a reaction. He seemed a bit uncertain when none of the women in the room quailed or began to weep.

"How do you plan to explain our deaths?" Leucretia asked.

"There are many cliffs nearby. Many coach accidents. Often the bodies are so mangled, there'd be no way of knowing if they had been shot first or not."

"Why would we be in a coach?" Eustace asked. "The ball is here."

Perhaps it would be best to tell Sommet the rest. Perhaps she could convince him to flee rather than face the consequences. "It's too late. I sent word again to the regent. He knows about your treason. If you kill us now it will look suspicious."

Sommet's face turned a mottled red. "Impossible. I would have known."

"Not if it was one of Wilhelm's servants rather than my own."

Sommet made no move to lower his gun. Neither did Leucretia.

"Suspicion is far different than proof." The duke motioned, and his servants drew weapons as well. "I can survive suspicion."

From the corner of her eye, Juliana saw Apple inching toward the table behind her. No one was paying attention to the young girl. Her fingers closed around a candlestick.

Her gaze lifted to Juliana's. She was ready on Juliana's sign.

Juliana shifted her gaze to Eustace, who hadn't armed herself, but the gleam in her eye said she was ready to act as well.

Juliana tried talking to Sommet once more. "What if someone hears the shot?"

"They are far below at the ball. And the servants will do nothing. Trust me."

Leucretia's gun was the only thing keeping them alive, but they'd been speaking so long that her arms had begun to tremble. They couldn't lose Leucretia's gun. The second Sommet's life wasn't at risk, they'd be dead.

Juliana stepped to Leucretia's side. "Hand me the gun."

"Don't," Sommet ordered.

But Sommet could do nothing to stop her.

Leucretia's hand might wobble, but the gun still pointed at Sommet and her finger still rested on the trigger. "Why should I trust that *you* won't shoot me?"

"Because I'd rather shoot Sommet."

Leucretia shrugged at that and allowed Juliana's hand to cover her own. "I never hated you, you know."

Juliana supposed it was a truce of sorts between them. She took the gun. It was only a lady's pistol, but she was armed.

Apple's eyes grew large the instant before glass exploded into the room. Juliana threw up her arms in instinctive protection, as did the others.

Ian vaulted through the window.

Wearing only—a loincloth made from flour sacks, and his boots?

Juliana didn't have time to wonder. She scrambled to train the gun on Sommet again. But Ian leaped past her, kicking out at the middle servant, landing a blow to the man's ribs and driving him to his knees.

Sommet fired at Ian, but missed, the ball slamming into his own wounded man.

The man screamed, collapsing the rest of the way to the ground, holding his stomach.

The footman nearest Eustace fell with a cry as well, and from the corner of her eye she could see Canterbury standing over him with a fireplace poker. When had he even entered?

But she didn't have time to wonder. The remaining guard was trembling wildly, his gun swinging from side to side. Ian reached for him but the gun fired. Smoke billowing from the muzzle.

A pained gasp came from behind her. She whirled about. Leucretia had been hit. A wet spot spread over her crimson gown. Eustace ran to her, but she gave Juliana a small head shake when she saw the wound.

No one stood between Apple and the door.

"Apple, get help!"

The girl darted around, ignoring a grab from the injured men at her skirts.

Juliana glanced back at her aunts again, but now a trickle of blood dripped from the corner of Leucretia's mouth.

The gun was wrenched from her hands.

Juliana whipped her head around to find Sommet holding Leucretia's gun.

"Over here, Sommet," Ian called. He'd picked up the downed man's gun. "You know I always thought you fought like a girl."

"Put the gun down or I will kill her."

"If you value your life you will put *your* gun down."

Sommet sneered. "No, I don't think I—"

Ian didn't wait for him to finish. He fired, the shot clean to the center of the duke's chest as Apple burst through the door with a group of elegantly dressed gentlemen behind her.

One of the gentlemen caught Sommet as his eyes rolled back and he slumped forward.

Everyone's gaze swung to where Ian still held the smoking pistol.

For an instant there was silence, then everyone spoke at once.

"He's killed him!" one of the new arrivals shouted. "He's murdered the duke."

"And the princess!"

Suddenly there were a dozen voices shouting, calling for his apprehension.

". . . the mad servant."

". . . killer. He shot the groom as . . ."

"Fetch the constable . . ."

Juliana tried to shout over the crowd but the men weren't listening. There were too many people in the room. She could only see Eustace weeping beside Leucretia.

She reached for Ian but he was being dragged toward the door. She fought her way to Ian's side, finally throwing herself bodily in front of them.

"He's my servant. I have a right to speak with him."

The men holding him froze.

She reached for him. She didn't care that all the assembled people saw her put her hand on his bare chest. He had bruises there. Cuts trickling blood from the broken glass.

"Why did you even break the window? I had the window open."

"Distraction. And I can't resist a good entrance."

"I'll have a hard time convincing them that you're not mad with your current clothing choice." Her voice quavered.

"It was a daring escape. It involved my feet and a nail from crate of onions. Spectacular even for me." Ian smiled sadly. "Abington!" he called over her shoulder.

The other duke appeared next to her.

"Keep her out of all of this," Ian ordered.

She shook off the other man's hand. "What? No!"

"Tell her how it will be," Ian said.

Abington took her arm again, more firmly this time. The crowd was beginning to agitate again. He had to shout so she could hear him. "A duke has been murdered. Someone must pay the price."

"Not you, Ian." Had he known this would happen when he pulled the trigger? But from the resignation in Ian's eyes he had.

"It was self-defense!" she screamed.

But the constable had come into the room, and he ordered the men to take Ian away. "Ian!"

"Take her, Abington," Ian called over his shoulder. "We have worked too hard to have her name linked to mine. If the government thinks she is in any way linked to this— You owe me a favor, Abington."

Abington swore. "I owe you nothing. You bloody owe me a dozen times over." But he grabbed Juliana and swung her into his arms, ignoring her thrashing and protests.

"Watch her arms, she has a decent swing," Ian said as they led him out the door.

Abington pinned her arms just as she was about to go for his nose. "She's overset," he told the others as he carried her from the room.

She craned her head around and she could see the group of men leading Ian down the corridor out of her sight. "Put me down," she ordered. "If I explain to them what happened—"

Abington sighed, then grunted as she dug her

elbow into his ribs. "Sommet was a powerful man with powerful friends."

"Sommet didn't have friends."

Abington tilted his head in acknowledgment of that. "But he had many associates who will not want to risk Sommet's dealings being revealed. Too many powerful men would look foolish. Or corrupt." Abington finally set her down. "They will want this settled quickly."

"They can't do that," she said.

"They do it all the time."

"I won't *let* them do it."

Abington slowly smiled. "That, Your Highness, is a completely different matter."

Chapter Forty-one

$\mathcal{I}$an stood before the magistrate, the heavy iron manacles digging into his wrists. This was what Juliana had reduced him to. He could have escaped seventeen ways over the past two days of his incarceration. He'd begun counting them to keep himself entertained.

But as soon as he escaped, Juliana would be lost to him. He'd become a wanted man. And a wanted man could never have Juliana. Could never marry her and have her growl at him in the mornings when he awoke her with a kiss. Could never stay by her side and protect her from all the foul things in the world she should never have to see.

So he stood here and faced the magistrate, a man who'd just made it clear he had no plans to believe a word Ian or his barrister said. Who thought the world had been plagued by Ian's existence for far too long.

He hadn't quite decided what he would do when he was sentenced to hang, but as long as there was any chance at all that he'd still be able to keep Juliana, he'd endure anything.

The courtroom was crowded around him, every seat filled with people who had come to gawk and heckle.

"The right honorable gentlemen of the jury will agree that this villain—"

The doors to the courtroom were thrown open.

Ian glanced back, then glanced back again, rising to his feet. His heart, his lungs, his brain—hell, every organ in his body—ceased to function.

Juliana. She'd come for him. She'd disobeyed everything he'd said and come for him.

Ian grinned.

His princess marched in wearing her crown and a full, gold gown fit for a coronation. Twenty soldiers marched in behind her.

The magistrate leaped to his feet, his white wig tilting on his head. "What is the meaning of this?"

Juliana strode forward until she stood directly in front of the blustering man. "I am Princess Juliana Castanova of Lenoria. The man you have on trial is my betrothed. Any further action of this court against him will be seen as an attack on our sovereignty and an act of war."

Well, that rather made keeping her name out of all this a moot point. The magistrate had to bang his gavel several dozen times before the courtroom quieted enough for him to speak. "This will not be tolerate—"

The soldiers behind her all drew their swords.

One of the guards was amazing small. Nearly the same size as his sword.

No, her sword. It was Apple, her hair tucked out of sight in her cap. And to her right was— No. Impossible. It was an incognito Prince Gregory.

Ian fought his grin. The front row of soldiers closest to the magistrate were Juliana's actual soldiers.

But the rest . . . Canterbury. The other members of the Trio.

"You will release him or we will take him by force."

"The man is a murderer."

Juliana lifted her chin. "Ian Maddox is a hero. He protected me at great risk to himself when the Duke of Sommet attacked and tried to kill me."

"That is an outrageous charge—"

"I will testify to it here and now. Ian Maddox killed the duke in his role as my minister of security. My aunts . . ." She swallowed. "Aunts will swear to it as well. Along with the Duke of Abington. If you have any further doubts, you can request an audience with your prince regent."

The magistrate's mouth opened, closed, then opened again.

She turned and her soldiers parted neatly to let her pass. She finally looked at Ian, her eyes blazing with determination and love. "Come, Mr. Maddox."

Ian didn't hesitate. He walked past his barrister and held out his shackled arms to the guard. The man looked helplessly at the magistrate, and when he didn't receive any direction, he fumbled for the key and unlocked them.

As soon as Ian reached her side, she marched them out of the court. No one tried to stop them.

The royal Lenorian coach was waiting outside. He helped her in, then leaped in after her, the door barely closing before the coachman had spurred the horses into a gallop.

"You—" Ian started, but his throat was suddenly too tight to speak.

You came for me? Too obvious. And too likely to induce weeping on his part.

You were incredible? Understatement.

Finally he managed, "That was the most bloody brilliant thing I have ever seen."

He pulled her onto his lap, ignoring the jumble of hoops and petticoats. Reveling in her broken breathing. Half excitement. Half laughter.

"Does that trump walking out of prison with the gaoler's hat?" she asked, her laughter finally emerging as sound. A beautiful sound full of hope. Love.

"You've elevated the Wraith to an everlasting legend."

She tried to frown but couldn't hold the expression. "Do you outrank me now, then?"

He smoothed a strand of hair away from her face. "No. Not when you've just proven yourself a goddess."

"No," she said. "I don't want to be a goddess. I can hardly manage being a princess."

"A queen," he corrected.

"Not yet. I may have Wilhelm's troops. But I still have to find a way to regain my country without bloodshed."

"Oh, I took care of that. Right before I allowed Sommet to capture me." Ian traced the confusion as it spread over her face. Her eyebrows rising, her jaw loosening. He'd made sure she would be all right no matter the outcome. "The French and the Spanish have agreed to accept you as ruler of Lenoria and have given up their claim to Lenorian land."

"What— How— The Spanish?"

"I figured out the details of Sommet's blackmail. The ambassador doesn't want anyone else to."

"The French."

"Bribes. Lot and lots of bribes. I'm bloody rich, you know."

She was watching him with awe, and he was already plotting the next few pleasurable things he could do to keep that look there. "I love you, you know," he said.

"I do know. I love you."

The words expanded in Ian's heart, obliterating all the lonely, hungry places. He pressed his cheek to hers. "Do I have to be king after I marry you?"

"No. I think you are officially the queen's consort."

"Far, far better. That has a naughty ring to it. Just promise me one thing," Ian said.

"What?"

"Promise me I won't have to have a double wedding with my butler."

Juliana grinned. "Don't worry. I think they might beat us to the altar."

"Ah, those impetuous old people."

"We will be old together someday." Her face grew serious. "I hope. Are you well? I worried about you in that prison. How are your wounds? Did they feed you enough? I had my cook—"

He caught her hand, stopping her from searching for whatever food she'd brought. "I'm not hungry."

"Did those words just come out of your mouth?"

He lowered lips to hers. "I don't need anything to fill my empty places but you."